DARK PLACES

MARGERY RAMSDEN

SPRINGBOARD FICTION

Published 1998 by **Springboard Fiction**
Yorkshire Art Circus, School Lane,
Glasshoughton, Castleford, WF10 4QH
Tel: 01977 550401
Fax: 01977 512819
e-mail: BOOKS@ARTCIRCUS.ORG.UK

© Text: Margery Ramsden, 1998
Editor: Mark Illis
Editorial assistant: Elsie Sykes

Support: Clare Conlon, Ian Daley, Isabel Galan, Lorna Hey

Cover Design: Paul Miller of Ergo Design
Cover Image taken from a painting by John Adams
© Photograph of Author: Kevin Reynolds
Printed by FM Repro, Liversedge

ISBN:1 901927 02 4
Classification: fiction

British Library Cataloguing in Publication Data.
A catalogue record for this book is available from the British Library.

Events and characters in this novel are imaginary. Similarity to real persons and events is coincidental.

Springboard is the fiction imprint of Yorkshire Art Circus. We are a unique book publisher. We work to increase access to writing and publishing and to develop new models of practice for arts in the community.
Please write to us for details of our full programme of workshops and our current book list.
Our Website is http://www.artcircus.org.uk
Yorkshire Art Circus is a registered charity No 1007443.

Yorkshire Art Circus is supported by:

For Tom

Chapter 1

It's all because of the heat, and the stench of the dung. It's because of the wool in my brother's lungs, the oil on his skin. And it's because of the cat that meows at our door day after day and drops mice on the cobbles of our yard. It's because of becauses.

Thomas has typhoid. It's in his sweat and on his breath, like the smell of damp paper. He's curled up on a blanket in the corner of the room watching the flickerings of burning coals through glazed eyes. His cheeks become puckered as he sucks the last of the juice from the skin of a crab apple. His hair is damp. And my feet are swollen and aching. But I'm listening, and he's talking about the dog that took up residence on a sack down the lane before the summer began. It is losing its fur and scratches its buttocks, in the heat of every afternoon, on the green, leaded railings.

Words are rolling around in the saliva cupped in his tongue. About the cat on the slag-heap with kittens the colour of a mink's skin. About the delicate state of his knees, because he's always worried about his knees. About his sixpence per month pay rise. How he's one of the men now, and Fosters's have agreed to whitewash the weaving shed twice each year. 'Something to do with the new law,' he says. I say nothing. Now he begins to ramble. Talks about a stirring in his loins, then a stunted dying infant, a black tree pushing through the stones at the end of the alley. 'Ale.' That's what he says. 'It needs a few jugs of ale soaking into its roots.'

Thomas has never partaken of ale. Never felt the need. Even at the age of fifteen. I place a damp cloth on his cheeks and hope he'll sleep. But he's talking. Still talking. Says between laboured breaths that pipes are being installed down Toftshaw Road and that now we'll have clean water, no need for the well or the stream. I smile at him because it's expected and, folding the palms of my hands around his toes, try to draw the heat of his feet. He's burning up. My brother, Thomas. The dreamer. The fighter. The bloody fool. The glare of the fire is making me drowsy. But not him. Nothing but his own body heat is bothering Thomas.

There's an unmuffled cough coming from the scullery. It's Mark of course, grass and mud still clinging to his boots. He's busy earning his wages and has never even bothered to bring me a posy. I would have liked that.

He touches the corner of my mouth, says 'You've been waiting for me.'

'No,' I snap. A lie. He knows it's a lie. He's no sympathy for anyone. I sense that, and it hurts me. Mark's tough, and something more. Something I haven't discovered yet.

He saunters into my living room, chewing on a chicken bone, wipes sweat from his forehead, then pulls Thomas's blanket up so that it covers the boy's neck. Then he boredly watches me squeeze water from a piece of muslin onto my brother's face and loosen the buttons of his shirt. And he's searching for a glimpse of my thighs as I lean forward. I know it. That's what attracted him to me. My legs. What attracted me to him was the hue of his eyes. Black. Sort of Irish-like. No great emotion between us yet. But who knows?

Thomas is still rambling. Mark rests a calloused hand on the splintered oak table and frowns. Tells me that time is short. That he's got to be back at Fosters' before dark to brush down the horses (or perhaps to serve some kitchen girl by removing his trousers, I'm thinking). If he's not back in time, he's telling me, he'll be called anything abominable, including the son of Lucifer. One of his exaggerations. His lies. I know that. But there's something about the bastard. I'd like us to be more important to each other, but we're not.

Life is life. Merely that. I'm a twenty six year old spinster, and for two years he's had the privilege of going under the weave of my skirt in the damp of the alley on quiet afternoons. So what does it matter? It's only crumbs. 'Go on then Mark,' I shrug. 'A devil of a life is this anyway.' Then I move across the stone to stir blackening carrots in a black pot on a steadily glowing fire. My duty. My duty to my brother. Jesus Christ, if Thomas is going to die, he's not going to depart on an empty stomach, not if I can prevent it. If I could prevent it he wouldn't depart at all. I've heard tales going around the town that the illness was due to flesh-consuming bugs in the air. Read all about them in the public library on its opening day. Know all about it. Have always wanted to rescue Thomas from them. All he's done in his life is mend neighbours boots in the pale of the dawn on the back stoop, and spend his days running like a madman through the roar of the weaving shed clutching spools of thread to give to the men who weave and spit.

'The boy doesn't look too bad to me,' says Mark.

'Doesn't he?' I ask.

He avoids my eyes. But I take a sharp intake of breath because I'm not as angry with him as I should be. I like the shape of his thighs and the memory of his breath on my forehead. Yet feel belittled by these thoughts, and angry. He is calling me darling. Talking twaddle. But why is he always calling me darling?

He spits into the coals and watches them sizzle then pulls on his waistcoat, and tosses a farthing onto my brother's blanket, before mumbling that he wishes him well. Then listens to the boy's ramblings for a few minutes. He turns to me.

'What the hell is the lad talking about?' and 'Why should he be trying to run down Fosters's anyway? One of the best mills in the country, that. Any fool can see that, burning up or not.'

'Oh, he has dreams,' I shrug, folding my arms and wishing that he didn't. Mark has no idea.

'You reckon that he really could be dying then? Know better than the doctor I paid for him to see I suppose.'

He scratches his right calf with the toe of his boot, pushing the heavy worsted against his skin. He looks uncomfortable. Weary. Bored, almost, yet wants to leave without annoying me. Unable to think of anything else to say we both turn back to stare at Thomas, who moves a hand to his cheek to feel the heat, like the sick do. His rambling turns into a tired whisper. Then he smiles at me, says 'Shit to bloody bosses.' He knows I'm tired of hearing it. He beckons me closer.

'Guess what?' he croaks. 'Guess who's just gone and shit himself?'

His breath smells of urine now, no sign of the sweetness of the apples.

'Well shit to everything,' I say, and don't know why I said it.

I've always warned Thomas to stay away from people who make utterances like that. Always. No excuse. I pull the exhausted apple peel from the sticky folds of skin on his neck, where it fell when chewing it for a moment became too hard for him, then sigh with relief when he dozes. The door closes quietly behind me.

Chapter 2

I wake up with the taste of stale Martini in my mouth and stare at a spider's web on the ceiling. It's broken, holding only the skeleton of one small fly. It's a strange dream I've had. One of sweat and the overwhelming colour brown. It's 1995 for God's sake, a time of anoraks and bottled water. A year of cats on heat and bulk-buying Kit-Kats. And I never had a brother named Thomas. Never had a brother at all. Never had anything. Except responsibilities. A family. A bloody family. Working class, licence-paying, satellite dish-owning, moaning and groaning family. My responsibility. I know all about the bind I'm in. But Rodney, my red-headed husband doesn't.

He turns over lazily in our well-sprung bed, inadvertently scratching one of my swollen ankles with a toenail. He looks like a child when he's not fully awake, one permanently bemused. Totally vulnerable and unaware. But that idea could just be the result of the tossing and turning of my imagination. I know that he's a shit really. He opens his eyes, sees the same skeletal fly that I do hanging from a thread on the magnolia painted ceiling.

He asks if I've taken my anti-menopausal tablets, and doesn't see me cringe. When I say 'No,' he yawns and scratches an armpit, mutters 'Hell of a wife you are.' Knows it annoys me. Well, it's meant to.

'What time is it?' he asks.

'How the hell should I know?' I say. 'Can't see the church clock from here.'

There's no church clock in miles of our house.

'I've no time for silliness,' he snaps. 'We've got to take every chance we can get, the likes of you and I.'

Neither of us have illusions. Never did. His voice is like Mark's in my dream. A voice of the shit in my head. Not his fault. Can't be. I'm not into all this Freud stuff. When you leave school at fifteen and live through stilettos and beehives and punk rot and rusted cars carrying dreadlocks and rave I think you learn not to take notice of stuff like that.

Well, I'm always thinking. It's a fault of mine.

Outside, the milkman is rattling unrinsed empty bottles together, and making an attempt to whistle. He complains to an early morning riser about the veins on his war-torn leg.

'I was at Dunkirk,' he's saying, but his voice is shaky and it doesn't ring true.

I press my thinning dentures against an eight o'clock cigarette, rolling its taste around my tongue, then push my hands inside my full-length nylon night-dress and finger the undersides of my breasts in search of all night mid-life hot sweat. I'm sticky alright. Tacky. Smelling of stale cheese. I remember waking and peering at the digital clock at 2am and counting the roses on the wallpaper, pale nicotine-stained yellow, like something from a bad, late-sixties television play. Then wondering if the fridge door had fallen off in the illogicality of the night, because it does that.

I think about the ink and pizza stained laundry in the pink plastic basket in the corner of the hall, and ignoring the screams of a labouring feral cat under a bush in the shadow of my clothes post, practice deep breathing. I know the truth. That I've got to get up. It's a bad morning. I can feel the reason in my swelling abdomen. It's clammy. Well past dawn. I haven't started to menstruate during the night. All that almost middle-aged lady's dark blood. So I suppose that's a blessing.

I should patter across the coldness of vinyl tiles, knock on the blue bedroom door and shout to my son that despite his fairly logical argument of yesterday evening, 'A tee-shirt is still only a fucking tee-shirt. And fuck to the label inside it.'

He'd put down his pot-noodle and, without looking at me, pulled off his socks and poked at his toenails, almost a nervous habit. He's so like his father that it disturbs me. Always did. Ever since the attendant midwife pointed out a brown birthmark on the boy's buttock, in exactly the same place as his dad's. I can't win. Can't ever win. I'm listening to Rod pretending to snore beside me, to the farting gases resulting from his last night's lager and take-away. Watching the tiny hairs from his nostrils sway in a steady stream of breath. Noses like that, pink and slightly pimpled, always belong to Rodneys, I muse. And what kind of name is that for a man to have, for Christ's sake? I tell myself to think about blue dolphins in a green sea. Because their image is supposed to be healing, soothing, for a short-sighted, pissed-off housewife on a predicted, ever predictable Monday in early light.

I let out a theatrical sigh, for the benefit of Rodney, but he doesn't hear it. Time to throw on my chocolate brown dressing gown, cringe towards the bathroom, then urinate a worrying yellow. Time to switch the kettle on in the primrose haze of the kitchen. I pick up the mail, pushed roughly through the letterbox to land on the rubber doormat like fallen birds. There's a green electricity bill and an invitation to Time-Share, some bumf about a Spanish holiday carrying the illustration of a girl adorned with plastic tits and blood red mouth grinning woodenly.

I throw the literature onto the kitchen table then, using a clean tea towel, wipe condensation from the window. The usual routine. I scratch my arse, examine my chewed down fingernails, light another cigarette, listen to precious silence and try to empty my mind. It's supposed to be helpful. The family stirs. Pads downstairs like a mini, reluctant parade. Daughter, Gaynor, in comprehensive blue. My son, fourteen years of age, long legged and pimpleless. Chewing on a Mars bar, and displaying eyelashes that a woman would kill for. But he has a boil on his neck that worries me.

The kids nod towards me in reluctant recognition, with more important things on their minds.

They're sometimes loveable. Loved. Aryan-looking and smug, already dreaming of a life of bank accounts and cars. I know the crack. It happens to all adolescents. Stupid, I may be, but not daft.

'Here's a pound each,' I say. 'Bugger off to school and live your life. I'm not well.'

Gavin winces, pushes grubby football shorts into his fraying schoolbag, says he's always being told to bugger off like it's an offering of a chocolate. And I wish I hadn't said that because every time I've bought him an Easter egg it's melted in my anorak pocket before I've had a chance to give it to him. No one can rely on me. I wonder if I've got an unwanted lump on either of my shrinking breasts, and check for that. It's supposed to be part of a routine.

Routine. If you've got no routine you've got nothing.

But I can't dwell on it now. My head hurts. Bloody cheap cider and frozen chips. That's what is causing it, no doubt. No excuses. But who the hell needs excuses anyway?

If I feel ill it's because my stomach is a sodding sewer. So what? Rodney slopes into the kitchen, his bare toes curling to grip the cushion floor. He's pushing freshly rinsed hair away from his remarkably unlined forehead and belching without self-consciousness. I used to admire him for the lack of that fault. Used to. Yet hate him now, and have done for a long time. Watched him con old women into buying miracle vacuum cleaners. The truth is he'd do almost anything to earn a buck. But I've always said nothing, so that I could eat without having to queue up at the Income Support, begging. I know that.

He hits on his egg with the usual silvery spoon, then grips his stomach as if it's going to burst, so I pass him the salt. Give him a few minutes to catch his breath because once he's fallen asleep he's comatose, and it takes him four frigging hours to become alive on a morning. Now is the time of day to act normal. Practical. I mutter that the vertebrae in my neck appear to be gone, that the dog has been sick all over the pure wool buttermilk rug in the lounge, and that the curtains need taking down and cleaning. Don't care if he listens.

His face shines patchily in the beams of sunlight pushing through the off-white, net curtains. I think I see the hint of a mole growing on his chin, and worry again, because worrying is supposed to be what I'm all about. Then shrug it off.

He tugs at his stonewashed jeans, tight below his belly. He hasn't looked at me yet. Then searches for his shoes on the brown half-paid-for carpet. Says that he's got blisters on his heels on account of the shape of the insteps. Nothing I can say to that. What does he want? Sympathy? He ought to go around town in my pissing Oxfam shirts, the prick, and see what that's like.

'For fuck's sake, poverty is poverty,' I mumble. 'And don't argue, because I don't want to get caught up in talking politics again. Neither of us know a frig about them. They shit in the same black pot, as my mum used to say.'

I don't remember her saying that. Don't remember a thing about her, but it sounds impressive. Rodney is banging the shell of his egg. Our eyes don't meet. 'You don't even like talking to me,' I say. 'Like I'm some slug, on the heel of your shoe. Left one or right? What does it matter?'

I ask that because he's always been a nit-picker. He's muttering to himself about what a burden I am, and the kids are still fastening trainers and packing their school lunches, busily deciding who's to have an orange since, neither of them desire the bloody pear. So I go upstairs to dress, and search for lumps in my armpits. Even become a contortionist to search for the telltale pink blobs I've read about, in the lacquer-stained dressing table mirror. There are none. Never were. Odd though. My ribs seem to be getting larger. Imagination. That's all it is. Imagination. It'll be my downfall, will that.

I'm listening for the mention of my name from the family below. There is none.

There's a tentative tap on the front door, the sound of heels in the hall. A hint of posing-type laughter. It's Sonia. Her of self-assurance. Her from across the street, the pattering feet of her little Jack Russell following on behind her. Temporary refugees from where gnomes cast nylon line for trout in the everlasting flora, and herbs in borders cling to their titles on lollipop sticks and grow.

I'm not in the mood for Sonia. My bones ache too much. My face is too unpainted. I go back downstairs. Rodney is still unwashed, unshaven, and asks what my rushing is all about. He should know better. There is no rushing. All that's wrong with me is a vague intolerance of a hot flush, for Christ's sake. How thick can a man get?

Sonia, it seems, is diplomatically ignoring the conversation. Stroking my cat, and sipping tea in a ladylike manner from a striped mug. And leaning back against a cushion in one of our second hand pine chairs, her arms folded across a cherry coloured sweat shirt. She's called, she explains, without embarrassment, to borrow eggs to feed the face of her toyboy lover. Everyone in the vicinity knows him, and either loves him or hates him, or watches him with owl's eyes.

But that's her business, I've been telling myself. Always her business. He's something worth beholding, though, I've had to admit to myself. Something boasting a penis. Someone permanently medallion clad, and keeping his hard-earned image. Dark, curly hair, the works. His swagger says he's easily the sexiest thing on earth, and he's going to make no bones about that. He is, he's kept insisting in the pubs, a truthful sort, a sort of perennial George Washington. Sonia always listened. Now it seems she's prattling on to Rod about Council Tax and such, because she knows he likes to think of himself as an expert on such matters.

Rod thinks he knows everything. He's above us somehow, even goes to the local horse fayre and brags that he's a better judge of the flesh than anyone else, which he isn't.

I'm searching through a cluttered, kitchen drawer for a clean comb to drag through my perm, and Sonia winks at me. Like hair is a feminine condition. She's haunting me. I can feel her smirk on my backbone. And unease. Well, you become more receptive during the early stages of a menopause, I'm telling myself. Then I feel even more uneasy because I'm not sure I've really reached that stage yet. And why should I want to? All I am is a confused shit.

Sonia is watching my reflection in the mirror, puffing on her cigarette, then she kicks Rod on the shins under the table. He's rattling on about his carburettor again. She glances at me knowingly as I turn towards her. Knows all about the crack. My drinking. So in turn I watch her. If this is the game, I'll play it. There's no choice.

'You shouldn't be sitting here contemplating your navel,' she tells Rod, in a practised, sexy voice. 'You've got a family to support, darling.'

My stranger of a husband looks to me for support. Gets none. Then stares through the window at the disinfected dustbin and falls into silence.

'And how are you, Laura?' Sonia asks me.

I don't like her condescending, supper dance voice, or her designer dresses. Why the hell we class each other as friends, I don't know. But I've got to answer. Say something. Convention demands it. It doesn't matter what I say. Well, I'm known as a nasty piece of work, anyway. Never baked scones or went to a parent/teacher meeting in my life. Never believed in that. Should have been teacher/pupil meetings. If that makes me an oddball, so what?

'You look miles away,' she purrs. 'I've just asked you a question. Don't you remember?'

What sort of a question? I'm wondering. She's confusing me. On purpose, I know that.

'What do you want? If you mean did Rod poke me close to death last night, then the answer is no,' I say. There's no reason why I should play her little games. No reason at all. 'Don't tease me Sonia, I'm feeling hung over and bloody minded. So what?'

I can sense the wheels going around in her brain. She's got to come out tops in the battle of intelligence, and probably will. But shit, why does she have to do it before breakfast? And what the fuck does it matter anyway? Any minute now she's going to ask me how my shuffling, slipper-wearing Dad is, out of politeness. Though the bitch knows damned well that he's going out of his mind, slowly and quietly, as expected. I try not to look at her. Rod is examining his knuckles, so there's no problem with him.

'Everyone hates well-meaning friends,' I'm murmuring. But this won't touch Sonia. She's not one for subtlety. She's as thick as my homemade custard. But a good listener, I'll give her that. I hate it when she puts on a posing act like this, it's the mark of a coward. Got to be. I decide to empty one per cent of my mind for her. Or is it one percent of nothing? Anything to get her off my back. The last thing I need right now is people. Supposedly well-meaning people. My ankles are swelling and my corns itch like buggery. 'I watched Sky at Night last night,' I say with the expected, supposedly modest shrug. 'It was quite interesting, especially if you want to know what a black hole is. Do you realise nobody knows what it is for certainty? Or is it for certain? It's all theory. All of it.'

That kills the conversation. It's meant to. I take my time refilling the kettle, and watch Rod's reflections in the cracked shaving mirror on the kitchen window-sill. He's glaring at me. I know the message he's trying to transmit to me well. 'It's going to be one of those days,' he's saying, self-consciously rubbing the stubble on his chin.

His face is sore. Even at the age of forty he still has acne. Must say something that, I'm thinking.

He's right of course. Today's going to be one of those hellishly bad days, I know it. I'll probably fall over some kid's bike in the street and Rod will most likely throw a moody because we don't talk anymore. But then we've nothing to talk about. That's the way I'm thinking. Life is painful. No doubt about it. Sonia appears to be feeling uncomfortable. She's picking non-existent fluff from her Marks & Spencer's skirt and giving out lady-like sighs. Then she stares at her thickly painted fingernails, and asks if I'm going down town to do some shopping today. I know what she's saying. I've lived across the road from her and prowled about with her for eight years. What she means is that she's certain she's got a thirst on larger than mine, and more immediate. She's asking if I'm going shopping via The Jug and Bottle. As it happens, I wouldn't mind a bit of shopping. I ought to pamper myself a little, buy some new shoes, but how can I when Rod keeps his wallet firmly pressed against his heart?

Rod is pretending not to notice. Or is it pretence? I don't know. I've never been able to work out just how bright he really is. He could be a genius slumming it. And that would make me one of the biggest bastards on earth for criticising his apparent love of soap-operas and sexual performance.

We loved each other once. The usual thing. The blue-black ribbon between love and hate, rewound so many times it doesn't hurt anymore. Maybe I'm such a pillock that I love him now, dandruff-covered shirt collars and all. There's been so much aggro between us that how the hell can I know?

Then I'm thinking what the hell does it matter?

Survival. That's what we're all about. And I'm a stupid bugger for letting myself become so maudlin. Sonia uncurls her legs, she doesn't like the silence, examines the scuff marks on the heels of her two-toned shoes, then says she'll see us both later, that she must have picked a bad time.

'Is there a good time?' I ask.

No answer.

She dons her mustard coloured jacket, searches the pockets in case she's been foolish enough to clog them with bus tickets and tab ends. That sort of thing wouldn't help her image at all. I'm watching her. 'It seems you're feeling a bit bloody-minded this morning,' she muses.

No answer is needed nor thought about. I'm thinking about this damned anal itch I've got. Filthy thing to think about. But facts of life are facts of life. She pulls at more non-existent fluff, this time from her sleeve, then walks out, eggs in a box, to be with her man.

Rod is looking at me, disgusted. Asks why I'm talking drivel and stares at me, disgusted, because he watches too much TV and thinks it's the thing to do. Melodrama always.

'You're in a cow of a mood,' he says.

His eyes suggest he considers me to be an idiot. No big deal. He's right of course. The bastard usually is. He comes from that kind of Yorkshire strain. Probably had a dog and hunted rabbits in his younger days, and knew better than to talk about it. Bought his mother embroidery kits.

I can't tell him that he's boring, because I don't know how sane I am, nor am I going to say that I don't need a sunken penis-brain like his moping around the house for days or months at a time. That would only reinforce his opinion that I'm a nasty bitch. Instead I inform him that I'm preoccupied. Have enough of a problem thinking about the old people. That I've got to visit Dad, the man with the well-fingered Teletext. Remote controllable. That I have to enquire if the old man has had his dentures fixed yet. Rod frowns and shrugs his shoulders as if he doesn't care. An act? I don't know. I've got to play stupid. Know the formula.

'Aren't I supposed to admit that I care about my father?' I turn on the hot water tap. Rod watches me fill a plastic bucket, fluoride essence mixing with essence of water mingled with mock disinfecting pine, then looks uncertainly at my hips as I push a recycled mop along the kitchen floor.

'Your old man's got hairs creeping down his nostrils, he's never even noticed. And he scratches his balls in public,' he adds. Then he examines my face in search of an expected reaction.

He gets none. So rises from the table. Then moves like an

overweight whippet towards the fridge. Purposefully. He opens it and the light from it gleams on the part of his shirt where a button should be but isn't. He commences to scrape the residue of shed lettuce leaves from the salad box.

That's Rodney. Always practical. Reasonable.

Unlike me, he saves things, rescues things. Knows what is what. He cleans things, hoards jam jars. Keeps asking why I throw every fucking thing away. Like we're going to live forever and everything matters. Jesus, he even gripes about spending money on the kids' school trips, arguing that they'll grow up and forget them.

He clears his throat then goes into the set scene.

'Your father is a thing going off of its head, like I've kept telling you.' I've heard all this before. So this is the story of our linked lives, I'm thinking.

'I can't understand why you worry about the old sod,' he continues. 'He never did a full day's work in the whole of his life. The bugger had more important things to do.'

'My father is an inventor,' I tell him. 'He created toys for me at a time they couldn't be bought, and mended wirelesses for women who were desperate to know about their desert-kidnapped bloody husbands, who probably shit themselves in some shag woman's Cairo hovel. That counts for something.'

'Counts for bloody what?'

How can I answer when I don't fucking know?'

Rod shrugs dramatically. Says all of this was fifty years ago and that I don't know what I'm talking about. He goes on to say that I'm not well, prematurely wrinkled, leather-skinned and vague, and that he has spotted cobwebs in corners of the kitchen. That he even found one in the bathroom.

'Not much to say then,' I mutter.

How could a person be as pissing narrow-minded as him? I've got pseudo-Indian and frozen prawns to grab from the grip of the freezer to defrost before lunch. I do it dutifully.

Rod would never even have thought of that. Women's work. 'That bed hasn't been bloody changed for a fortnight,' he says.

'So? You do it,' I say. 'I won't always be here to hang the washing.'

'What does that mean?' he asks.

'You tell me.'

But he's not listening, still thinking about his double-glazing commission, conning old ladies. Playing the game.

I'm thinking, not for the first time, that I should drop out of it. My chips are diminishing quickly.

I feel faint. Something to do with my age. The flags are cold beneath my feet. And the window is strange. Smaller. Some sort of sash dangling from it, and it's speckled with soot. Thomas is crying, Mark is by his side, arms folded.

'We all have our own cross,' he says. 'Pull yourself together Thomas.'

Then his voice echoes, fades, 'Thomas? Thomas?'

I scour the sink, rinse away Rod's Earl Grey tea leaves. Then wipe the formica on the fridge, and boil a kettle. No fool am I. Never have been. Steam scalds my fingers, hits the washable grape-patterned wallpaper, runs down it crookedly, like rain would on the pyramids of Egypt. I've read a lot about Egypt, I have. A lot about everything. I've kept telling Rod that, kept asking him to put down his newspaper, forget his itching armpits and tell me what he thinks about the Big Bang theory. He declines to answer such questions. Always. Doesn't even make a comment, except when he's in a good mood. Then he says that such preoccupations don't put bread on the table nor cream on a screaming baby's arse. (Must have read it somewhere). And what the chuff am I on about? What the fuck is this lateral thinking? He doesn't know. Neither do I, that's the shitty thing. No matter. No importance. Right now I'm doing some ironing, hot steel on man-made fibre, and wondering if the cat has fleas, because she's been scratching a lot lately. I love my cat. Of course I do. I'm starting on shirt collars and wondering why they won't uncurl. That matters.

Chapter 3

Once outside, the so-called fresh air hits the nicotine and the stale curry on my tongue. That's the way it is. I'm coated in washable anorak, and sniffing. I can hear a bird overhead screaming like it can't find water and won't give in.

The morning rush hour has gone. The bemused feral cat, the children kicking their heels in baby-buggies, and guys with hernias and egg sandwiches in plastic boxes coughing up their roll ups. It's still raining, as it has been for twelve hours, tapping on the poster-filled windows of Abdul's tobacconist's, and making the slate-loose rooftops the colour of chopped liver, preferably pig's. Now it's falling on me in my short grey jacket, and splashing.

There's not much to see. There's a green bus, stuck behind a glaring sign proclaiming Road Works, its driver dying for a cig. I can see it in the puckering of his cheeks. Some lad with a hood's loitering in hookey fashion outside a video shop on Norristhorpe Lane, a bag over his shoulder and a bacon sandwich in his hand. As I walk by, he takes off his hood, flattens down his crewcut and nods to me. And I'm thinking, it takes an idiot to know one, and what the hell can a kid like that know about life. Wouldn't even know about a fuck. And shouldn't. I pretend not to notice.

I'm pushing the toes of my shoes through the puddles. Wondering, like a pillock, where all the dandelions have gone. I've always liked dandelions. Bugger the daffodils, they're too fragile, temporary, I'm thinking, lighting a tab end under the awning of a newsagent's.

I once read a poem about daffodils, curled up with a cup of Complan with spiky pink rollers in my hair, because that was what a clever person was supposed to do in the sixties. That was the time of beehive hairdos. The distant past. But what the hell was the point of the past? Even dinosaurs had one. But what happened? They ended up as crocodile handbags. No point in dwelling on this bloody middle-aged mid-life crisis stuff when I'm supposed to go off my head. A family trait, that.

I walk on, then knock on the paint-chipped door of my father's semi-detached abode with all mod-cons. Could do it in my sleep, like smelling his grilled breakfast of never quite cooked kippers. Jammy bugger. He's even got Council-pruned conifers and a well maintained garden path, and an off-white number plate on his wall. Surely he couldn't want more? But he does, or says he does. Something to do with pretending to be old. This is respectable memory stuff. Like chewing cockles on a promenade and remembering black and white B-movies. Like pineapple jam from Woolworths. I glance at his stainless steel letter box. There's no pamphlets trapped in its mechanism so no problem. Inside, there's a sound from the past. When will I ever get rid of the bloody awful past? It's depressing me like hell. He's shuffling his fur-lined slippers along the foam-backed carpet. A sort of hedgehog-type hurrying because he's clipped his toenails and he's ready for the off. Because it's Monday. Blow-out day. The day I take Dad's right elbow into one of my washing-up hands and we can saunter like penguins down the hill to the amusement arcade. The day I ask if he's washed his underwear and we bet on the probability of bars and bells lighting up against the chance of four cheating cherries. All good fun really. A time for kicking up leaves on the verges of Mortimer Road, taking shortcuts down weed-breeding alleys of grey, littered with crisp packets, fruit flavoured condoms and long forgotten beer crates. He's still shuffling inside. I knock on his door again. What the fuck is taking him so long? Then hear a grunt, one hundred percent human, then the sound of the bolt being drawn back. The bugger shouts 'Who is it?' Then lets down the latch, opens the door and scowls at me. He mumbles through my silence something about him not winning a lottery that I said he would.

'I never did,' I swear.

He should know that I've never been into such stuff. But then, maybe he's been talking to my doppelganger, because anyone could have one. I'm into the supernatural and he knows it. So I say, 'Dad, not to worry, you and I couldn't win a point in a farting contest.'

My mouth is dry. Too dry. His face is too yellow. He can't blame me for all the faults in the world. Can't. Yet he blamed me for the lost Sooty puppet in sixty-one didn't he? The blockhead. I follow his bent back into the inexplicable mist of the kitchen. Didn't I scrub the thing out for him only the week before? Then I head like a moth towards the light coming from the window above the sink. Depressing place, this, and always has been. Dee and Dan, his black speckled goldfish, are swimming lethargically in expected dark water, in a pink plastic fruitbowl on the window-sill. Legally, I remind myself, because I'm not feeling too cracky, these creatures are mine. I won them at a fair I took my kids to. Out of duty. And then I gave the poor little goldfish to my dad. Tragic really. They need feeding, so I give them the crusts from the toast of Dad's long forgotten breakfast. Soft hearted, that's me. What else can I do? I can't change the world. Dad is a thoughtless shit at times. Most times, I'm thinking. And who does the old bugger think he is anyway? Christ, he can't even replace a fuse in a plug. Or so he says when he's feeling sorry for himself and has an empty sherry bottle and his salmon paste has gone off two days earlier than expected. All lies of course. He could remember to feed the goldfish. Just can't be bothered. Someone else can do the mundane things. That's the story of his life. Always acts as if his mind is elsewhere. Whether it has anywhere to go or not.

'I don't feel well,' I mutter. Can't locate the source. Expect sympathy.

'You look moody,' he says, heading towards the lounge.

'I'm sick,' I mumble.

'You're up the stick,' he calls back to me, confidently.

I suppose all men's brains work like that. Remarks like his just leave a peculiar type of numbness. Like chewing-gum gnawed for too long. I'm still in the kitchen, watching his dentures floating up and down in milky white liquid in a Crown Derby cup on top of an ancient, purring fridge. I'm caught in a web of boredom, self-pity and sameness. But the plastic teeth look vulnerable too.

Like everything else in his kitchen. There's a kind of hopelessness about it. Two pairs of Y-fronts are airing on the open oven door. They smell of chicken fat in urine, the cause being a long gone take-away. Probably one he purchased a few Saturdays ago on his way home from the off-licence then warmed up for his breakfast the following morning. I know him too well to have any illusions about him. And there's more to depress me. A fly turning to dust hanging from a thread in the corner of the room, an acrobatic corpse. So I search for other parasites. Find one on the armour of one of the four tins of sausage-stroke-beans next to a bulk buy of cornflakes inside his pantry. There's half a bottle of rum on a magnolia painted shelf in the shadows, nestling between his milkpans. There's always half a bottle of rum on a magnolia painted shelf, I remind myself, shutting the creaking door. A different brand every week. Don't know where he hides the full ones in case some bored and distant cousin should visit him for a cup of milky tea with leaves floating in it. They could think he's some eccentric old bastard with cash in his pillowcase. I don't care. What's his is his. Can't be fairer than that. The eggs on his kitchen worktop are the same ones that were there last week, and the week before. I just know it. Size one, brown, sell-by date blanked out. I've finished nosing. From the chill of the lounge he's prattling on about the virtues of oral contraception. Keeps up to date, does my dad. Listens to the radio a lot.

'For the last time, I'm not pregnant. Nor am I ever likely to be again,' I shout to him, pissed off by the silliness of his spouting.

'Can't do with your moods,' I hear him mumbling.

I take him his striped mug of Earl Grey tea. A sort of visitor's ritual. And watch him blow on it and then sip. Then he grows impatient with it, and goes back to stitching up the tobacco-stained hole in his trouser pocket, his hairy legs spread and a beach towel fastened tightly around a non-existent waist. He runs short of thread, tuts a bit, then narrows his eyes to thread a needle. Expects sympathy. I curl up with my varicose veins on the cold leather of a fifties pouffe and, opening the handbag, count what money I've got left, because it's important. Count the number of pages still left in my family benefit book. It's a habit. Nothing more. The electric fire, twenty years old, hums quietly and efficiently.

'Someone will have to trim my hair,' Dad is saying, tugging at his salt and pepper locks.

'It's a bugger. A feller shouldn't have to put up with so much hair. I never did last time.'

'What last time?'

He shrugs and then I shrug. Then he checks the TV Times to see what date it is, because he's got a thing about dates. Can't even remember what year it is lately. But I suppose it comes to us all.

'It's Monday,' I say quietly. 'You know. Soddin' Monday? The day that comes before Tuesday?'

'Too many of them,' he says.

'What?'

'Like I say, too many of them. They didn't used to come so quickly once. No fucking cars. That made the difference.'

'And I suppose you'd know would you?'

He grimaces, then examines his trouser pocket carefully. Brilliant eyesight, has my dad. Always did have.

'Time to get some air,' I say irritably. I've enough problems to contend with without this twaddle.

So he finishes dressing and dons his cap. The tartan one he bought on one of his more energetic days at a Methodist jumble sale. Then we go through the ritual of the shutting and locking of doors and listening to their creakings. There's the smell of wet grass involving our nostrils, reminding me of school playing fields where I had to stand, a motionless spectator, because I hadn't the eye co-ordination to play rounders. (The green-knicker-clad girls who could were bastards.) I mention this to Dad, and he makes no comment. I don't expect him to. He never wore green knickers with a tiny pocket to hold a handkerchief in his life. No way he can understand, I know that. I follow his athlete's feet along the pavements, and we look around us because there's nothing else to do, and nothing to talk about. Someone waiting at a bus stop down Aylesbury Avenue farts loudly. Dad and I catch the sound. Exchange unglaring glances as if to confirm our liberalism. I'm thinking that after a week apart father and sprog ought to have something worth mentioning. But Dad's on his sympathy searching kick. He tells me that he's put on an Elastoplast.

'On what?' I ask wearily.

'On an elbow,' says he, on account of it got grazed while he was trying to pull weeds from his garden. He probably fell down, warm and happily drunk, and caught his arm on a brick. He's wearing a frown on his egg-stained face. He thinks he's got problems. I've got swollen ankles, tender breasts bouncing in their sling. That tells me that a period is just about due. One bloody problem after another. It's all to do with this hangover thing.

He's muttering something about a chipmunk he's seen on a television documentary. He looks old even from the back. We pass the derelict mill we've passed a hundred times before, watch the dandelion seeds blowing in a warming breeze. It's an off-white, oblong building caressed by steadily growing weeds, its innards exposed to the elements through gaps where panes of glass used to be. There's a strong smell of marauding cats and the adjacent grey river. A rusted weaving loom lies discarded in front of the high gates, and a paint chipped sign, long fallen to the moss on the ground, proclaims that this was once the property of Foster's Textiles.

I feel uneasy. I've seen these words before. But this time they leap out at me. Tell me something.

Thomas worked there. But it was just a dream. No problem once you understand it. Still I shudder. The booze business is getting to me. Didn't realise it would happen to me so quickly. Hell of a whirlpool, the mind.

Dad says 'I need to buy some fishfingers,' then starts reminiscing about a long-dead mate of his who, one sunny morning, sent his pink-faced, polyester-clad wife out to buy fishfingers, then, locking the door behind him, went out and threw himself into the local dam. He took his spectacles off first and carefully rested them on the ground. Funny that. The bloke reminded Dad of a pink-eyed mouse.

'Seems he was something of a rat,' I say.

We keep on walking. The ritual. The amusement arcade is turquoise and orange. There's an unappetising odour of cheap, free coffee, and anorak-clad shoulders caught in the early morning drizzle drying out slowly. There's mutterings of 'Fuck its' and 'Damns' and 'Come on you money grabbing machine.' The usual crack. Always. There's a youth in Levi's with Golden Virginia roll ups counting change. There are mothers turned bottle-created auburn clutching cans of coke, refugees from the sixties. There's some bitch in a baby-blue skirt in the corner, holding her stomach. She's moaning because her head isn't quite there. I know her. Try to avoid her. She's tranquillised, recently divorced and world-weary. Waiting to win the lottery. Not my type of friend. Not my type at all. I smell bacon sandwiches, stacked up on paper plates on the formica snack bar for quick, and rightly expected, sale. I smell morose, engrossed lines of witches clutching tokens. Our town is known for witches. One was burned in sixteen-twenty for curing a kid's boil. I've read about it.

'I only come here because of you,' I tell Dad, sitting down at one of the three tables and giving him a paper cup of milky tea.

He's not listening, of course. He pulls his mind back from memories I can't imagine and shrugs his shoulders as if the air has suddenly gone cold. Then he calls me Alice. My mother's name. Now a dead, fading memory of a woman. Well, that's life. Maybe he's getting confused because she had the same wispy hair as I have. Or did have until cancer caught her breast and her locks fell out onto a striped hospital pillow-case one dawn. Dad sighs and sucks his fingernails. He's always doing that. They're pink and soft. Couldn't be softer without melting into his flesh.

'Remember when you were a kid?' he asks. And I'm thinking 'Here we go again.' The other half of his mind is in the here and now. Like mine always is when I'm ironing shirts, because if it wasn't I'd never hear the last about scorched collars. Adaptation. That's what it's all about. He's rummaging through his darned pockets for money for the bandit and comes up with a fistful, finely dusted in old, dry, tobacco. Everything he owns has a coating of stale tobacco dropped by trembling hands. (The fault of the sherry again).

'How could I forget about being a kid?' I sigh, because we've been through this conversation before. 'My potty training went well. I had a blue one. But look at me now.'

'You wanted to be a Sunbeam girl in the pantomime at the Alhambra. Damned silly ambition, if you ask me. But look at you now.'

'I just said that,' I say. Jesus, he can be a pain sometimes. I nod, then stand up to feed the most likely machines. Watch them flash. Try to change the subject.

'What about dreams? I mean the sleeping kind?'

He doesn't answer.

He's standing behind me and about to launch into one of his tales, I can tell. He screws up his untrained eyebrows tinged with dandruff from his crewcut. He doesn't care. Never was fashionable, Dad. He's trying to scratch his war-grazed ankle, in the process rubbing worn shoe against worn shoe. The dye has come out onto his white sports socks. He's got glazed eyes again, sort of pale ebony, and I know what is coming. No point in trying to stop it. But still I do. Well, it's in my nature.

'Look Dad, I love you, but let's not plunge into all the nostalgia stuff. I don't believe it's worthwhile any more than you do deep down. Besides, it's bloody boring.'

He hasn't been listening. 'You used to shut yourself inside our pantry,' he tells me.

'No more than a few metres across,' I tell him, because he's forgotten that bit.

He ignores me and continues. 'You little sod. Shouting that all who wouldn't believe would be damned, and letting all the bloody street know that you were a member of the Girls' Brigade and believed whatever the hell you believed. You could have become a bloody missionary.'

'I remember,' I mutter. Not much I can add, except 'I was only a fucking child.'

So I put more tokens into the slit on the bandit and carry on thinking. The past is no good. Gone. Merely dreams. Grooms with piles, mill-boys, hedgerow gooseberries, rickets, and scratches on knees caused by apple-scrumping, and uncontrollable limbs writhing in rags in corners of kitchens. Gone.

I'm starting to shudder. It's an old feeling. I always let my imagination gallop too far, with me and my hormones in tow. But I'm entitled. Everyone's entitled. I'm fucked by the past.

'Ok, so I'm slightly stupid. A numb bugger,' I say irritably. This is a bad move, because it makes the old guy feel superior. Important.

And I've still to get him home so that I can escape and live in the bloodshot madness of town for a while. An hour. Maybe four. I know what I'm doing. Or thought I did. But now I've given him carte-blanche to let his philosophy flow freer than Saxo. Hell of a bad day, is Monday.

We stand by a machine in the shadow of a doorway proclaiming in red letters that non-smoking is mandatory, insert, in turn, ten coins into a slot, dropping three cherries and one lemon, knowing the procedure. Computerised music plays. To Hold or not to Hold, that's the question. It's not important. I've gone home and smoked roll-ups instead of preferred ready-rolls on a Monday before, and been fucked without the price of a cider in my purse. Doesn't matter.

'This is important stuff,' Dad says wisely, inserting another 10p. He's still got one leg planted in the past. He's in a sort of old mucus area. He hasn't even noticed that I've won three pounds and my tongue is hanging out for sustenance. He's getting old.

'You had a boyfriend once,' he's telling me.

'Or two?' I suggest.

'They used to come to the door for you,' he says.

'Then they used to drop me, when they saw you peering through the curtains, Dad.'

Why am I doing this to him? The old sod is confused enough.

'We are both talking shit,' I say, then shrug.

He's still only half-listening and shrugs too.

'Remember that blind date you had, Laura? Some lad supposed to meet you outside of the Odeon and take you to see *The Sound of Music*?'

Now he's irritating me.

'The boy's name was Gill, and the film was *El Cid*.'

I'm wondering how he manages to remember that old chestnut. But it's not important.

Dad, as he often does, is becoming annoyed by the vagueness of his memories.

'The boy took one look at you waiting in the foyer, then hurried off rattling his car keys. You told me,' he says.

'That's a nothing from the past, Dad,' I say defensively. What is he trying to do to me? 'The past. All gone. The boy was embarrassed and his legs were obviously paining him. Sort of rickety, if I remember rightly.'

'You mean he had rickets, lass? They don't exist in this country. Not now.'

'No,' I tell him quietly. 'No, they don't.'

I wonder why I feel uneasy about the rattlings of an old man's mind and God, I could kill for a lager. It's the rickets comment that's getting to me. Thomas had rickets.

'Dad, laugh if you want, but I'm having strange dreams. Sort of misty.' I try to explain. 'They're real. I don't know how to describe them, but they're real. Sometimes I wake up in the middle of the night and wonder what I'm doing here. Like I'm in the wrong time. Like I'm something from a way-out library book.'

Here I am pouring my heart out to him, and he's looking at me blankly. It's an act. It's got to be.

'Like I feel I'm going mad,' I continue, 'but I know I'm not. It's difficult to explain.'

The old man is studiously offering me an inferiority trip with the well practised perplexity of his gaze. I don't know why he does that, but it doesn't work. Not anymore. Time to change the subject.

'Want any more custard creams?' I ask.

He doesn't answer. Maybe I'm expecting too much of him, viewing him through biased eyes. But he could be just as confused as I am. I know all about confusion. Great clouds of it burst unexpectedly.

'Your brain cells are dying and you don't know it,' I say nastily.

Hell of an awkward thing to deal with, is confusion.

'I'm asking if you think I'm going mad, Dad?'

At first he doesn't answer. Simply scowls at me. The scowl tells me no such question should be asked. Or it could be my imagination again.

'Nothing wrong with dreams, lass,' he says at last. His slightly hunched shoulders shudder, inside his faded, green jacket. 'Trouble is,' he adds, 'they're mostly nightmares.'

His expression is now genuinely puzzled. He asks me what date it is and grinds his dentures together when I tell him.

'It's coming around again,' he says suddenly. 'THAT date. No reason to remind you.'

No reason at all. I know what he's thinking about. Even if he doesn't realise how pointless the ritual is. The coming Friday and Christ, it flies around, is June the sixteenth, the date of our visits to Mum's graveside. The torture. When he drags me through his guilt. Don't know why he feels so guilty outliving her. Someone has to go first.

The ritual of striding through dry leaves, of ignoring condoms in the litter baskets, half-eaten sandwiches on paint-chipped memorial benches and dead or drying flowers. A time for nodding towards the ever-lurking vicar with the large feet and the lisp. That man is always silent. Either a genius or an embarrassed bed-wetter, Dad reckons.

Then we'll have to mutter what we can remember of The Lord's Prayer over the grave, then leave geraniums. After that Dad will tell me to fuck off and head for The Rose and Crown.

A nightmare, I'm thinking. The old man is always toffed up in his best herringbone jacket for such occasions and he'll be tanked up with whisky, of course.

'It makes sense,' he once told me.

I know where he hides the residue. Beneath the vests in his underwear drawer, for following day consumption. A day of self-loathing, no doubt. The whole thing is becoming bloody tedious. Not that the knowledge of his stupid secret matters. It wouldn't be a wise move to steal his booze or even water it down, I worked that out long ago.

There'd be hell to pay.

I pull my thoughts back to the present, to the sound of the clattering one-armed-bandits. No point in getting depressed about Friday until Friday. So I fasten my coat and tell Dad it's time to go home, pretending I haven't noticed him absently scratching his balls through his corduroy, egg-stained trousers. His mind is clouding faster than I thought it would. Surprise. And I'm feeling bloody minded and angry, and don't understand why, 'cos I never understand why. Time to try and get the old fool's mind working again. Duty, I suppose. Change the subject.

'When you keep your imagination in tow you're a good lass,' he yawns. 'Pity you married such a fucking idiot.'

I didn't hear him complain at the time. I didn't hear him say anything on my wedding day, but merely caught a glimpse of him through the corner of a bloodshot iris fidgeting on the edge of a chair, button-hole carnation wilting. He was sipping free Australian champagne in between gulps of his privately purchased Guinness.

Time to be honest.

'When Rodney and I married, I loved him,' I tell him, guiding him out of the amusement arcade into the summer drizzle. 'You don't like him because he's quiet. Introverted.'

'Secretive,' he grunts. 'And what does he do when he's out of your sight? Chats up shop assistants,' he adds abruptly, and looks startled as if he's just discovered the secret of life. 'Thou shouldn't trust him lass.'

I don't tell him that until boredom set in Rod was good in bed. But he must know the crack, surely. I'm not sure if I mean what I'm saying to him and not sure if he's listening. He's never listened before. He cocks his head to one side, looks like a chicken who glimpsed the chopper. Again, he drags his thoughts back from elsewhere. I glimpse that in the tick of his left eye. Then he's off again like a rambling child.

'You can't teach the working class to suck eggs, Alice,' and I can't follow his logic. If there is any.

So I ignite a cigarette and say, 'I wish you'd stop calling me by my mother's name. It makes you sound like an incestuous, dirty old man. My name is Laura. Laura Christine. Remember?'

Dad scratches the freckled flesh of what remains of his weathered forehead. He's following my thoughts, I know it, and trying to retrieve the word incestuous from his seventy year old memory bank. He fails but finds something else to talk about.

'When you was young there was always meat on the table.'

'Don't tell me,' I reply. 'You're talking about 'Daddy's going to bring me a rabbit's skin'.'

I know the nightmare of nursery rhymes. Always felt a compassion for Humpty Dumpty.

'And I bought you crab apples,' Dad is saying.

'Crab apples?'

'Yes, crab apples, amongst other things, and you were never short of something to read. I made sure of that.'

I'm not concerned with his last sentence. I'm still thinking about crab apples. Their sour, woody taste, the scent of captured rain seeping into blackening pips, whilst field vermin trudge through nearby rotting bracken. Did I ever eat them? I can't remember. But Thomas, if Thomas existed, ate this fruit. I know that. I can feel on my tongue what he felt, tainting his spittle. Time to think. Who the hell was Thomas? Thomas the imagined? The imaginable, touching the muslin of my sleeve? No answer because the whole bloody thing is ridiculous.

Yet I can feel him. The flesh of his fingers on mine. The touch of the non-existent. Feel the juice cooling the flush of his cheeks. Hear him describe its pungency to me as I wipe sweat from his buttocks. All romanticism of course. I've got to shrug myself back to reality, because there's nowhere else to go. Nowhere.

'When you were eight years old I went out and bought you some sandals. White ones,' Dad is saying when I pull myself back to listening. 'With rubber soles and two strong buckles. Workmanship. They lasted you for two years. So did that material stuff I got for you. Went to the newsagent's every Friday evening to get you that stuff, I did.'

I don't like to hurt him, but I always do, wondering what life would be like without honesty. Too big a question.

'There's more to life than rabbit stew and comics and shoes,' I say, wishing he wouldn't keep bringing up his age-distorted memories. It's Monday morning and my tongue is screaming for diversion. He should know that. There's no point in arguing with me. That he does know. No point in saying anything really. Flesh of his flesh? When did that ever matter? I'm on a downer. I won't say any more. Grab the old man by his left elbow. We shuffle through the mock Victorian precinct, smell the fresh, unleaded paintwork and the odour of disinfected buses and the pigeon pecked take-aways and listen to the other birds pecking on the peckings of sparrows.

I take Dad to his home, help him take his jacket off, settle him in front of a quiz on TV because that's what I'm supposed to do. I hand him his slippers then ask him.

'Know anything about Foster's mill? About the broken paving stones, and so on? About its history, maybe?'

He doesn't answer. So I clean his sink, flush a silverfish down the drain, flush out the remnants of carrots and specks of dandruff. Watch them flow anti-clockwise, then wonder why I bother. Father's got a sweat on. Doesn't look well. Some sort of fever.

'I haven't got any onions to go with my liver for lunch,' he calls, as his urine flows in the bathroom. 'Haven't got anything.'

'Foster's,' I growl at him, 'I'm asking about Foster's mill. The place is lodged in my mind. You must recall the bloody place. I know you do. Tell me you remember. You remember every place and every bloody thing. You keep telling me so.'

He says nothing.

I enter his lounge and look at the porcelain cats on his mantlepiece. They haven't been dusted for months. I know that. But they're watching. Always watching.

No point in worrying. I can hear a tap dripping, somewhere. Time I escaped. I've got a thirst on. Time to mutter goodbye and head for the Ramsden Ark, and its beers, wines and spirits. That's what it states on the sign over the door, and I believe it. Nothing much else to believe, I'm thinking, fastening my jacket. I need a drink. Excuses, excuses. Time to escape. And I'm good at that. Well, everybody has their own special talent.

Chapter 4

I'm alone, except for women carelessly dragging tartan shopping bags on wheels, dog excrement spinning round and round on worn rubber and leaving trails like snails. There are brown and white pigeons cooing on top of concrete lamp-posts, occasionally swooping on imaginary food, and a postman with a designer haircut doing a double shift and whistling something unrecognisable.

There's no-one stopping me and asking how my kids are, and looking disappointed when I can't come up with things like 'They've got leukaemia and rotten teeth.' There's nobody talking in my ear, meaning things, and the town-trapped air feels deceptively fresh. The towering, once grey buildings have, over the years, acquired their own special hue, and u.p.v.c. double glazing bought from men with sensible, correctly knotted ties and special discount forms. Their cavity-filled walls hold off the toxicants like the walls of experienced wombs.

Peace at last. Except for Thomas whispering from afar. But I can't make out the words. Should have no problem. No problem. I'm heading for the Jug and Bottle, to the continuation of the rotting of my liver, as a social worker would put it, if I was stupid enough to have one. But I haven't now. And why should I have one if I'm going off my trolley? Excuses again. I'm good at those.

The sign above the swing door shines like veins soaked in alcohol, casting its shadow over boys in jeans, pink raincoats, stray cats, business suits and plastic carrier bags stuffed with frozen fish and potato waffles. The town is spotted with areas of scaffolding, like an old dot to dot book, and long-legged lads with thin dogs. It's always like that in Huddersfield.

Toddlers are being dragged along pavements by denim clad mothers smoking Benson and Hedges. But there is still oxygen here, I tell myself. Freedom. Not everyone can be as manic as I am. There are worn, stone steps leading to the old carved door of the pub, worn down by generations of boots and shoes. I've got stilettos on, move soberly across the faded carpet to the oak of the public bar. I accept vodka on my tonsils and a weak smile from a Jamaican wearing a large gold watch and a sixties Beatles badge. I watch him lean against the juke-box wondering if what is said about the size of black men's penises is true. If it was, well it wouldn't matter to me. I've got past that. So I throw peanuts into my mouth and try to imagine the protein, taste the grit. It's not easy to get away from this sex thing, and I start to think that my knickers might not be too clean. And what would the ambulancemen think, should I, with a shit-stain in my knickers, have a heart-attack or get run over by a haulage truck? It's possible. Always possible. Supposing they saw my underwear? Daft thought really, but that's the way I've been brought up. Conditioning. There's always trouble with conditioning.

I'm wondering if I've missed something. Like the meaning of life. I can't come up with an answer. My mind is ticking over, and I'm wondering over what? I must have missed something. Like the meaning of life. These are ordinary thoughts. It must be an ordinary day.

I spy ex-postman, narrow-hipped Phil, moving proudly towards the bar. Phil of the charisma, who could sit with a pint of lager and drone on about the need for strong trade unions without sending people scurrying towards the door, and who now expects he'll become the manager of the local D.I.Y.

Fat chance. All charm and no practicality. If he assembled a rabbit hutch he'd forget to put a door in it, or if he built a display caravan out of matchsticks it would probably self-ignite. Still, he's always got his damned postman's pension to fall back on, and boy when he falls he falls. He's a man with friends. Friends who don't drink with him. Odd that, but who cares. Money is money.

He peers through the bottom of his bifocals and nods to me in recognition, as he slides his unexpectedly calloused hand across the lavender polished bar, towards my pink, laundry soaked digits. I like him in a perverse kind of way. He has a sort of basic knowledge I can accept without anger, and a twinkle that lights up the green of his eye at unexpected times. On the surface this pillock is a Mills and Boon character, but he's got more depth inside his head. Knows all about the hang-ups of skint housewives. Keeps telling me so, and bragging. But little boys are always little boys.

His adenoids are swollen, the result of mumps whilst bedecked in striped pyjamas and pom-pom slippers, perhaps. His shoes are tan coloured, old Italian style, and he has a new gold ring on the third finger of his right hand. A poser.

'It was a gift from a friend,' he kept telling everybody, implying, with a wink, that it was something more. So I analyse him, because I'm always analysing. He's ageing by balding, in an unconscious, desperate way, and has a gilded pendant strung around his neck, like some failed apprentice hangman's noose.

'Hello Princess,' he says to me, sipping his brandy. 'How's your dad?'

Then he raises an eyebrow, questioning. Remembers he gave me his address and asked me to visit him to partake of breakfast, last Tuesday, that he pressed a knee against mine under a beer stained table during a domino match at The Fleece.

He has a scar on his chin, strange eyes and this permanent smile saying he is destined for higher things, like aluminium ladders and stigmatas caused by half-inch brass nails. Yet he smells of something akin to the stench of dead horses. It is all to be put down to my imagination. I get a fleeting feeling that he could be Mark. I've had a lot of this stuff floating through my head lately. But Mark is only a shadow. Part of a dream, mixing with my indigestion, sauntering through a fog to an unknown kitchen to drop stolen cabbages at my feet. He's unreal, I'm telling myself, yet again. A face first imagined while I lay in the sweat of home and clutched, half-dozing, at candy striped sheets. He's a 'No big deal', a nothing. Like my muslin-shirted brother, Thomas, with the flyaway hair. Neither of them existed, for God's sake. Maybe I'm simply suffering a vitamin deficiency, I'm thinking. No boy sucks on apple skins below spiders' webs woven around low, rotting beams. No second-rate groom fumbles and fucks dying boy's sisters in sculleries. Except in third rate fiction. And that's what the figures in my nightmares are, a collection of no-ones. Just a fucking nuisance.

'So, what are you thinking about?' asks Phil.

So I tell him 'Nothing at all,' and sip my vodka and coke, dropping my change into the chasm of a pocket in my jacket, letting it mingle with the week's bus tickets and stubbed out cigarettes. I need all the change I can accumulate, because I've got to be practical, got to buy a squash for a Reader's Digest recipe, sanitary towels in case of occurrences, and thin sliced bread. Supermarket economy grade. Cheaper, and it lasts longer. Oh yes, I know all the tricks. Should do by now. Even if it is a bloody pain in the neck. No matter how Rod keeps moaning, I can still handle the grocery budget.

I lubricate my throat with brandy and Britvic and try to forget that I've married a stingy soul with dandruff and varicose veins, a car-grease and hedge-trimming man. I'm feeling quietly aggressive now, because drink always makes me feel quietly aggressive. But that's alright, because I haven't slit anyone's throat yet. Don't quite know why, unless I simply haven't got the balls.

I've had the kids with Rod, for heaven's sake. And more. Listened to his scratched sixties-type records. Fried his eggs. Had orgasms to coincide with his and feigned some. I've had him, and humped and groaned. Know the colour of his eyes. That he reckons he's got aristocratic blood in him somewhere. Know the cut of his Terylene trousers. Know all about men like him. Their unrealised vulnerability. That they mean well, and spend all their life with a disappointed expression on their faces. And that I'm a nasty piece of work for even thinking thoughts like these. That's what Rod would say if he could read my mind.

My preoccupation with words like periods and ozone worries him. As does the fluff and the occasional skeleton of a fly trapped in the grey of a web behind the toilet pedestal. I know that he aspires to owning an avocado bathroom suite. That he thinks that everybody should. This side of him makes me uneasy.

Not a safe line of thought for me to follow. I try to suck the remains of vodka soaked peanuts from underneath my thinning dentures.

'So what are you up to these days, Phil?' I ask, shrugging myself back to the presence of mock-brass horseshoes, nicotine-stained mirrors and elbows on lager-polished tables. I've got to do this. The preoccupation I've got with this dream thing is doing my head in. No point in dwelling on the pupils of the eyes of the fictitious

Mark, or mentally tracing the twist of his mouth caused by a fall from a horse.

I get caught up in things like that. Mad games that only mad people get caught up in, then spot too late and lose their kids to brat catchers. I have to pretend to be sane to keep my kids the same way. Even tread the rough cobbles on the slow road to tranquillisers. I want to piss again. Every time I have a drink and am expected to take part in a conversation, I always want to piss. Phil pushes fingers into the depths of the right pocket of his new, maroon jacket. This guy always was a fan of new clothes. That shows his insecurity. His need to bluff. He's still blowing smoke-rings towards the anaglypta of the low ceiling. Says he'll buy me another packet of peanuts and a brandy. Unlike Rod, he doesn't tell me the price and that somebody has to pay for it. I went to school with Phil, I remember. Remember he could never tie the laces of his plimsolls, and was at that time too serious to attract.

'I've heard all about your father on the grapevine,' he says. 'That his teeth are gone and he's not very well.'

'What the hell do you expect me to say about that bloody statement?' I ask him.

Then I smile sickly-sweetly to try and catch him off guard, and tell myself that there are plimsoll-clad plonkers like him born every minute, like ants on a dung heap. I ease my toes out of black, slingback shoes and glance at the corns, and watch the flickering of the fluorescent lighting above the head of a guy fingering his unfashionable ponytail then picking at his fingernails and pretending, with an expression of boredom, to be the ideal barman. All the staff here are on the make and I'm feeling tired, drained.

'Buy me another drink or not,' I tell Phil. 'It's what we're here for isn't it?' I'm being a bitch. A slightly tipsy bitch. Or am I? 'Just get me another drink Phil.' I sigh.

I don't want him to get the idea that I'm only here to meet him. The last thing I want now is a bit of cock or some man thinking I do, I never was unfaithful in the whole of my life. Besides, I'm struggling with a preoccupation. I've still got this picture of Mark in my mind. The bloody silly dream boy. I've got to shake it off. This is

Monday, like all Mondays. I'm here to meet supposedly confiding friends, crimson-dressed Sonia, who likes to hint about the abortion she had sixteen years ago and, with a shake of her head, says in bemusement, when she's had a few drinks, that she can't quite shake off the guilt. Then routinely goes on to talk about a facelift she is planning. Then sighs, smiling like a Persian cat, when I say I'd gladly kill for flawless skin like hers. All bunkum. But it's expected on our mornings out.

Then there's second-hand Beth, who sometimes sulks into her handbag under the pretence of searching for non-existent tissues, and talks about knitting patterns everytime there's a lull in the conversation. But she's a good friend. I know she is. I look at my watch. They'll be here, once they've escaped from the orange glow of the morning bingo sessions at the Mecca.

Sonia has been dropping hints that she'd like me to shorten one of her London bought skirts, and wants to ask my advice about the efficiency of her new man-made diaphragm. She's warned me about this on the phone. Fat chance. What she really means is that she wants to brag about her sex life and bingo wins. Lucky bitch. But she can't impress me. I used to go to bingo myself.

'I won the bloody game once, I recall,' I'm saying to Phil, without any previous reference. 'That day I teetered home legless with a Chinese take-away and a smile on my stupid face. That's if anyone can teeter home legless. I don't remember much more about it except that Rod stormed off down the dog track. It was a one off.'

He is yawning boredly. 'Your old father's no better then?' he asks. He's quite considerate really. It's a technique he's perfected to aid him in his seductions. He doesn't like anything that goes deeper than that. Just likes to have fun. Well what prematurely retired postman wouldn't?

'You know the old man's going down the drain,' I say, looking at the clock and suddenly feeling bored and old. 'You've met him often enough and talked to him enough to be able to take that on board. You must have. Be careful you don't go on to say something to hurt my feelings.'

But only fools like me are stupid enough to admit to having

feelings when they've had a few. If you do, the ale-captured audience stop fidgeting and stare, expect you to burst into tears and go away disappointed when you don't.

Phil's uncomfortable. Starts talking trade unions and politics. Switches his attention span from one subject to another even swifter than I do, occasionally dropping breath-freshening tablets into the healthy pink of his mouth.

He's looking at the printed pattern of strangely shaped leaves on my black and white blouse, trying to decide if I've got tits or not. But bottle fed babies are like that. He's stumbling his fingers on the table to the sound of an ancient Johnny Cash record selected from the juke-box by the landlord. Phil's gold ring gleams in the amber reflection of the lager.

I swallow down a barley wine, thinking Monday is benefit collection day so it's bound to be hellish. Then Sonia sways her hips through the smoke of the bar to the sound of some early drunk's wolf-whistle and some old biddy demanding an eleven a.m. shepherd's pie, pub lunch. I know the old girl. It's Gloria of the speckled face who keeps losing her purse and cadging drinks. Can't stand the bitch. There's nothing worse than deceit, I'm thinking.

Before she came into money, Sonia used to tread the pavements around here, frequented the Kirkgate pub. I know that. So what? She never actually kissed the Johns. She used to boast about that. Bloody stupid job for any woman to take on, anyway, even if she is a 'good sort' and helps folk out.

She's got Hungarian roots and principles. I understand that. Hell, I know what it's like to struggle through shit. Even understand her recently acquired obsession with bingo. A bit behind the times with their obsessions, are foreigners, right down to the third generation. She can't impress me. She's nearly fifty years old, ten years older than me, and hasn't got a single corn on her toes, she says.

Some people have all the luck. Some people make you sick and uneasy.

She's got Beth in tow. Beth of the sensible shoes and tentative shuffle. Beth of the fuzzy hair. Always follows on behind, does Beth. Behind her friends, behind her husband with his unlit pipe who looks like he's crawled out of the arches. Behind her children.

And she always carries her red, telescopic umbrella just in case.

'How's your hubby's book going on then?' I ask Beth, envying her expertly hand-knitted sweater with the little black cats on the front. 'He's pretending to write something about the First World War isn't he?'

She sits down and pulls her pleated skirt down over her knees to hide a blemish.

God, I can be a bitch sometimes. She looks uncomfortable and says I shouldn't have said that. She waits for her wine and lemonade and spreads her wide buttocks across the red leatherette and blushes. Then tells me defensively that her husband's brainchild hasn't reached the white of the paper yet but is all there in his mind.

'That's the way writers work,' she explains unconvincingly.

Nothing else to say on the subject.

Her unpainted lips are drawn tight in the ensuing silence. She doesn't believe what she's saying anymore than anybody else does. The feller she's married to is a failed con man. She knows it and protects him like a mother hen fearful of compulsory sterilisation. She shuffles her feet again beneath the wrought iron legs of the lager-stained table, then pretends to read the newly purchased magazine on her lap.

Sonia looks away from the guy she's flirting with to flash me a disapproving glance.

'Now then Laura, each to their own,' she says demurely.

'You should leave the oppressive bugger, Beth,' I say.

Beth scowls and tells me quietly that I don't know what love is. Then searches through the compartments of her blue, plastic purse because it's her round.

She seems worried. Must have put most of her housekeeping money into the slots of a flashing bandit in the bingo hall. Must have been searching for three triple bars. Must have been.

The stone inside the throbbing mass of my head softens a little. We're all human and stupidly hopeful. Got to be.

'I suppose we've all got our faults,' I mutter to myself softly. But the voice doesn't sound like mine.

Now I've made Beth feel miserable, and I feel guilty because I don't feel guilty.

Phil looks like he's about to fall asleep.

'I love my man,' Beth says, with uncharacteristic defensiveness.

'I'll stick by what I say.' I'm tired. Should be too tired to bother. For a moment Phil stirs and grins, says one should always stick by principles. Beth pretends not to hear, and Sonia grimaces, says I couldn't be more of a shit if I tried.

'You're having a bad day.' Phil nods to me knowingly.

'Tell me something worth knowing,' I grumble.

He whispers into my ear that Beth thinks she's in love and registers his amusement in the curving of his cheeks and the folding of his arms. Now's the time to speak. I've had an elephant's ration of courage juice so I do. Well, what in hell have I got to lose?

'Men think that a loving woman is someone who can suck his cock whilst smoking a cigarette and at the same time mop up his vomit from the cushion floor. No big deal. She's expected to be convinced that he's some sort of hero.'

'So where do you fit into all this, little Miss Smarty Pants?' he asks.

'I don't know,' I say. 'But I'm no lesbian, if that's what you're thinking, and if I was would it matter?'

Phil shakes his head. 'So here endeth your lecture before it starteth,' he says, and throws in an extra scowl for good measure. Then he grins again because he's well into the warmth of his sixth whisky.

Beth peers into the sunshine in her glass and says, in a quiet voice, that her husband John has promised to love and cherish and that she believes him, because she's supposed to. And forgets that it was only last week that she asked all and sundry and the launderette assistant and anyone she spied with a Filofax and popular breed of dog to help her to escape from him and move into a sheltered housing flat with her deckchairs and pot-plants. Oh, yes, I remember all that, and the scented blemish remover she applied inexpertly to disguise her black eye.

Beth is a real trouper, I'm thinking. And wishing I wasn't thinking. And I wonder how inadequate inadequacy gets, and does it extend to the shape of her toenails? Sonia is standing beside our table with her stomach held in by controlled breathing, because she doesn't like being out of the limelight. She's trying to catch my eye. No need. I've seen her.

'You managed to get away from Rod and the housework this morning then, Laura?' she asks in a purring voice not expecting an answer.

So I tell her to fuck off.

She looks appealingly around our party and balances a tray laden with drinks vulnerably and precariously on the north of her abdomen. Sonia is no amateur when it comes to the art of manipulation.

'Still having strange dreams then, Laura? What was it? Something to do with horses and typhoid and things?'

I don't answer.

'You really should seek some help,' she adds. 'I was driven absolutely crazy by an uncle with similar problems. Though obviously he was far crazier than you are.'

I'm concentrating on watching her, trying to make her feel as uneasy as she makes me feel. She's wearing a new eye shadow and still spouting something, finishing her every sentence, by purring 'Darling'. Almost a Hollywood thing.

With this, at least, she's out of date. The right thing to console myself with. Because it looks like the kind of morning when everyone in the civilised world is sauntering around trying to needle everybody else.

My fault. I probably started it, spread it from here to Siberia. I'm sober enough to realise that.

Sonia is a winner these days. Dressed in credit card silver. I'd give a hell of a lot to be in her shoes. Ready and able to bail out the boyfriend she's shacked up with. Him with his love of gambling.

Beth catches Sonia's wink of disapproval at my bitchiness.

Phil is playing footsy with me, saying, 'What is this dream thing all about then?' The leather of his toe-caps touching the plastic of mine. His breath reaches my forehead through the smoke.

I don't answer. I go to the toilet again, drop yellow wine and cool my cheeks against the tiles smelling of dettol, and ease off my shoes again. God these shoes hurt. They're tightening, darkening, alien.

I hear the rattling of wagons on Whit walk, the giggles of children and cheers of 'Thomas'. The floor feels cold. Cold.

Slowly, my mind swirling between flashing images and greyness, I switch round, breath deeper, hear a friendly voice. Not in the closet, but in the scullery.

Mark.

I'm teetering a little, can't understand why, but push open the closet door, and slowly make my way across the uneven flags of our weed-nurturing yard, push through the string of newly washed shirts and follow my nose to the smell of mutton stew in the kitchen.

Mark looks angry, is stiff in his best livery, his face held rigid. He doesn't even say good-day, and obviously has no inclination to stay a while. Not like the last time I saw him, in the stables, where he pressed me up against the door and lifted my skirt. The bolt dug into my side all the time he fucked me, pounding his body against mine. I still have the bruise under my ribs.

'It's that Thomas,' he growls. 'Spouting his mouth off on a day such as this. Encouraged by that fellow Bert. Outside the chapel.' He spits angrily. 'Why there of all places? Trouble makers. Everybody knows I come here. It reflects on me.' He smacks his thighs in frustration. 'You've got to go out and stop him,' he demands.

I'm still dizzy. And my long grey skirt feels cumbersome, too long.

Mark's voice isn't close enough. All wrong.

Everything's wrong.

'Well,' he asks. 'What are you going to do about it?'

'I don't know,' I find myself saying.

'Stop him,' he says. 'For both your sakes. Stop him.'

There's the sound of a door being rattled, the odour of burgers. The sound of Sonia's voice.

'Laura, I hope you're not spewing up in there.'

A mumble, 'Coming,' from me. My knees off the floor. A hand on the aluminium latch. Mine. Then the sight of her cherry lips and new Lycra sweater. 'Darling, I thought you'd died in there.'

I follow her back into the pseudo oak bar, still teetering.

The jukebox is playing loudly. One of those crazy Irishmen who've never seen Ireland is in again, tapping cigs and trying by telling jokes he's heard in the pub across the road to prove his superiority. I shake my head. Come back to reality surprisingly easily, and hear someone mention the Second World War, the second most popular topic of this time of day after social security.

I've got to test out my brain. I mention Hitler and that even that bastard must have been a child and pushed a hoop along the cobbles one Saturday afternoon when men dozed on verandas dangling braces. Then feel annoyed with myself.

My mouth is dry. No one understands what I'm talking about.

The record follows its given grooves. Blurts out something about a holiday seduction.

Beth, by some miracle, has managed to finance a round of double rum to go with the economy wine. She proudly swallows her's down in two gulps, because she's seen Sonia do the same and thinks it's expected. Then, with a wink at me, she offers me a packet of Camel cigarettes because I once told her I'd read in an advert in the Sunday Telegraph that Camels were considered to be the height of sophistication.

'Beth you must never listen to me,' I slur. 'Never.'

Then she natters on again. About how the cigarettes were extra toasted. And about how much she loved her uncle, who for months hid a cancer under grey blankets in a daffodil scented hospice.

I imagine his dentures floating in Dettol in a plastic beaker on his bedside cabinet, the printed, rose-covered Get Well cards signed 'You probably don't remember me, but my name's Charlie' arranged around his unopened packets of Jaffa Cakes.

She tells anyone within listening distance about the primrose-coloured walls on her uncle's ward, and about the wide-hipped nurse who wiped dribble from his chin. She can get very sentimental, can

Beth. Then she starts showing signs of itching, and scratches the freckles on her arm.

She orders another lager from a barmaid who's collecting glasses, and looks startled because she's got the nerve.

She shouts to all and sundry that the National Health Service is shit and that propped up in a proper geriatric ward, her uncle's tongue would never have fallen out into a Kleenex tissue while he sneezed and she watched.

No-one here states that they would ever wish to know that.

'Enough is enough,' is the consensus of sighs.

Sonia moves her right hip and it touches the thigh of a stool-based philosophy student. She slips the fiver she owes me under a beer mat, blinking against her contact lens. She catches my eye and we giggle, because there's not much else to do, and glance around at the blank faces at the bar, for the same reason.

Phil is still leaning against the bar, telling jokes he got from the Beano and the National Geographic. Which joke depends on the cut of the cardigans in his company.

He buys me half a lager. No surprise to me. Remarks on the curls in my hair and asks me if he can fuck me on his judo mat.

So I think of the consequences and ask, 'Supposing I say yes, and supposing you did? Then what?'

There's no answer.

I get out as sedately as I can. Breathing in the onion-type relishes of office workers' take-aways on the way. Time to move to the Rose and Crown. Do the rounds looking for cheap beer. Habit.

I'm wandering, supposedly window-shopping, staring at men's denim clad bottoms, wondering how my son has fared in the gymnastic exhibition he took part in today. Or was it yesterday? I don't know. I should know. I'm a bloody mother for fuck's sake. I'm feeling sorry for myself.

Phil's footsteps come up behind me, probably because he's got nothing else to do, as his transient girlfriend hasn't turned up for a lunch-time date.

Oh, what the hell does it matter?

He catches me and walks beside me, sucking peppermints. There is a silence, got to break it.

'My dad is beyond redemption,' I say, as we slope in the best way we can along the pavement.

Well, you've got to have something to talk about, and anyway I'm feeling lost.

Phil hesitates before answering then says. 'Perhaps you need a good fuck.' Because he thinks he's expected to, I suppose.

'It's nothing to do with that,' I say, keeping control. 'Nothing at all.'

The sky is a vague grey, tinge of a teatime pink. There's a chill.

Funny, I've never noticed white pigeons swooping the threatening-to-rumble sky before. Nor smelt sour apples on the plastic doors of the shops in the precinct. Nor felt so light-headed. The sound of the traffic fades into a rough purring. And Phil's voice becomes almost a whisper. His fingers, wrapped around my right elbow, don't feel like his anymore. There's an eerie firmness in this grip, so I realise I must be sloshed. No other explanation for it. So now I can talk crazy.

'I keep having strange dreams, did I tell you?'

'I should think you've told every other fucker in the world darling,' he says.

I ignore this remark. 'Sometimes, when I close my eyes, I hear a strange mumbling inside my head. Really hot. Like something is burning, like somebody is burning, then the people I feel moving around me aren't what they seem to be, aren't real. Like you right now.'

'Me? Who the chuff am I then?'

May as well carry on. 'I don't know. You look so familiar, and yet I feel you're someone else I met a handful of times. Someone harmless.'

'Oh, thanks a lot,' he says.

'I've decided I've got to work this out,' I slur. 'It's something to do with the boy in the textile mill.'

'You mean something like a haunting?'

I shake my shoulders. 'What I mean is I need a brandy.'

'Now you're talking sense,' he says agreeably.

'But no talk of judo mats,' I warn.

'Agreed,' he smiles. 'No talk of judo mats.'

We make it into the Rose and Crown and slump onto the new red upholstery.

Phil is watching me curiously, almost soberly. Second wind, no doubt. Says it's nice to get me alone for once.

'Look, Phil, I'm not going home with you. Now what shall we talk about? The NUM?'

'Don't mock me,' he frowns. 'Workers are important, and I know I'll win you round and get you to go home with me one day, that's no problem.' He sniffs. He presses an unusually large hand on mine. 'You'll come around to my way of thinking one day. You ought to try and stop living inside your own head like a rat in a trap and wasting time with pub morons uttering meaningless one liners. Loneliness, that's your problem.'

'Kettle calling the frying pan?'

'Could be,' he tells me. 'Try me, you won't regret it.'

Wish I knew why I can't bring myself to. Why I have to keep my distance when I don't want to.

I lean across the table close enough to see the light playing on his blonde stubble. 'I think you're bluffing.'

'Never, Princess,' he says, shaking his head.

Chapter 5

Someone walks through the mock-Victorian door and there's a chill, a familiar, unexplained scent.

It's Dad. In the pullover he's insisted on wearing without a break for the past three months. The one with the rabbit motif. I know it before he turns his head and I turn mine to meet his gaze.

It won't do will this. This is driving me crazy. He's pretending to look around the place like an innocent searching for salvation, and fooling no-one. Like the old, Methodist bastard that he is. He's grinding his dentures together, preoccupied for a moment with memories slowly enveloping him, then spots my home perm and saunters towards me, hands in his pockets, to show he still has masculinity, the expected but aged swagger. I pretend not to notice.

'Trouble at home,' he whispers, finally getting near enough to me to whisper in my ear.

'What kind of trouble?' I ask loudly. And I'm wondering which home? His or mine?

He shrugs his shoulders and parades a wooden smile, because he feels he's supposed to.

He's sheepish.

Not like Dad's usual behaviour, this. He normally doesn't miss an opportunity to spout anything out to anyone. He loves to spin his philosophy around denim-clad shoulders, around tightly clutched, denim shopping bags, and thin dogs on makeshift leads. He believes in free speech.

I'm thinking for the umpteenth time that this is not normal. But what is nowadays?

He's shifting the weight on his legs uneasily, complaining about feverish sweats. His hooded eyes dart around shiftily.

'Come on then, you old bugger,' I say. 'What the hell have you been up to now?'

He's got to have been up to something. I know the body language.

'You're not a closet flasher are you?'

It's a stupid question and I know it. Phil glares at me. Dad's body stench is caught in the heat of the silence. I'd never noticed his smell before. Perhaps because it evolved slowly and I never wanted to know.

'Well, come on, what are you talking about?'

And he says in suspiciously sober, yet slurred, words, that I don't care about him, that I don't remember the homemade jigsaws that he carved out for me on the kitchen table when things were in short supply.

'Never got a word of thanks from you,' he says.

Next could come the tears.

By now I'm pulling on my jacket and wishing I'd found time to mend its lining.

'You know I'm not a flasher,' he mutters, with a quivering of his lips.

I know nothing of the sort, I decide, intolerantly. He remembers everything inaccurately. Never did anything useful for me except change a bedroom light bulb then hide behind his newspaper. Never gave me any worthwhile advice or cuddles.

I can't trust him.

'I'm not a flasher,' he insists. 'You're not listening,' he says. 'Nobody listens.'

I can't tolerate this self-pitying stuff. His face shows three days of stubble, the remains of a lunchtime kipper, but no expression. I've no choice but to take him out of this place. And an uneasiness about him. A definite uneasiness.

We go through the swing of the door and hit the cooling air. Dad is coughing. Dad is always coughing, and won't take my advice to suck peppermint. He thinks he knows everything worth knowing. I've suggested that to him too many times to remember. But he won't listen. Any more than Thomas.....Thomas who?

I can't remember. Don't even want to make the effort. That would be the beer thinking. It wouldn't work.

We get through the door and the old man suddenly gets into the impressive rhythm of his stride, and without a word walks in front of me in the direction of his home. I should have expected his sudden moodiness, but I'm having too much of a problem balancing on the impractical heels of my shoes to be able to concentrate on anything else. I follow him automatically through the grey and brown of the streets, sometimes glancing at the pigeons.

Funny, I've got a fascination with pigeons. Always had. They know things don't they? Like where to go.

No point in mentioning this to Dad.

We cut through the familiar alley and stride over expected dog shit, and navigate through the river of cracked paving stones and Coca-Cola cans, through the breeze teasing the viaduct, to reach the varnish of his home.

I follow him into the once white kitchen, and watch him push off his still laced-up shoes, open a window with unsteady hands and silently feed his goldfish. Obviously he's getting back into a more steady mode.

The quiet is deafening. Obviously I've got to say something.

'This must be their first balanced meal of the week.'

No response. He pours and stirs my coffee, his hands still shaking.

'Can you smell the stale sherry?' He inspects my face for an answer. 'Or something more?'

I make no comment. Suddenly I don't want to know what this bastard knows or thinks he knows.

But he keeps on probing. Pushing. Prying. Now I've had enough.

'Are you saying you want me to come here more often and take care of you? Is that what you want?' I yell. 'Because if that's what you're telling me you know for a fuck that I can't take care of myself. I've got problems of my own.'

He's not listening. I knew he wouldn't. He shuffles from room to room, as if in search of something, then finally back into the lounge, and calmly winds up the cheap and unreliable clock he should have disposed of years ago. His words, when he speaks, have been carefully thought out. So how simple can he really be?

'I've got to go back down to the police station today,' he says.

'How do you mean back down?' I ask.

'Went yesterday,' he grunts. 'Got to go today with someone

who'll vouch for me. That's you.'

This is crazy. Crazy with bumps on. There's something in his eyes that looks familiar. Something from a dream.

'Come on then, you old bugger,' I say, 'What the hell have you been up to? You're not really a closet flasher, or something even more tacky are you?'

He winces. Says that he's an old man.

'That's pretty apparent, Dad, if you ask me.'

'You're not listening.' He clicks his dentures in frustration. 'Nobody listens.'

'The story of my life?' I suggest, glibly.

Dad checks on the safety of the safety pin holding the collapsed fly of his trousers together, and says, with a serious expression, the kind I've seen on half-moon faces of politicians on TV, that I've got it all wrong. That he got run in by the bluebottles yesterday because he sat on a bus.

I raise my eyebrows.

'They don't have a terminus now,' he explains. 'The damned buses don't go far enough. I wanted to go to Tong Hill cemetery to visit your mother. Her gravestone. To let her know we'd be visiting her on Friday. The bus driver said he didn't go there. Looks at me from beneath his turban, and says I've got dribble on my chin. He's got five children. He told me that.'

And I'm wondering where the relevance comes in.

'Then he tells me they've moved the soddin' cemetery. How can anyone move a cemetery? And how can I be threatened for sitting on a bottom deck? The bus used to go there. I know it did.'

'But it doesn't now,' I say quietly, resisting an urge to nervously wrap a strand of hair around my finger and twiddle with it.

'No,' he clicks his dentures again.

'They did move the graves, Dad, bones and all.' Why had I let that fact slip from my mind like that?' It was moved to a site overlooking the canal. Near where that new, red-brick church went up. Don't you remember reading about it in the newspaper? If it's any comfort to you, it's probably consecrated ground,' I add, as if it mattered to either of us.

We'd never been proper church-goers, any of us. The family's habit of getting a Christian burial was just a way of hedging our bets.

'You should have told me.' His fists are curled into balls that look like overbaked, misshapen, rock cakes. 'When I refused to get off the bus the bloody driver got the bloody police. Then the bloody policewoman treated me like a madman. I wanted to see my wife,' he says, raising his voice. 'Is that what a madman does? I ask you. Is it?' He shrugs. 'They blew it up out of all proportion.'

Then he launches into a tirade of shouts that a skeleton is a skeleton. That it's somebody's skeleton and that the authorities could get lost.

He doesn't notice me shaking my head.

'Crying for the moon,' I mutter.

Then he goes on about religion. He smells faintly of urine, and strongly of sherry. I can't leave him alone yet. I know that.

'Why didn't you tell me about this poxed-up situation before now?' I ask.

'Don't know,' he says.

Then I become my nasty old self. Because I know the impression he makes. He wouldn't have combed his hair before his jaunt, nor would he have fed the fish.

'You didn't go out in your old tartan slippers and with your fly unpinned?' I ask, cringing.

He tells me, 'Could have done,' and asks what sort of a daughter am I?

Getting ridiculous is this.

'For God's sake, Dad, you've got to get your head together. I can't carry you. Honestly I can't.'

The family is a mess. A mess I'm trying to sidestep. I feed him pea and ham packaged soup and proffer him six Jaffa cakes. Resist the urge to tell him I'm just as fucked up as he is.

'I know it hurts,' I say, 'but I've got to get away from this heaviness. I don't know if you can understand this.'

He can't. I know he can't. And I feel like a proper pillock. Daren't start on about the dream again. About Mark and Thomas. The old man simply wants to sleep. I can turn up at the cop hole with him. No problem. No big deal. First I'll let him eat his soup, and rest.

I quietly move. Silently close the old man's front gate. I've got to shelve him for a while. What about my life?

I breathe in the air.

I watch pigeons, then walk in the park, where chemicals smell of burning parchment and tar on the melt. No-one speaks to me. Rot, is all this stuff.

I'm sitting in Dad's only good armchair trying to put down a headache. It's been a hell of a depressing day. And now Dad's talking and talking and still can't believe he got it wrong. We needn't have made the journey to the police station at all. Only Dad could have been such a pillock brain that he should think that we had to. Only I could have been enough of a pillock brain to believe this.

'Look lass,' he says, 'you won't let them take me away will you?'

Despite all I've said, it only now occurs to me that I could be 'taken away' first and spoon-fed Valium on some white ward. I'm weary. A clapped out womb. Fingers on the end of two arms capable of manipulating nothing.

Once back at his pad I pushed off my unpolished shoes and slumped into the vagueness of the kitchen, then returned with a glass of milk and what remained of the Jaffa cakes I bought for him last week. Into the nicotine lounge, into the armchair.

He's scowling at me. 'You won't will you?'

'Well I'm ill myself,' I scream at him defensively. 'You know. A pale and drawn carcass? Ever heard the expression? I'm not a bloody saint.'

He finishes picking dried stuff from the upper caverns of his nostrils to look at me disapprovingly.

Whatever happened to the little girl with the ponytail? he's thinking. Well so am I.

'What do you expect of me?' I shout.

It would be nice if he expected nothing. Because that would mean he had a particle of wisdom lurking above the snot barrier. We always had blocked up noses, he and I. It's a family trait.

And wisdom? I'm asking myself. What's wisdom? I'm the one with silly nightmares. Not dreams. Not ambitions. But pointless nightmares. Something to do with the mist of the past when I haven't got a fog of a future.

'You don't look well,' he concedes.

'Well tell me about this nightmare I keep having.' I frown. 'You know something about it. I can sense it. Tell me about this damned mill I keep dreaming about.'

He shakes his head in feigned perplexity. 'I can't help you. If your mother was still here she'd probably be able to help you.'

I stare at him in disbelief. He's in an unusually serious mode.

'Dreams are dreams. Let's leave it at that. That's all they are.'

'Supposing I searched for information at the library?' I'm feeling desperate now. 'Supposing these aren't dreams, but recollections?'

'Recollections of what?' he asks irritably.

'I don't know. Some sort of tribal recollections? I just don't know.'

He's avoiding my eyes. Shakes his head, then tells me I must be suffering from some sort of indigestion caused by off-beat library books from shelves infested by the souls of half-eaten flies. Still thinks that he's a poet, on the days that he can think. But he can't expect me to swallow that whole.

What we should do now is think. Seriously. It's a fact of life. His bloodshot eyes advertise it. He's taking my words seriously. Hasn't tried to scratch his scrotum since we started talking.

'You're responsible for my existence,' I remind him, unfairly.

Then I go through what I've told him before. Told him while he's bitten into margarined crumpets, while he's examined the bunion on his left foot, while I've been ready to cry, because crying seemed more available than anything else.

'There's a boy in these dream things. A young boy with oil-stained trousers I can finger and still smell when I wake up. He keeps screaming through my sleep that someone's got to do something to stop it.'

Dad shows no mercy. 'Maybe the only one who should stop it is you,' he snaps. 'It's silly rubbish you're talking, girl. Now stop it. Just stop it.'

I glare at him. 'I believe you know Thomas. Could know more. And I believe I'm not mad. Think about it.'

Silence.

Now I need to get away from him. To kick through the nearby builder's rubble and go home, past the supermarket and dentist's white façade, to sniff the usual carpet freshener and tread on the familiar nylon pattern. Tell Rodney, 'Sorry, I'm late. But what the fuck should you expect?' I can't risk falling asleep in this old man's spare armchair. The feel of the velour is comforting, but there's something wrong.

I wish I could run the grooves of a finger along the tip of my mind and find out what it is.

The air outside, faintly tinged by night-stock, is changeable. The pavement slabs are dry and grey with age.

I wave towards Dad's kitchen window without turning to look. Know that he'll be there, staring through the dust on the pane of glass like an abandoned, bespectacled silverfish that has taken up residence where chip-pan fat calls to its followers.

This is a depressing business. But I expected it and am used to it. Dad. Lard. There's not much difference nowadays. I need to go home to a different voice. To the banter. The attractive prattle of my sixteen year old daughter. Just sprouting breasts. To taste the scent of my kids' blue and white, worn down trainers, the vibration of their words on my now perspiring skin. The children are mine aren't they? My flesh. For once, I've produced something and done it right. And I can talk to them. Love to talk to them.

But then there's that cloud hanging over me.

I can't sit at home embroidering chairback covers for them to rest their pubescently greasy heads against. I should have some part of my life not involved with the consequences of procreation. Jesus, my son is fourteen, almost old enough to stand on his own two feet, or my toes, and almost taller than me. It's getting to the point when he doesn't need me. So what then? Back to bingo and trying to bake sponge cakes in a delapidated oven. The meaning of life. Fuck it.

I'm asking myself these questions when I reach the door, and automatically spraying breath-freshener into my mouth. I can hear the sound of a voice scratched by use. And old Cliff Richards' brought from a car boot sale drifting down from above, and Coronation Street informing the lounge that trouble is afoot.

'So?' I ask Rodney as I kick off my shoes and push them underneath the kitchen table. 'How was your day?'

He's cooking a chicken stir-fry for supper. Makes sure that I know it.

I should be doing it.

'You're late,' he says.

'I did the pre-Christmas shopping bit, and that's it,' I say. 'I've got to be civilised, play the part. That's what you expect of me isn't it?'

He switches the hob off then sits down at the formica table to pretend to read his newspaper. Then sniffs.

'How was your father, then?' he asks, in a forced, matter of fact way. 'Still spouting his mouth off about the woes of the working classes?' Inexplicably he doesn't consider himself one of them. What I once considered to be an interesting reserve is a secret snobbery. I know that now.

I lower my fingers and scratch beneath the waistband of my skirt. There's no point in answering. He doesn't really want to know.

He concentrates on lighting one of his self-rationed cigarettes. Self-control. I think, God, that's annoying. And tell him so. And he says,

'Can't you find something to do?' and, 'Gaynor has gone and come home with some homework.'

Now I'm interested. Gaynor. I love Gaynor, despite her fat legs and the fact that when she's had a bad day she calls me an old cow. She's got her father's nose and my nature. They're the oil and I'm the troubled water. I'm in a maudlin mood again.

Rod can never understand that. But that's no reason why I can't speak.

'When she was young I used to scoop her into my arms and take her out to see the stars, treading over the weeds on the lawn. Some folk,' I say, glaring at him, 'would think that's fucking stupid. The stars didn't get to her. Not like they got to me. She was always hungry. Asked what was for supper. I remember looking at the set brown of her eyes, and thinking that all she'd ever want was to grow up and get some guy with an income to fuck her. It's wrong. Terribly wrong. With her trusting nature, she'll fall for it.'

Rod is staring at me and shaking his head, bemused. I ignore it.

'Experience should be passed on in the genes. Our daughter is a lovely girl,' I slur. 'Pimpled and wide-hipped, but lovely. But people don't look beneath the skin, and she'll be caught in a materialistic net like you. Don't you understand that?'

'Why don't you find something to do?'

'Find something to do?' I shout, near to tears. 'Give crab apples to young boys?'

Rod's losing his temper.

'You're talking about that shitty dream again,' he shouts. 'You're bloody mad, woman. Forget about it now, or you'll have us all bloody lunatics.'

He's right. I've got to stop it. To come back down to earth. Speak the same language. Behave normally. But what then?

'What do you expect me to do with my time?' I shout. 'Jigsaws? Hang washing out in the back yard? Should I stare at the wall like my grandmother? They took her away for that.'

He turns his back towards me. 'Maybe you should be taken away,' he mumbles.

But he doesn't mean that. Can't mean that. His shoulders stiffen.

'Let's go to bed, Rodney,' I say quietly.

'What?'

'Let's go to bed. Then I'll try to tell you about my bad dream. Or my obsession. Is it an obsession?'

He scowls. Then says I'm pissed. And I suppose I am. But I can't be totally useless because everyone has a use. That's plain reasoning, that is. So I pad across the kitchen floor in search of a cloth to wipe cigarette ash from the table.

'After all, that's what I'm here for,' I mutter. 'And to spoil the kids. They're not special. No kid is.'

He clips the excess from his fingernails and flicks crescent moons into the rubbish bin. I continue to wipe traces of ketchup from the table. And try not to let him catch a whiff of my breath. It's a hopeless task, I know. But this is marriage, no doubt. A thickening of the growing apart theory. Then I tell myself that the original growing together was no more than lust. I know it.

I watch Rod closely, because I know this particular trick of his. Psychological warfare. Soon he'll be pretending for minutes on end that I don't exist. He has many tricks. Subconscious. Always subconscious. I speak to him. Suddenly want to speak to him, thinking, well, we can't do without some sort of communication for the rest our lives.

'About these dreams,' I say, taking a deep breath. 'They're strange. Yet very real. Like I don't know who I am and don't know where I am. But they make me feel guilty. There are three men in them.'

'Like the three wise men from the East?' he snarls.

I'm not going to be put off. 'Don't be facetious.'

He's going to listen, whether he likes it or not.

'I can't shake it. But it's more than a dream,' I insist, 'I know it is. I knew or know the people in it. Don't you understand?'

Rodney is now pretending not to listen, reaches towards a cage hanging on a ceiling hook above the washer-stroke-dryer and lets the budgie out, watching its green feathers reflected from the windowpane.

He turns, but avoids my eyes. I can't decide if he's embarrassed for him or me.

'Speak to me,' I insist.

'It's probably something to do with all the alcohol you drink,' he mutters finally.

I look at his corduroy-clad buttocks and wonder why I want to grasp them, or if. Remember his breath on my ear lobes, then the floral patterned sheets, the morning stains. His question of long ago.

'What do you think is poking you, darling?'

It doesn't matter. It doesn't matter anymore.

'I'll take my alcoholic head to bed then.'

He nods, 'I'm staying up to watch a couple of videos. John Wayne.'

It figures. Horses, guns, and blood. Just his style.

'Goodnight then.'

There's no answer, so I creak up the stairs, my hand clutching the cold of the solid banister.

'A cold house is this,' I shout down. 'Too bloody cold to live in.'

The mattress is no warmer than the darkness of the room and the glass of stale water on the floor beside my bed, or the whirling of white lights behind my closed eyes.

Chapter 6

Thomas crouches over a commode in the corner of the red-walled scullery, clutching a piece of muslin round his genitals, coughing and defecating. His knees hurt too much for him to cross the ice in the yard to reach the closet. He stumbles back to his mattress in the room, shoulders hunched. There's the sound of the closing of the door. I'm wondering why he hasn't acknowledged my presence. Fatigue maybe.

I wriggle my naked toes uncomfortably on the cold floor slabs. So cold. Why is everything so cold? Then stare through the window, and listen to his almost instant snoring.

I'm expecting someone, but can't remember who because my head hurts, and my hands are smarting. I glance down at their redness. They're swollen and the wrong shape. Not mine. Frightening.

A shadow passes across the gloom of the backyard and moves a hand to casually brush some frost from the window pane. It can't be Mark. He's already visited today, my mind is misty but I can remember that, the smartness of his collar, dew in his hair, and that he swept out the yard for me, and fucked me with a smile on his face as I clung to the splintered table. That I could have said no. Should have. Didn't.

The shadow grows longer.

Jesus, it's big Bert tapping the door. I remember now, he left a message with Thomas that he wanted to visit me to speak of 'a matter of great importance.' Grand words from a trouble maker, a dangerous trouble maker, who impressed all the working boys, even Thomas, with his silly disruptive talk, including handing out barley sugar outside the pawn shop in the shadow of the mill. Where did he get the money to buy such treats, and distribute the leaflets that so impressed Thomas, who could read but few of the words?

I shouldn't want to know about such nonsense.

He lets himself in. Doesn't know about politeness. And scratches at the threadbare trousers covering his left calf with a right boot that still holds clay collected from the quarry he had to cross to get here, his bulk shutting out the light from the doorway.

'Well?' I ask. 'Come to talk to me about Thomas, I suppose. When are you going to leave the boys alone?'

'Come to warn you,' he says, looking me in the eyes and frowning, his eyebrows almost meeting in the middle. His skin is the colour of a young squirrel, and leathery. The skin of a harvest worker, who travelled from county to county. 'Word is that you're accommodating Mark, the master's lackey.'

'He's a friend,' I say defiantly. 'Not that it's any business of yours.'

'He's nobody's friend. Watch out for him and don't be fooled girl, you don't know the sneaky things he's done and will always do. Always puts himself first, that one.'

'What?'

But he's gone. Gone in a haze. I can smell stale tobacco and bacon. It's time to awake.

Desert Island Discs, cat scratching at the door, milk bottles rattling. Another day, another duty. I've got to face it. Better the soddin' devil.

I pad downstairs covered in night sweat, and cursing the cat who wipes his damp tail against my legs. I push it out of my way. Can't be ruled by a feline.

I'm me and only me. Got to put up with Gaynor's morning pouts, and having a long conversation with Gavin about his non-existent acne. In a stupor I send my kids off into the big world with packed lunches with relief. None of us like mornings.

It's time to visit Dad again.

He's depressed. I can tell by the slump to his shoulders in his green, ex-army cardigan that refuses to wear out, by his bitten down fingernails and the cheesy smell of his armpits when he taps his pipe on the mantelpiece. He could have been on the sherry all night, for all I know. And he's probably spent the daybreak hours clutching his duvet and trying to work out what the shapes created by nicotine on his Regency-type curtains meant to him.

Very keen on psychology is Dad.

He hasn't brushed his dentures. But not to worry, I tell myself.

Dad is Dad. The old bugger will live forever. Today he doesn't offer me biscuits. The kitchen stinks of overcooked chips, and he hasn't fed the goldfish again. But they are still moving, floating through green water warmed by sunlight purring through the kitchen window, like shadows of demented, midget sharks. Their mouths push out bubbles of puzzled panic. Soul mates.

I try not to disturb them, and step over a half-eaten pork pie inadvertently squashed into the surface of the tiled, kitchen floor.

'Alright,' I say, following him into the lounge of the ticking clock. 'What's the problem now?'

He sucks on his empty pipe, chewing the rosewood. I creep back into the kitchen, while he squints at the *Radio Times*, to make him tea, milky as he always likes it, then quietly go back in, clutching cups.

The gas fire hisses. He's staring at orange flames, and remembering. He says, 'Fires do that to you.' And I can't disagree. He's speaking quietly, as if he's in a doctor's waiting-room, and his words would be inaudible, were I standing nearer to the door.

'Are you well, Alice?'

It's unnerving to be constantly given my mother's name, but there's nothing I can do but pretend I haven't heard it.

He has a coughing fit, due to the roughness of cut-price tobacco, then seems to pull himself back to reality. He takes a deep breath then clears his throat, again.

'I've got a social worker coming to visit me in the morning. Government orders.'

'So?'

His bottom lip is quivering. 'She'll be a she.' The old sorry-for-myself routine. He's watched a lot of television.

I nod. Because I can't think of anything else to do.

'And have red fingernails,' he continues, 'and be dressed in tweed. And probably she'll have one of those plastic card things.'

'So?' I say again.

'You know what I mean,' he snaps.

'Of course I do. It's about deciding the matter of your competence.' No point in lying.

I'm trying to imagine him in some Council-protected, communal lounge, with cardiganed women on chairs lining plush walls, and air smelling of urine burst from too long waiting bladders. Then there's this vision of some matron dressed in green boasting a narrow waist and asking if he's content.

I can't see him in this environment, somehow. All he needs is peace and someone to make sure he hasn't set the settee on fire. Not too much to ask. He should have peace. An idealist, that's me, but I shrug his problems off my skin. It's a question of survival. Today is Tuesday, so I've arrived armed with sausage rolls and sherry, and some cheese I found languishing in a container behind the tomatoes in the fridge.

Tuesday is an occasion for a slight blow-out. For Dad and I, and Beth, and perfume-covered Sonia. It's because we are all pig sick. A good excuse for a meeting, if ever there was one.

Dad doesn't look well. He doesn't even laugh when I mention the National Lottery thing anymore. His eyes are caterpillar-yellow, and glazed, and his abdomen is obviously shrinking. Bad signs.

'You should stop thinking too much Dad,' I tell him. Knowing, instinctively, that he can't. 'Our only real problem,' I say, feeling like a politician, 'is lack of money.' I don't believe what I'm saying. 'And we're not going to get any. None of us. We know it. So where's the problem?' By now I'm in full flow. 'You think you've got it bad? I've got kids to worry about. Kids who don't know what the fuck life is all about. Top that if you can.' Well, early morning boozing does that to you. Still I continue. 'Take my son, great boy, he is. Knows all about designer labels, senses that a T-shirt is only a T-shirt is only a T-shirt.'

I'm losing the drift of what I'm trying to say, and still tasting the early morning vodka on the back of my throat, and trying to convince myself that I'm entitled. But life is like this, I decide, blowing on my tea. It's knowing that a sticky pink diaphragm can stick to your flesh without subtleness on mornings before you've even had a chance to taste your scrambled eggs. I tell Dad this, whilst trying to comb a parting into his thinning, salt and pepper hair.

He scowls at me in disgust, and asks if I'm talking about scrambled eggs or scrambled heads.

No chance to answer.

There's a knock at the door. It's Sonia, in costume jewellery and bright red angora. She's brought vol-au-vents and half a bottle of supermarket brandy. Doubtless she drank the other half whilst lounging, this morning, in a bubble bath. She strides over the doorstep without even wiping her feet. Says she's fucked up and that if her guy doesn't pull his socks up and stop his midnight bouts of gambling down at the Greek's place he'd better stop thinking about pulling his trousers down on her Axminster in the mornings. But what should she expect from a boy fifteen years her junior?

I shrug. It's hard to think of something to say to such a question. But I manage it. 'The only thing he's probably brilliant at is being a squirmer,' I tell her, guessing that she's not really listening, but it doesn't matter. 'There's something about him that should be off-limits. Though I can't think what its name is. It would be impolite of me to call him a pillock.'

'At least he has a job of sorts,' she tells me haughtily.

But what the hell does it matter anyway?

Sonia, fucked up or not, always manages to dress in expensive clothing. She gets no sympathy from me. Hell, she's not even menopausal yet. She's well tanked up, I can tell. So can Dad. Even though he does seem to be preoccupied with scratching his crotch through the polyester trousers he bought from mail-order. He looks her straight in the nose, because he's small, like me, and she's a five foot ten inch failed model. Until recently, she had a Cleopatra type haircut with the expected fringe as crooked as Council house guttering.

Dad's dying to talk. 'I was carted off to the cop-hole, yesterday, because I was vague,' he tells her, expecting an illuminating answer.

Sonia is startled. Says nothing. So to break the silence I tell the old man that life is life. It's like that. And ask what the hell he's frightened of anyway? All of this is nonsense to Sonia's ears. She's kept her self-contained brain down ever since she stopped coming Johns, and that was years ago. She's forgotten what real life is like, I suppose.

Good grief, she's probably spent her early morning trying to calculate how long it takes to roast a chicken. Not much else can get to her now.

She side-tracks him. Tells him that the weather is lovely for the time of year, leans back and scratches her shoulder blades against the vine print wallpaper. She grunts with relief. Then, disgusted, Dad goes off for a pee.

And it's then that she tells me that Phil's been invited to our dominoes, on the proviso that he brings Irish Whisky, a favourite tipple of hers. Then I ask her what she's playing at, because it's expected of me. Got a great hang-up about doing what's expected, I have.

'We're boozing pals,' I remind her, 'and Phil is not a proper one.'

'A proper what?' she asks demurely, casually floating into the lounge and thrusting before her the scent of musk. Not the real thing, of course, always keen on chemical substitutes, is my friend. No surprise.

So I tell her that this is something like a pissing knitting circle and that Phil is only an invader. And that I don't accept invasions gladly.

It's all shit I'm talking. And Sonia knows it. She sits down, crosses her legs, reaches inside her sweater to scratch her left breast, then pretends to look shocked when I notice. Then she gives me the guilt trip. Tut-tuts about Dad, he of the hand-knitted cardigans. So I glare, and mean business.

'Christ, you're touchy,' she says, jumping to her feet.

She clears scraps of old toast and blobs of dried shoe-polish from the once polished table and shudders uncomfortably when the old man's green budgerigar, encaged in a home on a hook above the television set, sings a deep-throated dirge.

Sonia's feet are hurting inside her narrow shoes. I know that look, can see it in the tiny lines surrounding her eyes. She's bored. Tired of waiting. My whole life is made up of waiting, I want to tell her but don't. What's the point in talking to thick heads like hers?

I pour myself another sherry.

This woman hasn't a clue what I'm thinking, I'm thinking, because it takes one neurotic to recognise another. We act politely.

Are well aware of the consequences of not doing so in Dad's presence. He's leaning against the sideboard and watching us.

My tongue is as dry as I imagine the Gobi to be.

Dad is scowling. He hadn't expected a lot of company and has probably sneaked into the bedroom to put on a clean shirt. The last thing he wants is three women and a strange man descending on his home. So he says so.

Surprise. Surprise.

'Well yes, I can understand that, I think.' I say with what I hope is construed as an air of thoughtfulness, because I was brought up to be respectful.

Of course, this doesn't mean a thing. We're only here because this is a good, discreet place to play dominoes. Especially when all we want to do is get half-pissed.

I retire to the grey of the bathroom and apply lipstick, because Phil is coming. And, plonker or not, a man is worth flirting with. Life could be simple at times. Like pulling wings off butterflies. It's all about satisfaction, I'm telling myself, trying to peer into the mirror. About temporary comfort.

I remind myself that it's time I went back to the doctor's surgery to get some Valium and perhaps a repeat prescription for Dad.

He needs it more than I do. Men are kids anyway, I think. And they've hurt me often enough.

I feel like a nasty piece of work, and it doesn't make sense. So I start to think about Rod and his habit of undressing in the dark, poking, as he calls it, then saying he's got to go, disappearing downstairs to watch some waited-for canned soap. No sense in that, either. No logic. No answer to dreams. Not enough to even bring sherry tears to my eyes.

Great mistake, this depressive track of thought, I decide.

Time to go back into the sittingroom and sip coffee-stroke-chicory. I'm feeling too sorry for myself.

'Shacking up with a guy because you're grateful to him doesn't work,' I tell Sonia, suddenly. Thinking about her toyboy, the pretentious way he holds his cigarettes and the shape of his thighs. Didn't his mother once work for the television company, soldering red to black wires and carrying a beehive on her head? She was too intent on sucking spearmint chewing gum and worrying about faulty condoms to give a fuck for her kids. She was a nasty piece of work.

And so am I, I'm thinking, pouring myself another drink. Wouldn't trust a God if I won him on the National soddin' Lottery. A bit of a philosopher in all of us. It's taken me twenty years and two Caesarean sections, and a hell of a lot of shopping and shit and bleeding and smiles to find that experiences make you that way.

And I need another drink. No big deal. What the hell? Nobody's perfect.

'Where for Heaven's sake, is Beth?' I ask. 'She told me she'd be here.' I give Sonia a weak grin, and then examine the thin coating of polish on Dad's lounge table, contemplating its age. When he snuffs it, it has to be left to someone to take care of.

There's an awkward silence.

'Beth is probably up to her armpits in soap suds, or fucking her life away on her Axminster staircarpet,' I say, not quite believing it. And I'm annoyed with myself because I shouldn't have said it. But no big deal, again.

Then I realise I'm letting my mind get side-tracked, so I start to watch Sonia, because that's what I'm about. A nosy bitch. But I know exactly what she's up to. With studied absent mindedness, she's hitching up her herringbone patterned skirt and showing her knees, clad in outdated American tan, to Dad.

A waste of time, that.

He's fumbling to fasten the button on his shirt collar. He's old, and at this stage couldn't stick his cock anywhere six miles wide, let alone up Sonia who must, mistakenly, think he's got a fortune hidden away in his pillow-case. He's an old man with shrunken balls, for God's sake.

I go into the kitchen to feed the fish, looking decidedly pink. The fish and me. Then Sonia shouts out that she's dying for some 'reasonable' refreshments.

What she means is that she'd kill for a Bacardi and Coke, or for cider, or either.

I know the feeling. So I wash a few chipped teacups, look at their fading, blue, pattern. Each one is identical. I remember that my mother had a thing about willow-patterned pottery.

It's gone now, the shadow of my mother in the corner of this kitchen. When you're dead you are dead, or become part of a dream, perhaps. Like Thomas, with his strange, camphor-odoured breath.

And who the fuck can say that he never existed anyway? Or that I exist?

I look at my reflection through a grease-tainted window, and apply Sunset Beige to my eyelids, to compete with Sonia's Midnight Grey.

Here we are, both of us on the search.

On the search for what?

Another drink and I may not ask such a question, I decide. Reality is too harsh and big a question to ponder at this time on a morning. I've got a bigger question. What to do about the problem of a dad dressed in tweed, sporting worn-down dentures.

It's sad. Too right it's sad.

The old boy is struggling on Income Support, buying cabbages for their bulk. He's shrunken, and dying, and can't face it. The usual crack, and he must have had some whisky.

He's trying to conjure up some guts. As I would in his place. He can't envisage the possibility of throwing himself under a metallic blue, Intercity train. Knows that Paracetamol destroys only the liver and not the man, and that dangling a neck from nylon rope from a light bulb is painful and the sign of an exhibitionist.

I feel like I should cry for him or kick him in the teeth.

Sonia doesn't notice any of this. Can't feel the vibes.

Well she wouldn't. Too busy worrying about what went on or could in the future go on between her legs. Or am I being unfair? Always a question I'm ready to answer. Even if the answer is 'Of course you fucking are'. Well I don't have to accept it. Just the possibility.

Sonia purses her lips, reminds me that Phil always fancied me. That some men have a thing about wide-hipped ladies.

'So, what time is Phil turning up here?' I ask casually.

There's a certain unvoiced competition between me and Sonia

when it comes to the stud of Bradfield.

But it's all fun. Isn't it?

My mind goes back to sorting the problems of Dad, and questioning if it does need solving, because the man is going back to being a baby again. But my baby? God forbid. The whole thought is grotesque. Like a Van Gogh painting. A congealed conglomerate of something or other. I love spinning long words inside my head. It's something to do whilst standing in bus queues or watching plonkers like Sonia tapping their pointed fingernails on paintwork.

My madness is something to do with genes. It's also to do with duty.

Sad. But what can I do? I ask Sonia who peers at me blankly, doesn't want to know what I'm talking about.

'We can play dominoes,' she purrs through her smoke-rings.

The nicotine hits the pot cats arranged around the fireplace.

'Why not?' I ask or slur.

It is Sonia's turn to shuffle the pieces uncomfortably. She says she's cold.

I agree. Despite her constant prattling, there's an aura of loneliness about the place. Very susceptible to auras, am I. Once saw a ghost of a workmate, can see it in my mind now, and that was without a single glass of sherry.

Dad's still sitting in his basket chair and grinding his teeth. He's switched the TV set on, pictures and no sound, and he's staring at the people opening and closing their mouths like his kitchen goldfish. Almost a sadistic pursuit.

He clutches the arms of his chair. 'So, who is this Phil we're expecting?' he grunts.

So I say something meant to be reassuring. 'Phil is a good laugh. Phil can cohabit and not notice that the woman hasn't cleaned behind the lavatory pedestal, as long as her bosoms smell of roses.'

Don't know why the hell I'm sticking up for the plonker. He's a prime target for Aids or a mermaid dressed in a white coat and sporting a thermometer.

'Phil is a nobody,' I shrug after a little thought.

'I need another drink,' Sonia whines.

I'm not really listening. But start to follow my imagination again. That bloody cesspool, as Rod calls it, when rinsing car-oil or garden soil from his hands. He keeps telling me things. Like Dad's brain is slowly melting, and that this fact has to be faced. That I can't face this and it may be hereditary perhaps.

I'm on my day out, have to shrug off the idea I've got that I'm stuck with a husband who said that after the first flush of sex I never listened, nor knew my place. I think he has an idea that I should be a blank sheet of paper ready to be typed upon.

I keep telling him things. Like the ozone layer doesn't exist, that the issue is more important than a silk scarf from the Co-op that loses it's colour in a cool wash, short spin cycle. That I'd like to be invisible, along with my kids, the only people I'd die for. That I know I'm there to take care of them and he knows I'd like to cry.

Then he tells me not to worry. That he'll take care of me, and hasn't he always?

And I know it's a ploy and let him fuck me.

I tell Sonia this. And she informs me, quite demurely, that I'm pissed, and that I only need a man with a hard-on to set me right. And I can't believe that she believes that.

I tell her that she's talking rubbish, then shuffle the dominoes and ask 'Where the fuck is Phil?'

'He's another piss artist, I expect,' mutters Dad, removing remnants of bacon from the gaps between his bottom teeth with a needle. 'That's what you all are. You're nothing more.'

He puts down the needle and examines the soles of his old leather slippers. Stares at them in search of slime, in case he's picked up a dog's shit when he went outdoors to deposit empty plum-tomato cans in the dustbin.

There's a slow, steady knock at the door.

It's Beth. Who else could such a timid knock belong to?

She's in her pink. A jumble-sale purchased, nineteen-seventies, duster coat.

Dad and I exchange glances. God, she's letting herself go, that woman, it won't be long before she's wandering about doing her necessaries with crimson, knitted hats on her head that pass as teacosies.

But she's good hearted, is Beth, saves money off the price of Brillo pads by cutting out coupons from the pages of *Woman's Realm*. Even makes a Woolworth's pair of tights last three months. She's what I should be. I think.

She's got sad eyes, has Beth. Always had sad eyes. With small, amber specks in the corner of each.

She walks in silently, deposits a pack of pre-cooked sausage-rolls onto the table and asks what this meeting is all about because had she been using her brain, she could have been at the launderette by now.

Sonia seems to show concern and tells her that we meet here for fun and asks what the hell else does she expect?

'It's all about breaking the monotony, dear,' she tells her.

Dad unexpectedly nods and says 'Everyone should have some free time.'

I can't believe he said that, but anything is possible. He sniffs at her, as if that is how he obtains knowledge. I've got sensitive nostrils of my own. Can catch the scent of middle-aged menstruation in the air. I'm thinking about this and wondering why nobody else notices it or mentions it. Then the fuse blows on Dad's old kettle, discharging fumes of burning rubber.

He goes into the kitchen and then comes back with a perplexed expression on his face. He calls me Alice again. Well it figures. Leopards don't change.

Finally, he joins us at the table and narrates his latest, unfortunate adventure. Struggling, with emotionally charged words, to explain his encounter with the Sikh bus driver. Like a small boy trying to talk away failed examinations. He says the bus has no soul, and never stopped where it was supposed to. And that, after the journey, he never found my mother's grave. No sign of it at all. All this after him having plodded through the bus station clutching daffodils.

Maybe we're supposed to cry.

I stare at him, expressionless, and bite into a soggy custard cream. Well, he deserves to be treated like an idiot. He never thought much of my mother when she was alive. I can't imagine that he even made any inquiry of her, apart from making sure she hadn't lost the silver bracelet he bought her for their second wedding anniversary. The gift being a result of an aberration on his part, after a ten to one shot on the horses at Goodwood on a sunny Saturday. A rare event, I was told. The family legend tells that he pushed my pram out into late frost and bought me an angora bonnet that day.

'Daddy's going to buy me a rabbit skin,' I mumble to him, remembering. But nobody present makes sense of it. Everyone ignores me. Expected.

Sonia is raising her eyebrows and asking the question 'Who's got double six?' Then there's a clutching of dominoes.

Sonia is smiling at me. Or is it smirking? She knows me a lot better than she lets on. I can't understand how. Hers is a history of semi-detached and cars.

'How's married life, dear?' she asks of me.

Prides herself on living over the proverbial brush, does Sonia, and comfortably. She doesn't realise it hasn't been considered daring since the early sixties. But she's got a hell of a lot of gold chains out of her man for enduring this supposed guilt trip.

'Married life is the same as it was yesterday,' I frown. 'I'm still doing the laundry.'

I expect her to wince and look away, but she smiles demurely. Seems to have a patent on 'demure'.

Now there's silence. We wait.

Phil doesn't knock on my father's door. He simply opens it and walks in. To prove he's civilised he coughs to announce his arrival, then thrusts supermarket chocolates into Dad's hand, and produces a bottle of gin from a plastic carrier-bag. Then removes his maroon jacket to display a lime-green shirt and a Burton's tie.

He looks at us confidently, then asks 'Why the invitation? Why the occasion, then? A meeting of bored housewives looking for a possible stripper?'

He laughs, and we're supposed to join in. Sonia does. Hedging her bets, I suppose.

I picture Phil alone, bending over a gas-ring and burning his lunchtime soup, then looking at his clock and wishing he could hear real fucking voices. The picture fits. Wasn't meant to be alone. Was meant to head a cause. Something simple and sexy, like 'Free Martian prostitutes from the Lebanon'.

Now I feel smug.

'Of course we're bored housewives. Aren't you? Your little scam job in the D.I.Y. makes no difference. You're what I am. Practice being a piss artist,' I say.

No one blinks. We're all here for the same reason.

Now there's a lull in the conversation. Sonia shuffles the dominoes. Again. Beth nervously runs her fingers along the bits and bats in her big, brown handbag. In search of a dry-cleaning redemption ticket, she says.

It's odd, I'm thinking, there's only me seems to realise that Beth is here. Maybe she's a spectre, like bloody brother Thomas. So I down another drink. Keep my eyelids open. And my wits. Phil is wondering which one of us ladies he can entice home to cock-suck him on his judo mat. That's his game alright.

There's half-hearted communal discussion on the price of Ambrosia creamed rice. Then a strange kind of footsy game under the table. Or am I imagining it? Could be.

And I say, for lack of anything else to say, that it's a bugger about Russia, that I heard something vague about it on the radio this morning whilst shaving my corns. Nobody's interested, of course. Had I thought they would be I never would have said it. Would have talked about the abundance of dolphins in the Bermuda triangle instead. Don't know why I'm being so nasty, unless it's something to do with the ozone layer.

Dad is staring at the wallpaper, counting vine-strangled roses.

Phil is staring at me. No big deal. Nothing new.

Domino time.

Two hours later the bastard winks at me, offers a cigarette, then nods towards the door.

I nod back because I'm buggered and don't care and I'm tired of hearing about the unhygienic habits of Beth's new Yorkshire terrier puppy. Can't think why it's not interesting. Must have something seriously wrong with me.

'Time to get away,' I mumble. 'Time to go home.'

Then I'm walking, clip-clop of metal heels, like a horse. I can feel air in my lungs resting on tar.

Someone's holding me up. Phil, of course. We saunter past the playing fields, feel the smell of wet grass, long ignored, watch a fawn coloured whippet with a limp chew hopefully on a cherry flavoured condom, shrug our shoulders in the steadily settling frost.

Depression. Can't have any effect on me. That stuff. Never could.

Phil squints through his rain sprinkled, gold-rimmed spectacles and holds my hand because he's got a reputation to keep up. He doesn't sense my depression at all. But, after all is said and done, it's only due to my irritable bloody hormones. He doesn't notice the moon. It's the colour of peaches. Strange for this time of year.

He's talking of tits. Says 'Thou art the best.'

Words like that are out of character. The said phrase would be Mark's, in the dream, or perhaps Thomas's, had he survived. But he didn't survive anyway. Did he? Never really was. Imagination. All of it.

'I feel sad and don't know why,' I tell Phil. 'But, I'm feeling sad about something that could have happened years go. But I can't know, can I? Perhaps I'm crazy.'

He's not listening.

'I could be a fucking reincarnation. It all seems so real. But I've read a lot of books. It could be an influence imposed on me by my subconscious.'

He appears not to be listening to me. Doesn't even hear our heels crunch the frosted, dying weeds as we cut across the playing fields, or smell the storm moving down from the moors. I shrug my shoulders and think 'So what?' It's only water, sheet lightning. Nothing more important than that. In hospitals people are dying, spitting out tongues onto well bleached handkerchiefs while old women clutching paper bags of satsumas stand helplessly by their beds. Important. Stuff like that. Especially when you're feeling weepy.

I try to tell him this.

'It doesn't make sense does it?' I ask. 'You're listening to the madness of a middle-aged lady who ain't no lady and hallucinates.'

We pass underneath a flickering street lamp and I watch his face, fine boned, sunken cheeked, tinted yellow by a struggling late evening.

'Perhaps I could be psychic,' I suggest. 'Stupid, but psychic.'

This makes no impression on him.

I'm thinking that I may have a migraine coming on. Feel colours tightening like fragile metal bands around my chest, sounds attacking my eyes. Grab onto paint-chipped railing for support, and drop my take-away sweet and sour.

Phil, whom I've known for millions of soot stained years, still doesn't notice or hear.

'Thomas,' I whisper to myself. 'I can almost hear Thomas.'

'Who?' asks Phil, loosening his grip around my waist.

'Thomas,' I repeat. 'You don't believe me do you?'

'Who the hell is Thomas?'

I don't answer. Thomas is only a whisper. A scent. A touch of racial memory perhaps. I've read so many weird library books that they aren't weird anymore. I don't know what to think.

Thomas, illusion or not, is crying out. He's hurting.

'Do you think I'm mad?' I mumble. But I'm not really asking Phil. 'Maybe pain imprints itself on its surroundings,' I think out loud.

This time the man hears me. 'You're in pain? When you're in pain you've got to do something about it.'

'Like what?'

He grips my elbow and leads me towards the deserted cricket pavilion. His warm breath hits the coolness of my short ones.

'What you need is a good fuck,' he says. And, standing in the shadow of a padlocked shed, I let his fingers discover the gusset of my panties, printed, floral things, bought at a sale price of one pound ninety-nine. Know that they can quickly find their way inside of me. Prodding. Wriggling. Poking. Pushing. Higher and higher.

And that's all I want from him. His fingers.

Right on cue he yanks down my tights and runs his tongue along my clitoris while I pretend to swim in a candy-pink haze. Been drinking all day haven't I? I'm pissed off. That's why I'm letting him do this, I reason. He could be anyone with a penis. But he's not.

Wood, splintering from the shed, grazes the back of my neck, but doesn't break the skin. The pressure isn't strong enough. I whisper to Phil that he's the only guy I've let touch me 'down there' since I got married twenty years ago, apart from Rod, of course.

Rod smelled of horses.

Phil smells of horses.

Perhaps most men smell of horses.

I push his hand high so that I can feel his thumb pressing against my pelvic bone. I can't see his eyes in the gloom.

'I'm drunk out of my skull, OK?' I'm starting to cry and don't know why, mascara running down my cheeks. There's a chill between my shoulderblades. There's a thrusting.

More thrusting.

And Thomas is crying. I hear him. He wants to get out. Wants both of us to get out.

'There's mice and rats eating through my skin,' he screams through my dizziness and I can almost see him writhing in delirium on a pile of rags. 'And there's pollen burning me. The pollen will get us. Drive us mad.'

'Twaddle. Absolute twaddle.' My mind screams back.

He's still calling out, his words punctuated by spluttering as droplets of bile run from the corner of his mouth. The reflection of a flickering fire paints wings on his face.

'They'll get us,' he shouts hoarsely. 'The flames!'

Then he's fading, like the shadow of a weakened cloud.

I open my eyes. Shudder.

Find Phil's semen in my hand. Feel the wind around my knees. And the warmth of camphor on my left cheek. Imagination. It's all imagination. No-one hears Thomas but me. He doesn't exist. All that exists is here and now, I remind myself.

'Thank you Mark, for nothing,' I find myself saying, hitching down the hem of my skirt, in readiness for pulling my heels homewards across the overgrown turf. 'I'm not into these games and it can't happen again,' I add.

'Just who in the hell is Mark?' asks Phil, as he wipes the palms of my hands on a tissue. 'I'm Phil, Phil, my drunken old friend, remember? And what on Earth was all your talk about horses all the time I was trying to fuck you meant to mean?'

I look at him and shake my head. 'Can't remember.'

'You must need a few sedatives.'

'Yes, I need sedatives,' I say impassively. 'I'm tired.'

If I'm mad I want no-one else to believe it. Not yet. Not until I can't hide it any longer. I've got kids taking school exams next year. And a non-existent brother, Thomas, whispering through my brain like a foraging worm, and sometimes Mark, a dreaded and senseless Mark.

I'm simply too high on alcohol, I suppose.

A cobweb inside my mind holds skeletons of aphids, that's all I've got. It should be ignored. I try to laugh. Then reach for a hand.

Phil slowly guides me through the dampness of the housing estate. He keep shrugging his shoulders uneasily, and cracking a few jokes to try to get himself into character. By the time we reach the corner of the avenue he's psyched himself up again. He's good, amusing old Phil. Says he understands I may have guilt feelings. Hasn't a clue.

I say nothing, because I've got to practise that.

And then he tells me that he knows I've got to prove my respectability. Something to do with my upbringing. 'Nurture,' he calls it, and then uses one of my favourite phrases. 'I've read a lot of library books.' Tries to get me to smile.

He doesn't understand. I know how his mind works. If he can't cheer me up with so-called humorous banter, he'll try little bluffing, back-handed compliments. And he does. If I want to visit his home tomorrow, he tells me, he'll drag me into his bedroom, pull his sunflower patterned curtains, take off his spectacles, and fuck me blind. I don't let him see he's raised a scowl. Don't want to look at him.

There's a tale going around that he's got the largest dick in

England. But I don't know. A joke is merely a joke. A poke is just a poke. Has to be, for peace of mind.

I run the toes of my worn-down shoes on the grass verge. The ground's becoming more frosted. Unusual for the time of year. There's a three-legged dog rubbing its spine on the rusting fence in a useless effort to rid itself of a family of tics.

There's the expected stench of fish and chips in the air. And two youths suddenly appear from the east to walk in front of us in blue anoraks, discussing a girl with outdated, spiky hair. They whisper about anal sex together, in an effort to shock, then work-training schemes. The usual.

Thomas would never have done that to a girl, I know he wouldn't.

A red Fiesta hurries past us. And a bright star or planet hovers over the darkened Bull's Head.

Then Phil says, unexpectedly, that he thinks I'm lonely.

Because I've had sherry and I'm haunted by this bloody dream thing I burst into tears again. Of course I'm lonely, for fuck's sake. I married a man out of gratitude two decades ago. He was a bloody gardener, a lover of carburettors, a man with unconquerable inhibitions who undressed in the dark and thought that we should play mothers and fathers with a polish spray and a duster.

While we're walking, Phil respecting my silence, I come to a conclusion. Perhaps I AM a bloody chain-smoking witch, fucked up and pissed. Phil suggests I should cheer up because gloom is bad for the nervous system. But he's got more sense than to believe that, I'm hoping. He's keen to find some bushes so that he can feel my tits and push his pelvis against me again.

I don't want that. Not in this weather, besides (the thoughts hit me and now I feel cold again), Thomas, were he here, would disapprove. Probably spit out the crusts of bread he chewed on each day.

'What are you thinking about?' Phil asks, taking a tighter grip on my hand.

What am I thinking about? Thomas. I'm not going to start that conversation again. So the sensible thing, the only thing, is to come up with something else.

I tell Phil that The Big Bang Theory doesn't make a lot of sense to me and that I like the idea of a superior being-type-thing, even if it is a manifestation of the inner-consciousness. I know he isn't listening when he sighs, and I'm glad about this. Hiding madness is difficult enough. But his sighs are not as judgmental as Rod's. More like disappointment tinged with a little disappointment.

'I like clever women like you,' he sniffs. 'You must have a bit of something inside your head.'

I don't disillusion him. Let him see my ankle in the moonlight and the stream of yellow from a streetlamp, giving them a sort of psychedelic appeal. Make sure he notices. It was easy enough for him to invade my body, but no fucker invades my mind. I'm sobering a little.

'You'll do for me darling,' he says. 'No questions asked or answered.'

I write down his address and agree to meet him tomorrow.

What I want now is to get home to Rod. Out of a vague stirring of better the devil you know.

It's evening. Don't know how it's got to evening. There's been too few moving clouds, too few street sweepers whirling brown leaves up with brushes of olive green. I could have been at my father's for half a day. More. I don't know.

My husband hears my footsteps on the garden path. Doesn't acknowledge this when I open the back door and teeter into the kitchen. I glance at the back of his head and spot a faint nod. He knows I'm here.

'I'm what's known as the family shit,' I slur. 'And what's even more exciting is that I get illusions. DEAD people.'

He doesn't flinch. Perhaps he's been practising. He's leaning over the cooker and frying chips. I haven't deterred him, I know.

'The kids are in bed,' he mutters, still not turning towards me. 'They were grumbling because I can't cook a good poached egg. I broke the yolks.' Now his voice is getting louder, less controlled. 'I broke every yolk I dropped into the pan.'

God forgive me, I'm glad about this.

'Why didn't you drop a little vinegar into the water for solidifying purposes?' I yawn.

Silence.

I'm not behaving as I should. I know that. Nothing else to say.

Chapter 7

Sleep was uneventful. It's today again. Somehow I got to bed. There's yellow-topped milk on the doorstep again. I give the kids their dinner money again and ask about their geometry exams.

Strange quirk of fate that. Different class groups. Same subject. Sibling playing against sibling. At one time it wouldn't bother me, but now. It's almost as if there's something sinister going on.

'Just trust in your heredity darling,' I tell Gavin. 'Anything to do with logic we get it in the end. Just use your head and not mine. You've got the answers in your blood. It's the gene thing.'

'The stuff doesn't work,' says Gavin, then suddenly asks why I go out so much.

'There's something wrong with my head, sweetheart,' I say. 'A sort of unhappiness.'

'You mean clinical depression,' he says firmly, still looking for signs of acne in the mirror above the kitchen sink.

Watches too much TV does Gavin. Then he says he thinks he's found a spot.

Gaynor says, 'It's pointless mum.'

And I say, 'What is? Geometry? Or the spot?' I know that either way she's right.

She's full of questions. Still full of questions, thankfully. It's apparent by the way she keeps pushing her blonde fringe away from prematurely furrowed eyebrows. She pushes a copy of *True Romances* into her school bag, then glances at me daringly as, dressing gown wrapped around me, I cross my legs, lean an elbow on the kitchen table and light another cigarette.

'Why do you and Dad keep snapping at each other?' she asks.

Still believes in this romance stuff doesn't she?

'I can't answer that because I really don't know,' I say.

But she can't take that in. Doesn't know enough, nor trust enough yet. She turns her back to pour a second helping of cereal into a chipped Pyrex dish, in silence. I'm expecting too much of her. Yet I feel vaguely disappointed and wonder who the romantic is, her or me?

Gavin's been listening. Says he doesn't care who snaps at who as long as he can have some pot noodles.

He's not untouched by what's going on around him any more than his sister is.

'I'm just a hopeless, incompetent mother,' I say. 'Don't take any notice of me.'

The frightening thing is they want to.

Phil shafts me in his oddly shaped bedroom then asks if I enjoyed his cock, then throws a sheepskin coat smelling of aftershave over me. I scratch my toenails on the thick, floral patterned mattress and say I'm a happily married woman, because I'm supposed to, and toss in a cynical smile for good measure. Hell, I've got to act the part. Then I doze. Feel the chill. Then I'm drifting in a haze, listening to my own breathing. The feel of the bedding is all wrong. Then gone. Why is it gone? There's a sudden blackness.

Thomas drags his cold feet along the stone floor of the kitchen, grasping a corner of the splintered, wooden table for support. Says we've got to get out, that he's read that the air is no good, and there's plenty of work for strong boys on the Southern farms now that the weather is changing.

I open my mouth to say he's not strong, that it's obvious, but there's no voice there. And I'm fighting down a panic. I can't let him know that. Am I real or not? There's something strange. Something wrong.

'I'm here,' I shout, fighting down an inexplicable fear. 'I'm here!' I'm standing like a statue in front of him.

There's a moment of silence.

Thomas looks at me questioningly, then shrugs off curiosity and coughs. The sound of his breathing is slightly noisier than the ticking of the clock on the shelf. His feet, obviously as cold as the stone slabs on the floor. His eyes say he can't distinguish the temperatures. I move towards him and hug him, because I have to, arms around lean shoulders. Then I see Mark pressing his familiar grinning face against the dust on the outside of the small window pane. There's something odd about his eyes. Something disturbing.

Thomas follows my gaze and stiffens, and his thin arms, wrapped around my waist, grip me tighter.

'It's the groom,' he mutters, 'that bastard groom. He'll bewitch you. Don't listen.' His grip becomes like a vice, and I'm fighting, fighting for breath.

Suddenly I'm spinning. I reach up an arm and grip the hook holding onions to the grime on the ceiling. 'I'm dying,' I yell, my lungs struggling to pull in air oddly thin. The picture and feel of Thomas melts, like a negative photograph exposed to sunlight.

Then there's a mist around me. Cold air. A fog. A nothingness. Someone is calling my name. Again. Yet again. I awake. But can still feel the heat of a pulsating wrist and the pressure of sweat-covered arms on my spine.

'I'll be back,' I find myself screaming. Know that I'll be back.

Phil is flicking his fingers against my cheeks and suggesting fashionable decaffeinated.

The sun is shining through polyester curtains.

He pulls on greying boxer-shorts and says 'How about eggs and bacon?'

His eyes are not Mark's. I know that. Don't I? My lungs drag in the steadily thickening air. A dream. That's all I've had. A dream like an episode of a soap opera. Nothing more. But a dream of dimming eyes. Phil pretends not to notice me shudder. Doesn't know where I've been. How can he? Doesn't realise he's got a mad woman on his hands. He pulls the sheepskin coat up to cover my neck in a satisfied gesture of consideration, or because a middle-aged body doesn't look as attractive after drinking from sunrise to sunset. I've no illusions about that at least. And yank it up to conceal my head. I'm cold.

'You've been drinking too long. Can't stand it like the rest of us. Ought to give it up.'

'I'm always cold when I'm naked,' I mutter. No surprise. That's the problem, the cold.

The coldness makes me dream of Thomas. And Thomas doesn't exist. Never did. I press the palms of my hands against the tightening heat in the middle of my spine.

Phil asks if I'm alright and I say, 'That's a bloody silly question.' And look at his eyes again. Just checking. He's not Mark the groom. Of course he's not the groom. My muscles relax and the heat in my spine fades. Goes where bloody alcoholic dreams go.

'I've got these faces in my head,' I explain. 'These smiles.'

I grasp his hand. Need to clutch something. And feel his sweat on my life-line. Then smell the mixture of peppermint and nicotine on his warm breath. Look up at the bare lightbulb.

'Sometimes people like me go crazy,' I say, searching for a response on his face.

He doesn't listen. Possibly hasn't got the time.

What's time?

That evening Rod and I routinely park our carcasses in the local pub. The done thing. He's informed me of that many times. He groans because he hadn't realised that it's quiz night. And the light is hurting my eyes so I complain. Loudly. Doesn't like complaints, does Rod.

There's a smell of salted peanuts and pine disinfectant recently poured enthusiastically over the carpet. And a lone moth crawling without energy across a small window.

'This place is nothing short of soddin' rubbish, if you ask me,' says Rod.

I gape into the amber nectar in my glass and say nothing. I've had plenty of practice. There's nothing I can say that he'll try to understand, I decide.

I'm thinking about the times I gripped his hand, almost always to try to dispel his lingering disapproval of the times I rested my face against his chest, without prior warning, in search of peace. Of the times I gripped his penis because I felt randy. Of the times I asked him if he loved me. Of the times he hesitated and then said 'Course I do, silly bugger. But there's a time and a place. You should know it.'

'Know my place,' I mumble. Then there is silence. Accustomed to silence, me and Rod.

I try to smooth out the creases in my unironed skirt, know he won't notice and, out of boredom, examine the display of car-boot sale bought glassware on a shelf above the bar, listen to the computerised humming of the flashing one-armed bandit.

Rod is telling me about a faulty starter-motor, then about an oil leak, and that his sister, Audrey, has dyed her thinning hair again, that she always did steal all of his conkers and that she's a pillock with no TV licence and has just gone into debt so that she can have a fridge-freezer with an automatic light. I nod.

'Time for another drink,' I suggest. Then tell him I've got cramp due to the period shit. He looks away. Rubs his hands together, embarrassed. 'Not my business.'

I can't bring myself to concentrate upon him. Can't look any longer. We're living a farce anyway.

'Any way you look at it,' I mumble.

I shift my gaze to a poster on the wall advertising an American lager. It makes no impression. Then towards the girl wearing black tights who's trying to chat up a boy in blue denim and displaying a crew-cut and a ring adorning his right earlobe. Old hat. That's all it is.

I start to think of some weirdo called Edward Lear because, being a weirdo myself, I like him. Something in one of his poems had a ring in its nose, but I can't remember what. Need another drink.

I think of my kids, a boy who thinks a man is a man, and a daughter who watches too much telly. After implying that she's lost her virginity she's come to the conclusion that a girl is a girl, so she should get what she can get. She never said that she felt this way. Had to find out for myself.

My fault, it has to be. And I've even started grinding my teeth again. Kids. Frigging question marks. That's all they are.

Rod buys me cheese and onion crisps, reads the racing results on Teletext. Remarks that the fine hairs above my top lip are nicotine-stained. He reaches over and slips a fiver into my jacket pocket for the purchase of bingo tickets. Some sort of bribe meant to zip up my lips, I believe. And tell him so.

'You think you're some sort of macho-man,' I say. 'I loved you once.' My words come out as little more than a whisper, but he hears them and shrugs.

'Laura, don't start spouting all that emotional shit again. Not in public. I've always been tolerant, and there's always been food on the table.'

And I say, 'So there has,' and wonder if I should tell him about Phil sticking his tongue and his cock inside of me. I'm not sure it really happened now. Or tell him about the dream. Or either. Or neither. I can't do it. It's not proper. Doesn't gel with my Fair Isle cardigan.

We're sat among the bronze of a Bass pub. Watching the rum and the cigarette smoke tainting Regency striped curtains, and the black shirts and swaying jeans of the locals, Rod's mates. Our mates. Now is not the time to rock the boat.

He's sipping his Cola and glancing at his highly-polished shoes. Could be contemplating the renewal of well-worn radials, or greenfly, or an unmentioned boil in his groin, or quantum physics. No way I can know.

'Do you ever have dreams?' I ask. 'I mean REAL dreams?'

He winces, like he's heard all this before. I don't recall bringing the subject up before, but must have done. I feel like gripping his arm to feel heat from his flesh working its way through unshrinkable cotton to reluctantly lick my fingers. But that wouldn't do. Someone could be watching, and then he'd grimace all the more.

I'm tapping the edge of my wedding ring onto the cool of a half-pint glass and nodding politely at women with wine and cashew nuts, and I'm wondering if there's enough chicken portions in the freezer at home to supply my brood with another cook-in-sauce supper. My mind darts bluntly, with a strange reasoning, as it always does when I've had a few drinks. The tongue is loosening. I can't stop it, so I stare at Rod's scarred nose and say, 'Our so-called marriage is a farce. It's the truth.'

So he says, 'It's all in your imagination, and if you think it's all over then you go. Because I won't.'

So I sigh and let the matter drop because I'm scared. I'm a schizophrenic. Must be. Half of me is wanting to tear his eyes out.

We gulp our last drink in silence then go out into the chill, treading the crispness.

An aged, half-blind white cat approaches us, glances up dispassionately then turns away. There's a windblown seagull resting and preening on the bonnet of our second-hand car. It moves away reluctantly then sits on the small brick wall and stares at us with slight interest, winter drizzle glistening on the unusual mottling of its wings.

It's only got one eye. Rod notices that and then asks if I fancy fish and chips. He should know better than that.

'It's not my scene,' comes the growl. I'm tired. Going to bed as soon as I get home.

Usual scenario.

'How's your dad?' he asks, out of guilt, when he finally climbs into the driving seat with his special and twice.

'He's mad.' I hope I'm exaggerating.

He nods grimly, informs me that what can't be helped can't be helped. 'Nature is nature. No-one can stop the march of time. And that's that. Simple isn't it.'

We go home.

It's almost dawn when the phone rings.

Dad is under arrest, I'm informed, and that is that. No way out. No excuse. He doesn't know the time of day, I'm told.

Rod stands beside me in his boxer shorts, looking for all the world as if he'd thought it would be the secret police phoning. It strikes me it must be a struggle for him to live with me, on account of me not fitting in. His eyes are criticising me while I slur into the mouthpiece shouting 'What makes you coppers such fucking experts anyway? Blood is thicker than thicker. Haven't you heard that?'

When I replace the receiver Rod says, gently for him, that my old feller was never right in the head. That this knowledge is there for anyone to see.

He points a finger at me to push home his point as if he expects it to really work, then, inexplicably, reminds me that my father didn't even wear a tie to our wedding reception. I don't remember it. Don't remember a thing about it.

'That says a lot,' he says. 'Blood will out.' Then he hands me three pound coins so that I can pay for a taxi.

'I've got to visit Dad, to find out what the Christ is going on,' I tell him. I almost feel guilty for touching his fingertips to take the cash.

'Laura?' He calls out as, having thrown a track-suit on, I reach the door. 'You've got to sort yourself out. You know that.'

'And pride?' I yell back at him. 'What about pride? Do I dump it?'

His thrown look says 'Yes.'

Chapter 8

It's almost daylight, yet I'm standing under a fluorescent light looking down onto a dark oak desk in a police station, and catching the smell of government supplied worsted dampened by night rain.

Dad shifts his feet. It is hard to imagine legs beneath his trousers.

A Sergeant chewing on a eucalyptus tablet yawns, and tells me that Dad was arrested in the early hours outside the green door of the Kirkgate Inn. That the old man was barefoot, whistling and abusive.

'He kept going on about the war,' he adds with a shrug, 'and shouting something about some woman he calls Alice.'

His smirk tells me he's thinking about Alice in Wonderland.

'That was my mum, he was talking about,' I explain quietly. 'Is that a crime? Even an old man should be allowed a guilt trip.' I'm tired out of my skull.

Dad's upset. He's led into a small back room to sip tea.

'He needs attending to,' the officer says when we're alone, because that's the type of thing he's been taught to say. 'We can't go on rescuing him like this. He shouldn't be out on his own.'

I feel a shadow behind me, blotting out the dawn light attempting to warm up the window. A familiar scent. A surprise. It's Phil, still smelling of lager, but now looking wide-eyed with interest.

'A novel situation, this,' he's saying. 'I found your old man leaning against a pub door and shouting like his head was about to burst. I couldn't leave him to closing-time muggers. Then the cops turned up. Like they do.' He gestures perplexity with his hands. 'All I could do was accompany him here. Needs someone with a clear head, does a situation like this.'

'Thanks a pile of shit,' I say. Then pick up a pen on a chain and sign to say I'll take temporary responsibility for the old man who managed to spawn me.

Dad shuffles out of a door smelling of fresh, government paint. A custard cream clasped between the third finger and thumb of his left hand. He hunches his shoulders, so that the old, green army cardigan he always wears tightens on his stooped spine.

He's tensing his jaw, and top denture gnaws bottom denture. He's forgotten to put some socks on and hasn't combed his hair. It's unlike him. Always a great one for doing the conventional things, my dad. But things change. People change.

He looks down at my sling-backed shoes, without seeing, like a schoolboy in contrition, and says that he's no excuse for his behaviour, like he's supposed to. Then adds that he simply had the idea that someone must know where my mother is. That she embroidered clover patterns on handkerchiefs and loved to wear green. Like that's supposed to mean something. He continues to ramble on.

'She knew the names of all the birds visiting her garden. And had bad feet all of her life, God bless her.'

'You never thought much about her when she was alive,' I snap, fighting memories of him reeling home from the pub with cold cod and chips in his pocket, and a grin saying it didn't matter. A man was a man. I remember her silence too.

'No-one like her should be forgotten.' He shakes his head, his voice deepening with every word, like the soundtrack of a BBC drama.

Do I remember her, is the next question. Of course I remember mother.

She was the one given to histrionics, and lending neighbours tea, and velvet curtains. The one who dutifully shed tears for friends who had husbands in the infirmary with cancerous tongues falling out into tissues, or brothers with syphilis, diagnosed late. She was the one who, once teatime was over, undressed in the lounge and scratched at her purple nipples in front of her unthought about offspring, then covered herself in floral winceyette. The one who cooked dumplings and was slightly unhinged, according to Granny. Mother was the one who spread-eagled her legs so that her ankles touched the arms of the moquette settee, and rubbed zinc and castor oil cream around her quim. The one for sighing and watching her children, wondering with a sort of pride if we knew she'd been fucked the night before, wondering if we knew what it meant. My brother and I did.

No doubt about it, we weren't little innocent mice. Children brought up on Crawshaw Estate weren't. That's why my brother pissed off to Australia as soon as he had the chance.

Father was the simple one, or pretended to be. It always annoyed me that, his deceit. But he couldn't change light bulbs or handle a tally man, so perhaps I was wrong. Mother was the one who never let him know he was being conned, and felt embarrassed about it. She'd married beneath herself, that was for sure. I can't stop myself snapping at him. Telling him if anyone has a pillock for a father, I have.

'And what the hell are you playing at, you haven't even bothered to have a shave.'

The taste in my mouth is like a cross between a soup kitchen and cut price petrol. And my feet hurt like they've never kissed slippers. There's the sound of strengthening drizzle hitting the kidney coloured rooftops.

Phil clutches my father's elbow and fights off a yawn. 'The old man is looking jaundiced,' he tells me, 'and that hole in his cardigan is a disgrace to mankind. It needs binning.'

'What? The cardigan? Or mankind?'

He knows it's too early in the day to expect me to talk sense.

Rod would have glared at me, not understood. His mother darned everything. Did do, until the day she fell over and died, whilst tending to her herb garden or making fresh bread or root ginger beer, or something. The family were like that.

'I don't feel well,' Dad mutters.

'Neither do I,' I say.

'Things aren't like they should be,' he adds, obviously addressing himself.

A pigeon crosses his path with a McDonald's fry in its mouth.

'You've got to thank Phil for taking care of me,' he tells me, almost stumbling off the pavement.

Funny, I hadn't realised how frail he'd become.

'Thanks Phil,' I say.

'I'm telling you I don't feel good,' Dad stresses.

'I don't feel good either,' I say again. And wonder why I'm playing this game.

There's a slowly spinning ball of fog inside my head. When I speak my tongue feels heavy. The words taste alien, wrapped in an invisible fur. Yet there's no reason for it. I haven't overdosed on vodka for weeks. I know it. I feel faint. Like this is yet another dream.

I find myself murmuring. Thomas used to say 'Things aren't like they should be.' My legs feel like diver's weights. Muscles stretching the blotchy covering of skin. There's a sudden increase in the surrounding chill. Yet I'm alright, and stone-cold, bloody sober. No explanation for this but a mind blowout.

'Who are you talking about then?' Dad asks me. 'Who the piss is Thomas? You keep going on about this Thomas.' He turns his head and looks at me. So does Phil. 'One of your fancy men, then?' the old man continues.

I tell him wearily that I don't know. I look at the carrier bags of dusters and Kit-Kats of early morning office cleaners scurrying to rub semi-polished desks, spray-kill flies from the tiles of urinals. Feel nauseous in the dawn. Don't know what I've said. Nor why. Only know it's rubbish.

We lapse into silence. All three of us having falling blood-sugar levels. It's six o'clock cringing under a pale morning of a sky. And we're trying to stretch up from last night's ale.

An insomniac woman with sagging bosoms and inexplicably wet hair rustles her pink mackintosh towards us, unknowing, and unthinking. Then accidentally bangs the war-torn wheels of her tartan shopping trolley against the swelling on my ankles. There's something about her face that I recognise. Something I can't put my finger on. The three of us walk on, morosely.

A number fifty-nine bus manages to miss our bodies because the Jamaican driver stops chewing his sandwich and jams on the brakes. He peers through his dust-covered window and screws up the right side of his mouth in slight surprise. It takes no more for me than a glance at the fading whites of his sexy eyes to bring up the realisation that he's become accustomed to this town. That he knows the greyness, the yuppies, the psoriasis sufferers, and the pink-cheeked drunks on Station Corner.

He winks at me as if to say he's accustomed to what he's accustomed to see, and believes in the whole soddin' set-up.

'Something to do with his religion, perhaps,' says Phil.

We must be familiar to the man, people like me accompanying old men in torn, green cardigans, stiletto-clad dreamers of nightmares. He's a no-one. A buyer of salted potatoes and sweetfish.

I wink at him, then feel stupid.

We weave our way along the pavements, making silly remarks.

Phil says, 'Do you remember that when we were kids we thought if you stepped on the cracks between the slabs a witch would get you, Hansel and Gretal style?'

I say, 'I remember when there were no pavements at all,' which, of course they both ignore, like the Victorian statues of has-beens on Foster Square.

There's a cool breeze licking the back of our legs. The old man scratches his arse through lined corduroy and believes the act's not been noticed. Asks me again:

'Who the fuck is Thomas?'

He's been asking that a lot lately. Because I've been talking to him a lot, thinking someone's got to listen. Totally naive, that's me.

Phil winks at me, uneasily, but shoots out a faint smile because he's used to playing the part of the clown. Then says, 'You're looking awfully pale, girl. Could be pregnant.'

So I snap that I'm only listening. Don't tell him I can smell insects lazing in nests of yellow hay or the rain on the excrement on steep, cobbled streets, or taste in my mouth a cocktail of overcooked pigs' trotters and worsteds and sweat and fear. I've got to show some semblance of sanity.

I've got to stay real, ask, 'Who's got change for the bus, then?' Because I've got to get home. I know I have. Definitely have.

But the fog in my mind hasn't completely gone. It's gathering momentum, blocking my eyesight. There's a sudden greyness and the steadily diminishing voice of Phil in my ear. A stench of urine floating from the kerbside. Someone invisible tugging on my anti-dandruff shampooed hair. A feeling that part of me is falling, leaving the rest to a nightmare.

Then I'm struggling to recognise a voice. Any voice. I do.

'I'll pay for breakfast,' whispers Phil, not noticing my confusion.

I recognise the warmth of his peppermint breath on the lobe of my left ear, the macho-type concern. Think that I'm going off him. Know that he's an anarchist, and that fiddling the tax office is easy for him, and money no great problem. Easy. I've got to concentrate on the mundane.

'Maybe you've got a touch of migraine,' he frowns.

'Yes, that's it,' I say eagerly. 'A touch of migraine. Where you see flashing lights and stuff.'

I'm lying, but what the hell does it matter.

'You're too tired to care,' Phil says, wisely.

He keeps a tight grip on Dad's right elbow, turns his face towards me again as we walk past Woolworth's, waves a hand in front of my face and says 'Hello, are you there?' As if he hasn't seen me before. He's watching. Then suggests that we go to El Greco's Continental Cafe for the two pounds per head, midweek breakfast, guaranteed English.

He holds open the plate-glass door of the cafe.

Then I feel the heat of his fingertips on my left wrist. I know it's only a game for him.

Dad is nodding. Then he's nodding again, as he blows on his frothy coffee and shifts his body weight from one leg to another because of the pain of his ancient corns. He's attention seeking. Wanting to talk about his clouded version of last night's adventure. His strategy doesn't work. His mind is becoming too muddled to be able to concentrate for most of the time.

The beginnings of senile dementia? Maybe it runs in the family. I shudder because I hadn't realised that I could become as hard as this. I'm staring at the coffee cup to avoid Phil's gaze. He's questioning everybody's questioning. No banter from me. Well known for banter, I am.

I shift my gaze to the anaglypta wallpaper, then towards the slightly used, silver-plated juke-box in the corner. One that still holds Elvis Presley and Neil Diamond.

No-one senses how dizzy I feel, and no more questions are asked.

Plates of sausage, beans and extra-fried bread are banged down on our egg-stained table by a hand with a rose tattoo. The bacon in this cafe is red and scrupulously clean. The waiters, at all times, have tea-towels draped over their arms, pretend to be sophisticated, and they always know the phone numbers of the local taxi companies. The usual crack. Nothing exciting. Nothing exciting in this town except what goes on in my head.

We eat in fluorescent-soaked silence. Then Dad, still gnawing on a slice of slightly cooked toast, curls his fingers over mine, for no reason I can understand, and squeezes them tightly. Then watches the whiteness creep over my knuckles. He's trying to be friendly because he's an old man and hasn't got far to go. I know that. But there's a real urgency there. Not a pleading. He's too proud for that.

I'm munching absently on a dry digestive biscuit and feeling a weight drag on my womb. I've got to begin menstruating soon. Got to. That would explain everything. It's hormones I'm at the mercy of. Hell, I know the score. That's the reason for the tears. The temporary madness. Got to reason things out.

Dad's prattling voice is suddenly softer than it's been for weeks, as if he's rising from some strange form of fog I'm struggling to keep out of.

'Where among the hounds of hell is Thomas, then?' he asks me again.

I'm feeling faint. Have never felt as faint before, not even flinched when a midwife unwittingly flaunted black-painted fingernails and the smell of vegetarian curry in front of me whilst I lay gasping on a hospital bed pushing an afterbirth out onto waterproof sheeting. Not even when, one crawling, midge-bitten summer's afternoon, my dog licked his gangly legs then haemorrhaged his stomach out while I sat, portraying shock in my garden chair, thinking that could happen to me.

Then I picked up the lifeless body, and dumped it in the dustbin. No big deal.

I'd almost forgotten about that incident. Yet it is coming back to me in full force now, the memory of the only death I've ever witnessed, along with a totally unconnected smell of apples.

I feel even more faint. Can no longer take in the aroma of the espresso coffee.

The proprietor, in white tie and designer stubble, is resting his elbows on the formica of the counter and staring at me.

Nothing seems real any longer. And the fog in my mind is thickening swiftly. My arms are becoming numb, numbness is crawling from my shoulders like an anaesthetic. A handbag bounces from my lap and bounces against a table leg. I follow, there's no way to stop myself. Then my shoulderblades are touching the warmth of the floor. Faint voices turn into nothing. My Dad's here somewhere. I can feel his presence, smell that infernal peppermint on his breath.

Smells, always smells. I'm somewhere else. Have to be somewhere else. Don't know, for a moment, who I am.

I can discern children swearing and skipping by an open window. I'm standing there, trying to cool my face, my hands pressed against a long skirt of unbleached linen, passed down to me from an old neighbour. My hair is drawn back, fastened with two large grips, and pulling against my skull.

I stand there for a long time, my naked feet cooling on the stone, scullery floor. That is what I wanted them to do. It reduces the inexplicable swelling in my ankles. The air is that of damp October, yet I know that we've just had a heatwave. And know that I've got a toothache. The kind with long-standing abscesses that people say a hot needle will break. All nonsense. It's not important. I know what's right and what isn't.

It's getting darker. A shadow creeps across the wall, and there's a distorted reflection of a face coming from the bottom of my best copper pan hooked on the wall. There's a small spider crawling along the yellowing lace of my bodice in an attempt to escape the dust-filled air fleeing from the nearby brickworks. I've never seen the specks, nor looked for them. But Thomas says he has and they're there and that animals don't like them. Thomas is a romantic fool. Always has been.

I turn to face my nervously silent brother standing in the doorway nervously fighting the urge to cough up phlegm. Nervous. That's my brother. Can't be described any other way. He catches my frown, but doesn't mention it.

His boots are worn down around the edges, by the rough, dry earth on his journey home. His fists are clenched, as they always are when he's swallowing back words, ready to bubble like scrag of mutton in beef fat. His eyes are large with excitement so I try to stop it bursting. He's not fit enough to become excited.

'I noticed the air hung low today,' I say casually. 'No chill, merely a faint scent of lanolin.'

He's not listening.

'I've done nothing all day. Nothing but stand here by the window,' I say desperately. 'Can't remember what I've been thinking of, nor why.'

My forehead is clammy and I feel a weakness in my arms. A weakness uncalled for. He's going to tell me what he's got to tell me. Knows I don't want to know.

'We've gone and done it, sis. Done it. The men and I.'

A vein throbs in his neck because he thinks he's brought good news. His exhilaration is like an odour crawling across the floor. I can't cope with this. I wipe my hands on my skirt and force myself to wonder if I've managed to scrub the chicken fat I spilled yesterday, from the uneven tiles. Wish I could remember. But today I feel vague, like the curse is coming on and the unsteadiness of the weather is doing nothing to help my wellbeing.

He's looking at me, perplexed about what he perceives to be my lack of interest. I've made his news seem minor. I didn't mean to.

'We've only got to work in the weaving from six until four now,' he says, shaking his head. 'I thought that would please you. It means I'll be home early. You'd like me to be here to run my share of errands, wouldn't you?'

He's bemused. And I feel a pang of guilt. His excitement is like an odour and perspiration is running down his cheeks, twisting like a grass snake around his lips. His weekend treat of aniseed balls is on the heat of his breath.

He suddenly shows me his wire-torn hands, hands that he's been hiding behind his back. They're old and beaten, lank, dead prey. He's been scouring the scrub on his way home and caught a rabbit, using nothing more than stones and string and his 'secret' as he calls it.

'But it did have a lame leg,' he adds with modesty.

Blood drips from its still damp, brown fur onto the grime of the floor. He puts it onto the splintered table, then pushes down his collar and shows his yellowing teeth in a sheepish grin, as if in a promise that we'll always get by because he's the man of the house. I hate it that he thinks like that. He should be out courting, somewhere. But he's got beautiful teeth. Beautiful teeth worth counting. None of them gone. None of them.

I've been standing so still for so long that I feel stiff. Weak.

He supports me while I look around and try to straighten up my spine. Always caring, is Thomas. But there's something wrong. I can't concentrate. The room is strange and I can't understand why. It's too cold, and too brown. And the ceiling is too low.

I think I hear a murmuring.

'Were you speaking to me just now, Thomas?'

He shakes his head. Clearly doesn't know I'm afraid of madness. Can't understand, mercifully. It would scare the guts out of him were I to be taken to an asylum. As for me? I don't think I'm bothered. I don't know where I am or what I'm doing at times, find myself shaking a mattress I've already shaken or damping down the fire twice.

Thomas is looking at me with concern and brushing the dust from my apron, then touches the tightening muscles on the back of my neck. Seems proud. Says he knows all about women's problems.

'You've been suffering from them vapours again,' he says. 'Not many lads nowadays have sisters who take to the vapours. It's a sign of class, like.'

I clutch his hand, feel him flinch as my grip touches abrasions caused by the cutting edge of the belts of the machines and the whip of the wool.

'Bert is the one to thank for our decrease in hours,' he tells me, with a firmness given to the young.

'Bert?'

'You know Bert,' he insists, 'he helps us lads. Stands up to Foster's men and even your man Mark.'

'Mark?' I am fighting off tiredness. This is an old story. Thomas never took to Mark. Said he kept his distance too often.

'We're talked about every time you let him come here, woman. Don't you understand?'

All I can do is shake my head. He's too young to know. Too young to know anything. I reach up and touch his cheeks. They're hot. Too hot. Another attack of fever perhaps.

'I know you're sorry, because you're always sorry. But things will be alright,' Thomas promises me. 'They'll be alright.'

Then a voice inside my head bounces from my eardrums. Not mine. Too deep to be mine.

'Give her a vodka.'

Vodka?

What the hell is vodka?

Then comes a familiar chill. I can almost spell it backwards. Wonder if I should do. Then a breeze licking the badly stitched hem of my dark grey skirt. Screaming in my head asking for rum and peanuts, screeching 'Where is the phone?' and 'How about a taxi?'

There's a slight sensation that fingers are tapping on my cheek. I close my eyes.

Thomas is still gripping me. He spits onto the beige-coloured rag he's pulled from his pocket, then uses it to wipe the dirt from his trousers.

'That rabbit was a really strong buck,' he grins mischievously, like a boy done for scrumping apples.

He doesn't notice my unease. But why should I care? He's my brother. Clad in appropriate brown, but still my brother, of the same flesh as I, living in the same place as I. He never mentions it, but he knows as well as I do that our parents died within months of each other of an illness to do with genitals. Something dirty. It has to be something dirty.

He crouches on the floor because he's comfortable that way, while I lean against the wall and watch the flames of the fire. Somehow I've managed to keep a blaze going all day. Without reason, I'm telling myself, shuddering. Nothing but a vague sense of coldness.

A voice of a familiar grey-faced man floats from across the street. I know him well. He'll be pulling a rickety cart, almost empty. I return to the window and watch him. Thomas has no more to say. And the gloom seems to be deepening.

There's a docker in a wide, cracked belt swaggering along the cobbles, shouting to someone he thinks is hurrying ahead, to go to hell and stay there. Then he spots a face in a window.

'Fuck it, woman. You promised to buy me a jug brimming over. I'm not going to be a fist-fucker for you for nothing. You're mad, woman. Don't you understand?'

The face disappears.

I'm trying to concentrate on their conversation because they're neighbours of mine. But it's difficult. There are whisperers in my mind, whirling nonsensical, talking cars. What is cars?

I don't let on to Thomas.

There's a lamp of panic in my lungs. Growing. It and I. 'Thomas?' I say, pleadingly, as he helps me back to my chair.

'What?' He wipes his hands on a sleeve of my lavender coloured blouse.

'Supposing we die?' I frown. 'I've never thought of that before. But now I'm thinking. Just supposing?'

His thin lips turn into a pout and while he studies his answer he scratches his armpits.

'You mean when we die,' he corrects me, trying to hide his annoyance. 'I'm not well, and you know it.'

The poor boy is fucking dying. I know it and he knows it. And yet, thoughtlessly I've now jumped into his mind. Stomp. Stomp. Loaded him with ifs as if he was a donkey from the fair.

I'm feeling more drowsy than ever. He reaches up his arms and tries to shake my shoulders, his eyes showing incomprehension. A moth that has been slumbering on the window-sill moves from its damp bed and touches my hair.

'Listen to me, girl. We've got a ten hour day.' Thomas is shouting. 'A ten hour day. That means I'll be home a lot to help. And all you can do is go into one of your dreams. Don't do this to me.' Then he says that he's going to go to the new Mechanics Institute.

'They teach boys,' he stresses. 'Then when I've learned things we'll be rich. Understand it, girl. Understand. When I've learned things we'll be able to get out of here, go to the hills, the seaside maybe. Even to Borneo. I've read about Borneo. It's green as far as the eye can see. You'll like that.'

His voice is enthusiastic. Manic almost. He can't stop talking.

I watch the slow curving of his lips as he's speaking. Ignore the gurgling of washing on the boil. I like his smile. It's the only smile I can trust won't hurt me. But his thoughts are deceiving him. That's what thoughts do.

He should know that, should recall the smile of the woman who got him to visit her cottage to cut down the weeds in her garden, and then shouted 'Thief'. Like I recalled a smile from Mark when he pulled his cock from my quim screaming and smelling of horses then thrust it up my arse.

But Thomas trusted a smile. Always would. Too much hope. That is what Thomas has got. Too much hope and a torn shirt and head lice. I can't tell him. Daren't. He's still talking. This time, about blackberries ripening in the cracks of the viaduct.

'How's that for a surprise at this time of the year?' But he's told me this many times.

He's watching me. Timidly presses the coolness of his fingers onto my flushed cheeks in search of some reaction. Then, satisfied that I'm still conscious, removes them.

His mind is flitting about and his expression suddenly darkens in bemusement. 'I visited the graveyard today. While I was chasing a rabbit,' he explains, in answer to my raised eyebrows. 'It's full of pots containing flowers.' He looked amazed. 'Special flowers, I mean. The likes of their colours you won't see growing around here. And there were tombstones and stone surrounds, fancy pebbles, the kind that people pay for.'

'You mean that you would like such stupid things,' I mutter, annoyed. I don't get a response.

I'm just so tired. Too tired to see and hear. Or perhaps I'm dying.

Talking about it has tempted fate. I'm too weary to care. I hear a voice calling me again. Tugging. Tugging.

My brother's hand moves away from mine. And I try, without success to call his name through the thirst of my throat. Feel the heat from the weakening glow of the fire on my skin.

'Touch me, you bastard. Touch me.' Not my voice. Not mine.

I think I've pissed myself and burnt a hole in my jacket with a dropped cigarette.

Someone's pressing my shoulders back to stop me rocking.

'You KNOW where you are,' Phil is saying. 'You're sitting in a red, plastic chair in a cafe, with a bump on your head. You KNOW where you are.'

I don't want to use my voice. Am not sure that I've got one or want one. My nostrils suck in the odour of mushy peas and the air of fresh nicotine. Phil is pressing his thumbs on the back of my neck, holding my head between my knees. It feels like he'll do it forever. That my future view of life will be of primrose coloured, lino tiles forever.

I know something about tiles. The colder kind. He releases his grip slowly and glances around the El Greco in slight embarrassment. Then clears his throat and signals to the white clad Greek crinkly-haired counter hand that we need some more coffee.

Sensation is coming back into my legs. I can feel the blood reluctantly warming the backs of my toenails, pumping through channels.

'So?' Phil asks me, glancing at his watch, 'What was the point of pretending to be comatose?'

'What?'

'Exactly that. What?' He raises the padded shoulders of his off-white suit into the air. 'You know what you've done? Your father is over in the corner feeding coins into a robbing bandit like there's no tomorrow and possibly no today. He's as worried as a womb-stitched rabbit on heat.'

'About what?'

'About you, silly bitch.'

I clutch my elbows. Can't answer. I've got to have time to think. I need to think. Work my pounding head out. Clean it up. Maybe I'm having some sort of withdrawal symptoms and just sort of wandered off. Sane or insane.

'I've got to know, for fuck's sake,' I say out loud.

'What the hell is happening to you?' Phil asks. 'There's no simpler question so answer it.'

Simple? He's just another pillock brains isn't he?

The coffee burns my tongue and I ignite a cigarette with trembling hands, watching the glow on the disposable lighter. And thinking. Supposing I told this guy that I wandered off into the past, a past I didn't believe existed? Suppose I tried to explain about Thomas the unexplainable?

He would tell Dad and then Dad would go out of his way to call at the betting shop on Saturday morning to give Rod the nod and the wink, and before I knew it I'd be whisked off into some sort of drying-out ward. A soul-destroying place stinking of Dettol and chicken soup, where people in white coats stand behind you in huge lounges on bingo nights waiting for you to either pee yourself or slit your wrists.

So I take Phil's left hand between both of mine, try not to sound pleading because I'm a survivor. Veins are poking my temples and my tongue is as dry as a newly purchased Brillo pad. And tastes like it, tinged with aniseed balls.

Why aniseed balls?

Now I've got to make sense. And know I have to. But I feel nervous. Vague. Can't concentrate, not even on the young fly crawling along the checked cloth covering the table.

Phil drops a cigarette in front of me then asks the question again. Gently this time. 'What's wrong with you, angel?'

So I say, 'Sorry Mark, I can't tell you.'

And he glares at me. Watches me shiver as I realise what my hormones have said. He says he's not called Mark and never has been. Figures, really. It's time to change the subject. But the panic rising as a fur ball in my throat has its own voice, like something from a horror B movie. Whispers. Suggests. Shouts.

'I'm going fucking mad,' I proclaim angrily. 'Don't you know? Can't you see it in my eyes?'

He fingers the old, sixties cravat worn loosely around his neck, his eyes matching the green of the paisley. Then coughs, quietly. Presses three fingers onto the right shoulder of my jacket, and makes sure one of his knees is touching mine under the table.

'I've got a few fresh prawns dying for it, and a bottle of Barcardi at home,' he whispers. 'We could talk or something. And that will help.'

He must think I was born about the same time as the micro-chip.

'So that will sort my head out?' I snap. 'That's your answer is it? How will you explain that to your girlfriend who works at the bakeries? Won't, I suppose. After all, there's nothing to tell is there? Often entertain mad women at your place do you?'

Phil shrugs. Offers the explanation he thinks I am expecting, 'You're too bogged down in domesticity, Princess. I've seen it before. All that family stuff. Causes stress, does that. So you're frustrated and run down. Understandable.'

For a guy who admits to having spent time finger-fucking for a living, to never having been pissed off or married, he seems to think he knows a lot. He's got things on his mind.

'My kitchen floor is made for a good blow-out between you and I. You need that,' he says. 'You know you do. You've got to be sorted out somehow. By someone. And I care for you. Care for everyone. I'm your knight on a white charger.'

I don't give him the backlash from my tongue that he deserves. I'm too exhausted, know that sooner or later the fun has to stop, if only for a while.

'There's got to be something more,' I say out loud. 'Always has been.' I can smell my own naivety.

'Like an oil leak in your Rod's old car, I suppose? Or maybe you've given in to him and joined an embroidery circle?'

I wince, because there are some things, like venom, we do have in common. We're linked. Like a viper and an adder fleeing from a mongoose.

He offers me what he says is his last cigarette, but I know he's still got two unopened packets in his pocket. He gets them from his brother who fiddles the supermarket till during his Saturday job. Neither of them can be trusted. Phil and his ilk always rock the boat. Bastards with designer stubble who, when trouble comes, curl up into hedgehog-type balls and withdraw until the fog goes.

All to do with images. Like Rod, hiding beneath a prescribed veneer. I've worked that out for myself, I have. Nothing to choose between the Devil and the sea. Destroyers. Honest madness can't destroy. Only pretentiously sane people can. I've read enough obscure library books to know that.

'I don't need your kitchen floor Cushion-floor to fuck on,' I tell him.

'So?' he says. 'Just come home with me.'

Now it's my turn to shake my head. Instinct. That's what I've got. Plenty of instinct.

'I'll come home with you someday,' I say bluntly. 'Some Easter, perhaps, but not now. All we have between us is ... I can't think of the appropriate word.'

I've pondered on situations like this before, know the pattern of the brainwaves, wonder if I've got a thrush infection and could transfer it, then side-step my mind to think about the boil on Rod's neck. I don't need a 'bit on the side'. But there's always the problem of Rod's pink-shirted dart's night, of him walking off into the cool of Wednesday sunsets. Me, then, masturbating in the floral-curtained bedroom, afterwards rising to fry chips. Then him coming home sullen, preoccupied, forgetting to say hello. Only sods would do that.

Then there's the thought of my kids, slightly acned, only slightly hungry, with the same nose as him, and acid words inherited from me, and my mother's liking for sighs.

They're my flesh, for heaven's sake, but alien, and prematurely preoccupying themselves.

I've no illusions. No illusions at all.

'So I'm bogged down with bleedin' domesticity,' I admit to Phil. Or could be admitting to myself. I'm not sure who I'm talking to. Cursing at. 'Nobody talks to me,' I say suddenly. 'Nobody tells me anything.' Except the people inside my head, I'm thinking.

I chew slowly on a doughnut pressed into my hand because it's thought I need sustenance, and wonder, for a moment, if my lapses into fantasy are as pale as those of a child playing with catalogue cut-outs of smartly dressed people.

But fantasising then was voluntary. And now? Not now.

Phil brings me more coffee and has the sense to say nothing.

Dad's still in the room. I can sense him.

This is hyper-sensitivity, I tell myself. I've got to do something with my soul. Maybe I should buy some multi-vitamins and make an excuse to go, stay with one of my arthritic aunts in Scarborough for a while. The ones with nice smiles and floral patterned teapots and picture frames decorated in plastic resin and seashells. The twins who cried into handkerchiefs because of husbands amputated in the desert in a long gone war.

They stock their fridges with Colas and Lasagnes, give me hot water bottles and Aspirin, bemusedly wrap me in pink blankets and, on warm days, introduce me to delphiniums and bingo.

Kind-hearted souls.

God, what a bitch I am, I'm thinking.

People died, but what does it matter? I can still take out compound interest loans, buy red shoes and dive headlong into whisky. Why not? It's the kind of behaviour expected of a menopausal twat.

Can't explain all this to Phil. Wouldn't want to. He's flown from my nastiness, muttering that I need time to sober up. Now he's exchanging banter with two Irishmen at the corner of the counter and studying the cigarette machine, because he has a thing about machines.

Dad's staring out of the window towards the bus station, watching the green buses snail by, and some homeless guy selling magazines on a corner. The back of the old man's neck is glistening in sweat. It's always glistening in sweat, I remember.

He wants to go home to slippers and goldfish and Teletext, I know he does. Where he can assemble his jigsaws under the light of a pink plastic lamp and swear at his corns. He created the jigsaw himself, years ago, using a fret-saw and flour glue and snow scenes from Christmas cards.

Clever man, once, my dad. Could leap from conversation to conversation. Doesn't say much nowadays. Doesn't take part in real conversation.

'My fucking feet hurt,' he suddenly says. Loudly.

So there you are, I tell myself. He's spoken.

Then he turns towards me. Comes up with a topic I don't want him to. Not bothered about hurting people's feelings, is Dad. Not bothered at all. 'Who is this fucking Mark, then?' He points a finger at me accusingly. 'You mentioned him, so answer.' Just like pulling wings off a butterfly, this game he's playing now. Playing it like cold fingertips stroking my spine. I wish he hadn't done that. He's pricking the bit of my mind that is still me. I'm his mad daughter and without knowing it he's trying to push me over the edge, is that it?

'Not now, Dad,' I warn. 'I've just had a silly dream.'

I'm looking around me because people are listening. This is a place to find people listening.

'Whatever you've heard me say, there's no such person as Mark Thorne.'

I jump, visibly. What in the land of fuck am I saying?

He doesn't miss the signs. Senile or not, he's ruthless. As ruthless as ever. Doesn't know or wouldn't know why, even when given the option.

'You're attention-seeking. You've been out reading headstones,' he says, disgusted. 'Been loitering around the graveyard and it's gotten to you.'

'What?'

'Thorne,' he says irritably. 'You've learned all about Thorne, you bastard. The fool who obeyed his masters. The one who locked some kids inside the mill. Saw them burn, he did. Used horses to keep their families away from the gates. You've read all about it in the library,' he accuses loudly. 'That's what you've done. The worst bastard that ever was in our family, him. And you can't let well enough alone.' He raises his voice. 'Hero-worship him, do you?'

He's more coherent than normal. Too coherent.

'I don't know what you're talking about, Dad,' I shout. 'Know nothing about it. Why can't you leave me alone?' My mouth is dry. And there's nothing I can think about. Nothing I can make sense of.

He clicks his worn dentures together, it sounds like tupperware dishes hitting tupperware bowls, then sits down at the other side of the table, the heels of his shoes squeaking as he pushes the metal chair legs against them. He's slowing down, even more than I am, and probably has the same kind of arthritis. Genes. That's all that's down to. He clutches his elbows like a comfort blanket because he's in a mood. I know the signs. Know he can't, at present, be reasoned with.

Phil shuffles his leather soles and comes to stand behind him, crinkling the cellophane he's tearing from his cigarette packet. He coughs loudly and signals with a tilt of the head to look through the window. He looks guilty because he perceives he's important. Guilty of something in his imagination.

'It's Sonia,' he hisses to me. 'Your mate Sonia on her way in for morning coffee. Say nothing.'

What he really means is don't tell her I tried to get you to suck my cock, otherwise she might let her tongue slip off the news in front of Rod someday.

He doesn't know me. Doesn't know me at all, does Phil.

'She could think that there's something going on between us,' he says.

'Then she'd be wrong,' I say. 'Wouldn't she?'

Dad is still muttering. But his ramblings have to go onto the back burner for a while.

When Sonia is out and about no-one gets time to ramble, or think. She guides her hips in. Then she orders a lemon tea, winks at the counter assistant, because one never knows who one might meet one when one is in difficult financial circumstances.

She sits next to me, giving out the perfume of poppies, then folds her legs, tells me that she just happened to be passing and spied me through the plate-glass. 'I've been for emergency dental surgery, my dear. You know how exhausting that is. By the way, how are your children?'

Why the hell does she keep asking me that? She's no kid-lover. Told me, one day, over glasses of sherry, that she was sterilised at the age of twenty-nine in case of 'mistakes'. I need to get out. Need some fresh air. My head is still throbbing. And asking. I can't stop it asking.

There's no-one to speak to. I can't talk to Dad. He of the Harris Tweed jacket worn from 1974. Can't do with his shitty talk about my crazy dreams. Not just now.

Phil brushes non-existent dust from his jacket and offers to take him home, show him where the pavements are.

'Laura and me will see you're ok,' he suggests, and clearly can't see I'm working up a satisfying, bloody-minded mood and don't want to take part in this charade. He doesn't recognise the vibes.

Well, he can't get too involved can he? Hasn't got the guts.

Sonia yawns, tells me she's feeling weary.

'I'm not falling for all this pretend friendship fuck,' I tell her. 'No. I'm going out and may be a little while.' Like Oates, I'm thinking. My deserts of snow are the gutters littered with residue of McDonalds cheeseburgers in a bun with pickle.

'Ok,' she says, her mind jumping quickly from one boring thing to another. 'If you spot some of them cut-price Tampons in Boots window on the way just pop in and get me some, and I'll give you the money later. Or get me something from the delicatessen selling that lovely Polish cake with the apples inside.'

She claps her hands in anticipation, like a trained Shirley Temple, expects her act to be swallowed. 'I promise you I'll reimburse you.'

I don't answer.

Phil offers Dad another cigarette, hands one to me without speaking. Then takes Dad's arm. My father is looking tired. Confused again, angry because his vagueness comes and goes and he can't do anything to control it. But he knows. When his mind is not preoccupied with incontinence pads and gas bills he knows. He's told me that often. Knows where he is and what he is. Sometimes, even what he's talking about.

Chapter 9

I'm alone. And it's quiet here in my brain. Even the town's pigeons have walked around me.

Phil has taken Dad back to the old man's semi-detached as a favour to me and I've nothing to worry about. So why do I feel uneasy?

I've had a few drinks in the warmth of The Pheasant with no reason to speak if I didn't want to. And most of the time I didn't want to. I've met Rock-Bottom Tommy there, who owed me a lager and bought me one. Then I bought raffle tickets for The Big Breakfast to be drawn on Saturday, and purchased one of the fresh cheese sandwiches.

Everything is normal. No need to worry.

I'm walking. Right now, I'm walking. The wind rustles my badly-permed hair and leaves lick my worn down, tan shoes. I've already had an emergency pee behind some bushes. And listened. Listened for voices. Because that's what graveyards are all about.

This cemetery is clean. Well swept. Well planted with daffodils.

Don't know what I'm doing here. I've been conned again. By Dad's mind again. I've had a few private vodkas and should have known better than to follow this line. Dad never said anything, merely suggested by gestures. Could be something to do with genes, and I ought to be sick of pissing genes dropping blood and ammonia all over the soddin' place.

I'm digging fingernails into my pockets in search of tab ends and searching for Mark Thorne's grave. That's the sort of piss artist I am.

Alright, so I feel relaxed. I'm reacting to Dad's reaction to tranquillisers. That's all I'm doing.

There's nothing here. Nothing but weeds and birds pecking at dog shit, and blackness.

It's a wrong time to go for a walk. Time to go home, to sit silently in the moquette chair by the side of the TV. Try not to breathe on my children, and I could always change the bedding.

I need to change the bedding.

My heels click on the uneven Tarmac. The Council never mends roads on our estate. That has been long understood. Too many Jamaicans here, too many Walkmans, too many boarded up shops, too many too manys. And people are worn down.

I'm becoming manic now, I realise. Depressed. For no good reason.

My cat runs through the rain-soaked gate to greet me and wipes its tail on my calves. It smells of semen. I know it. Know the story. Can even guess which tom has been up to it on the moss of the garden, pushing out its barbs. Cat's penises all have barbs to stop the queen running. I know about it. Read about it in a book.

I come to a halt. Stand as still as I can.

Cat walks away, unnerved by my silence. I could have comforted it, but shitting hell, how many plonkers can I carry?

Rod is standing in the kitchen with an egg-poaching pan in his hand. Frowns, when I walk in, as if he's been waiting. I can hear my daughter's voice upstairs, her self-conscious giggle, and suspect she's looking at the flickering of some Australian soap on her portable. Shout up 'Good on you mate.' Don't mean it.

It's almost five o'clock. And Rod asks, 'Where the chuff have you been?' Knows where. 'You've been with your chuffing Dad again, down town. All you're bothered about is your chuffing Dad.'

I'm too tired to argue. Not interested. And I realise that that should worry me.

I watch his pelvis as he moves efficiently around the room collecting dishes and emptying ashtrays. Wait for him to say something meaningful. He doesn't. He's got a sulk on. Steam from the kettle bathes the beige nylon curtains, and a lone silverfish scurries underneath the fridge. But for the purr of the lightbulb and Rod's dramatic sighs, there is silence.

The best thing I can do, I decide, is to kick off my shoes in the hall and go to bed. Have an early night wrapped in duvet and listen to the echoes of his grumblings through the muffling of the walls and cool my ankles on the candy-striped sheets.

'It's too early to go to bed,' he mutters, as I slip off my blue jacket and throw it onto the back of a kitchen chair. 'You're not right in your head,' he adds. Then winces, as if he didn't mean it.

Too late for reconciliations now. His breath, skimming the top of my head, is warm, leaves an aura of Kit-Kats and nicotine.

Going upstairs is easy.

I curl up on the mattress and cling to a pink pillow-case, wishing that my ill-fitting dentures wouldn't make me dribble on the bedding during the night. They will, of course, they always do. Rod persuaded me to have my teeth extracted the last time I was pregnant because due to my condition it wouldn't cost anything. 'Better now than later,' he said. God, what a fool I am. Now here I am, toothless, relying on plastic.

Doesn't know what he's done to me, does he? Never knows what he does to me. He's almost the past. Doesn't understand.

I hear his footsteps on the stairs. The worn-down slippers. His coughing hitting the badly painted walls. Then he's leaning over me, the odour of the aftershave his sister bought him last Christmas hitting my nostrils.

'Enough is enough,' he says. 'You're drunk again. You know you're drunk.'

He doesn't reach out to touch me. Nor smile.

'Well fuck me,' I say nastily. 'Go on and fuck me if you dare. But you already have, haven't you, with your words and your damned silly spit?'

He looks horrified.

'You're a sorry little bastard,' I say, shaking my head. 'A mean little man playing house. Don't you know that? We've got nothing. Nothing,' I slur. 'And I'm supposed to be your wife.'

Why won't he touch me? Listen to me, then speak and mean it?

He turns his back to me, looks around the room as if he hasn't seen it before and is not impressed. Then runs a finger along the embroidered cover on the dressing-table. He's avoiding his reflection in the mirror, and mine, and pretending not to listen.

'So when did you last dust this place?' he says, 'Go into the bathroom and you'll find a damned great cobweb behind the toilet pedestal. I noticed that yesterday.'

'So?' I ask. 'Spiders have to eat don't they?' What the hell is he trying to do to me? 'I'm your fucking wife,' I scream, 'talk to me.'

'Show me a fucking wife,' he suggests quietly, 'and I might talk.'

I pretend not to feel the sting. I've had children to him, pointed out the pimples on his back, washed stains from his underpants. Screamed loudly and screamed quietly. What more can he want?

'Am I your wife or aren't I? You haven't even asked me where I've been or what's happened. We're strangers.'

I've only just realised that myself.

'Shit knows or cares,' he says. There's nothing in his eyes. Nothing that I know.

He walks quietly downstairs. I hear the click of a television switch. The voice of Channel 4 News.

When I lug my heavy suitcase downstairs he says nothing. Nothing to say.

'I'm still the same person you married,' I say.

But I'm not am I? I don't bake sponge cakes anymore, or listen to his talk of carburettors, or feel happy about undressing in the dark. We always undress in the dark. Not bloody normal at our age.

'We've no reason to stay together now, see,' I tell him, as he throws me a disbelieving smirk. 'No reason at all. Unless you can give me one.'

There may be something I haven't thought of. Or could you put your arms around me, or cease fucking me in the dark then pretending it hasn't happened?

'Whoever taught you that fuck is a dirty word anyway?'

I'm close to getting into full flow and he knows it. Close to taking down the wall clock, because it's mine. Probably the only bloody thing in this house that is. Paid for out of my bingo winnings.

Rod goes into the bathroom and bolts the door behind him. 'Self-preservation,' I snarl. I can hear slow steady brush strokes on the wall, as he goes on with the decorating he started yesterday. I call his name but he doesn't answer. Conversation over.

The kids are in the pink and blue of their rooms, Gavin listening to the buzz of his computer and probably squeezing a fresh spot like a typical adolescent, and Gaynor screaming at the dog to get down from her bed. Her voice is even angrier than normal. The walls in this house are thin enough for me to know that.

They know that I'm going, but expect me back. Like Rod expects me to crawl back. That's it, I realise, the bastard expects me to return with a proverbial tail between proverbial legs and a promise to knuckle under.

'I'll be back to collect the kids tomorrow,' I shout, slamming the door behind me. 'I'll be back.'

Now I'm standing at the gate and catching my breath, waiting for him to come running after me because I've read too many Mills and Boons and that would make me safe again. Stupid bugger, I am. I've nowhere to go. Nowhere except to Beth and Fred's large semi-detached down Cherry Lane. Can't stay with Sonia of the plucked eyebrows and sixties record collection. Her designer-bearded toy boy wouldn't like the intrusion.

There's a large slug in front of my garden gate. Got to be stepped over gingerly.

But there's a bigger problem. I'm disenfranchised because of my stubbornness. Yes, that's the word. Disenfranchised. And can't even spell it.

Alone. No big deal.

Sonia is watching me from across the street, her red paint-chipped fingernails holding back the crisp white net of expensive, lounge curtains. The spasmodic tic in her right eye, which she once boasted to me was 'Psychosomatic, darling', is visible, even from here.

Her buxom figure disappears from sight for a moment. Then she's standing in the doorway, beckoning to me.

She volunteers uneasy concern in a nervous voice.

'But perhaps you were being hasty with Rod,' She says, when I explain. 'It was a very short and sweet argument you had, wasn't it?'

'And trivial?' I volunteer. She's searching her memory bank for words.

'The question is are you alright?' she says, as if she's just been a witness at a séance.

'I can't be,' I say. 'I've just pissed up a marriage. And if you're waiting for me to shed frigging tears, forget it.'

She's got the skin of a rhino, this woman. There's a theatrical sigh. 'Better to find out about it now rather than later,' she purrs, watching my heels crunch over the gravel. I haven't washed my face. She can see that. My mascara is running.

I'm wondering if she's gloating, but tell myself I don't really care. I've ousted myself by being bloody-minded. That's what I've done. She nods, as if she understands what I've been trying to say. 'I'll keep my eye on your family for you,' she promises.

So I say, 'I hope it's not the eye with a tic.' And wonder why I'm hanging on to frivolity. I could kick myself in the cunt. Can't keep away from sarcasm can I?

'A good night's sleep, that's what you need,' she advises. And I shudder. 'Maybe if you kept off the liquor,' she suggests.

There's a cool breeze blowing. There's a mange-suffering mongrel following me across the footpath on the sport's field, stopping occasionally to rub the blood-stained itch from its naked skin on splintered fences. In front of me some Afro-Caribbean kids disgustedly kick a glue can into the shadow of a broken bench. Well, they can't be all bad.

The bulging Co-op carrier bags holding my underwear seem heavy, the handles hurting my fingers. I've made a right fool of myself this time and no mistake. I haven't even bought anything worth having with me.

Beth, clad in a turquoise dressing-gown, opens her door and looks at me, startled. I'm the last visitor she would have wished for. And I know it.

The Town Hall clock down in the valley strikes ten and echoes around our ears.

'Well?' she says.

'Well?' I say.

She invites me into the kitchen decorated with ceramic hens holding wooden spoons, and Brillo pads and eggs. It smells of good quality coffee and the remains of slowly cooked dumplings. She offers me instant Horlicks.

'Sorry I've no tea,' she says.

'Hot, sweet tea for shock,' I mutter.

'What?'

'Never mind.'

She means well. Always good-hearted, Beth. Then her husband Fred walks into the room, smelling only slightly of best bitter. He looks at me suspiciously, then mutters that he got caught up in a game of dominoes at the Catholic club.

Beth nods nervously towards me, then towards him. 'Laura's left Rod,' she tells him. 'Something to do with intolerable situations.'

Fred sniffs.

'And she's staying with us for a while,' Beth says with a stubbornness that surprises me. I never knew she had it in her. It was a statement she made. Not a question. Fred's taken off-guard. He kicks of his shoes, for something to do, and then flinches. Drags half a bottle of sherry from a cluttered cupboard.

'I expect you two want to stay up for half the night talking girl's talk,' he mumbles.

Then takes his plate of hot stew from the oven and carries it from the kitchen into the shades of gold in the sitting room, to watch the snooker finals.

Beth looks at me uneasily. 'He doesn't like a crisis. They upset his stomach,' she explains loyally. And I think she probably believes that.

'Who the fucking hell does like a crisis?' I say, because I'm expected to.

I try to imagine Beth and Fred cuddling up in bed together. Can't.

I've had a bad night in Beth's spare room, dreaming of half eaten apples and running through the streets barefoot. Everybody dreams of running barefoot. Something to do with inadequacies, I've read. But there were other things I dreamt of. Horses, and gates, and shouting, and a strong smell of camphor. Can't remember smelling camphor before, but I know what it is. Then there's a face, broad lipped, voiceless, but warning me by rapid contortions.

Warning me of what?

Jesus, it's doing my head in.

Then there's a hand shaking me. Holding me. Clutching my shoulder. I open my eyes to see the mottled face of Beth displaying a concern that's touching.

'Phil's on the phone for you,' she says, 'Something to do with your dad. He phoned Rod and he said you might be here.'

I nod. 'At least it confirms that my husband didn't suspect that I'd jumped into a dam, out of despair.'

Stupid thing to say. It would have been obvious to him that I hadn't contemplated a swift end once he'd noticed that I'd taken the Income Support book out of the kitchen drawer. And he would have checked that alright. It would have been the first thing he did, check that, and then search under the bed for half-empty vodka bottles. Never could tell if I was sober or drunk, could Rod. Never.

'I don't suppose Rod sent his love?' I say flatly.

Beth looks at me blankly. Offers me cornflakes if I can get downstairs in ten minutes, and the loan of a clean blouse. Her mind is already working on something else. 'You've got to be careful,' she warns, 'very careful.'

It's clear she's spent a semi-sleepless night worrying about me. And she's obviously not as thick brained as I thought.

'You could lose everything,' she says.

'Perhaps I already have. But supposing I've found something?' I ask, clutching at straws. Clutching at straws as always.

I meet Phil in the bus station. He's looking slightly embarrassed.

'Your dad says he's frightened he'll be taken into soddin' care,' he says, as if he's memorised the words. 'I can't think why he telephoned me. I've ploughed halfway through the phone book to find you.'

'That's because Dad likes you,' I nod. 'Can't think why. He wouldn't rear up in your company like he does in Rod's.'

But what the hell does it matter? Dad's got a really strange way of thinking about folks. A frightening way.

'What are you doing staying at old Beth's place, anyway?' Phil yawns.

'Just need a break,' I say.

I'm a coward, I tell myself, as Phil and I walk through the town sharing a fag. More than a coward. I'm a loser.

Phil is looking at his watch. 'I've got this fantastic woman to meet at eleven o'clock, a real goer.'

'How real is she, then?' I ask. 'Aren't you tired of struggling to be the eternal, horny bachelor?'

'Nobody gets tired of struggling, sweetheart. Otherwise they may as well take up embroidery. They wouldn't be real.'

How real is Phil I wonder, with his keep-your-distance smile, his graduated pension and leather trousers, and suntanned balding head? How real am I with my psoriasis? How real is anything? How real is Thomas?

Shit to Thomas. And to Mark? Though he isn't real he was one of the biggest bastards to ever walk this earth. Yet in dreams I loved him. A shadow in my imagination. So why do I keep doing this to myself?

I've got to voice it. 'I've got a strange kind of hangover,' I explain. 'If I told you about it you wouldn't believe me.'

Thankfully, Phil doesn't pursue this. Merely looks at his watch again, then remarks on the weather. 'We don't normally get weather as pleasant as this, darling. Not nowadays.'

'We did once,' I say with certainty. 'A good run of ten years.'

'You studied history then?'

'Sort of,' I shrug.

There's a car outside my father's door, a red Marina, and the front door is open. The overgrown, amber-tinted hedges surrounding his lawn waft in the breeze, and the Spring wind and early morning drizzle disinfect the threadbare, grey carpet in the hall.

Phil and I exchange glances.

The anaglypta on the wall is damp to the touch, and Dad's raised voice echoes through the caves of the memorabilia clutter of his good back room.

I push the door too gently and grab Phil's elbow, then guide us in.

'I don't know what I'm doing here,' he mutters.

'Neither does Dad,' I say. Then instantly regret it. 'I'm sorry, Phil, I should be grateful.'

There's a social worker ensconced on the faded cream of the embroidered covers of his settee, gingerly sipping tea from a chipped, white mug. Knows what she's here for. Asks Dad what year it is, and does he know the name of the current President of the United States?

'Well, it's not the peanut baron,' he says. 'Yon got a hole in his head.'

This doesn't help him.

She turns towards me when she sees we've walked in, and smiles sweetly, closes her folder.

'Your father is doing well for his age,' she ventures. 'But...'

'But what?'

'Well, he's a little vague isn't he?'

'So were Hitler and Churchill,' I say, 'but they still had a fucking dog fight.' Then I wish that I hadn't said it. All I've got is uninformed rubbish. I know it.

Phil clears his throat. 'What exactly are you here for?' he asks her.

Then she uncrosses her legs, removes the glacier mint from her mouth, wraps it in a tissue pulled from her handbag and tells me 'The gentleman has been a little confused of late, wandering around in short sleeves in the cold of the night.'

'Well, it's a free country,' says Phil, to his credit.

She pushes grey hair from her forehead, and sighs.

'You don't understand. He's getting to be quite a character. And with his bronchitis. And there's always the danger of malnutrition.'

'I'm not eating bloody salads,' Dad screams suddenly, clenching his fists in agitation. 'Not bloody salads, nor bloody poached rabbit, nor crab apples. Had enough of them. I've had enough of them!'

My mouth is suddenly dry. 'Dad, why did you mention crab apples?'

He's beginning to look confused. Hesitates for a moment. 'The peel hurts my throat, God damn it. They burned it. Right through the gullet, the bastards. Yon Mark's fault.'

'When?' I ask firmly. 'Dad, just who are you talking about anyway?'

He leans forward, his hunched back moving from the crocheted cushion of his chair. He doesn't answer. Doesn't know. Of course he doesn't. He's tired. Hugs his knees, his skin yellow under the dimming lightbulb.

'I'm not Mark,' he mumbles.

'Repeat that,' I tell him firmly.

'I'm not Mark,' he says louder.

I can hear the ticking of the clock, Phil's embarrassed coughing.

The social worker glances at me questioningly, says she's duty bound to put in a report. 'The elderly need more care of course.' She carefully replaces her pen into the pocket of her mohair jacket. Suggests a visit from a home help and a doctor would be useful. 'Your father's problem is general ageing, of course,' she says, stupidly. 'That's his affliction and he tells me that.'

And I'm thinking what a stupid cunt.

'Something to do with his date of birth is it?' I snap.

'His heart valves aren't as strong as they should be,' she explains. 'Perhaps he once had rheumatic fever.'

'Or typhoid? Or typhus?' I find myself saying.

Now she's looking at her watch. 'Anyway, I'm sure we can sort something out.'

Phil takes the hint from my eyes. Escorts her to the door. Tries to break the tension by talking about the weather. Knows all the rules, God bless him.

Dad's staring, glazed-eyed, into the fire. Doesn't want to talk.

'Just what?' I snap at him. 'Just what were you rambling on about just now? Do you want them to place you in a home where you'll get incontinence pads and kippers?'

He winces, but doesn't answer.

He finally looks me full in the face. Questioningly, innocently, almost. And minus his dentures because he probably left them on a bus somewhere. He won't stop aimlessly travelling around on buses. In a search, he's told me. A search for what?

'You opened this can of worms, so explain yourself,' I persist. 'Who is Mark?'

Yet I'm frightened that he will. Can. That we're two crazies together. It happens. Something in the genes. But we can't be experiencing the same waking dreams. I imagine that his eyes meet mine. 'Speak sense for once,' I spit.

All the time I've been trying to explain what's happening to me, he's pretended to be perplexed. When the names Thomas and Mark sprung involuntarily to my lips he pretended to be bewildered. How could he do this to me?

He shakes his head, as if to shake my question off. It won't work.

'I've got to know, Dad. Who is Mark? Mark Thorne, I believe you once said?'

He grinds his hard gums together, the tiny lines around his mouth deepening, then frowns. Seems to mentally shake himself, trying to lose vulnerability. He stares again at the fireplace.

'It's just rubbish. Geriatric rubbish, girl,' he growls.

'Like my dreams?' Is that what they are? Geriatric? Listen to me, Dad, I've got to know. It's making me ill. Do you understand? I'm drinking more and more shit to try to forget this nightmare. Sometimes it even comes when I'm brushing my teeth, for fuck's sake, or when I'm washing the kid's clothes.'

He's got to understand what this is doing to me. 'It's making me lose everything that matters to me. And you know all about it. I know you do.'

His gaze stays on the fireplace. And he begins to rock backwards and forwards, like a child without its comfort blanket. His paisley cardigan tightens around the blades of his shoulders.

All I can do is sigh, 'So all this is hereditary? Madness, is it?'

Phil has come back into the room, must have been standing there for a while, says 'You'd better switch the old man's central heating on, then come back tomorrow with some groceries. Nothing to be done now. He's dropped into another world, can't you see?'

'I've been there myself,' I say quietly.

I stand up and start to leave with Phil, my feet crunching on spilt cat litter on the carpet, but I can still hear Dad's whisper.

'I let your mother die.'

'What?'

'I let your mother die.'

'That's rubbish and you know it,' I say.

Jesus, what sort of hell-hole am I living in?

Phil pulls at my coat sleeve. 'Let's go,' he says, 'just let's go. The old chap's had enough upset for one day.'

I'm watching Dad's eyes as he turns. There's an emptiness there. An uneasy acceptance.

'Look at me properly and talk to me,' I plead, nervously folding my arms.

He won't.

'You didn't kill mum,' I say, annoyed. 'Understand? You didn't.'

Phil's embarrassment is increasing. I can feel it in the warmth of his hand. 'For God's sake, leave it, Laura. He's not well. Needs to be left in peace for a while.'

I snap back, 'How do you know? Read people's minds, do you? So I ask too many questions.' I know exactly what he's saying. 'But this is nothing to do with you.'

'Nothing,' he shrugs.

If he peers at his watch again I'll scream, I'm thinking. Dad loosens his grip on the arms of his chair and closes his eyes. Sleeping. Or pretending? There's no way I can get through to him. Not now. I let Phil lead me out.

'I feel guilty about leaving him alone,' I mutter, 'but if I keep holding his hand he'll expect me to do it forever. I had an auntie like that.'

He catches me catching him looking at his watch. 'The old man's had enough,' he repeats, as we walk down the street.

'And Mark?'

Phil doesn't know what I'm talking about. But Dad clearly did. He also knows about Thomas and his one-time diet of apples. I know he does. And more. There's got to be something more.

Yet, people don't share dreams. It's as simple as that, I tell myself, again. 'I want to make a detour via the cemetery,' I say.

'You're kidding.'

'Am I?'

Nothing there. Nothing but gravestones too weathered to read. And what am I searching for anyway? Perhaps voices rustling through the leaves, like on a television horror movie.

Phil plays the gentleman, wraps his jacket around my shoulders. Says, 'Come on, I'll take you back to where you came from.'

'Via your flat?'

'If you wish.'

Night comes quickly, and dawn slowly. Again, and yet again. I'm finding myself wondering what day it is, and if it really matters. And why my children don't phone. Pride perhaps. Like the same sort of distorted pride that caused me to walk out on them. Because that's what I did, I keep telling myself, then wondering where the nearest bottle is because I've never been breast-fed. They haven't either. Hell, it's a mess.

Chapter 10

The weather's changing, becoming warmer, and I'm beginning to feel like a dog that's forgotten to moult, in my long camel-hair coat, the only coat I took with me when I left Rod. And I'm worried and bored. Bored with staying with Beth. Avoiding her husband as he heads for the bathroom to use the shaving soap. Avoiding stepping on her ridiculously light coloured home-made rug in the hall. Avoiding talking about Rod.

I'm worried. Worried because Phil said he'd phone today and hasn't. Hasn't all week. The only crutch I've got. Worried because I've visited Dad's house twice during the last week, leaving Beth to do the washing up, and shouted through his letterbox.

Today I try again. No answer.

'He went off for a walk, luv,' a neighbour in a tartan skirt tells me, wearing yellow kitchen gloves and pulling up garden weeds.

'When?' I ask, leaning against her fence.

'Can't rightly say. Could have been this morning. Or yesterday. He's always going out nowadays. He wasn't half mumbling to himself though. Strange guy ain't he?'

I'm in no rush to get back to Cherry Avenue, and the infernal ticking of Beth's knitting needles against Lincoln green wool. She's creating yet another sweater for Fred. This time one with a polar bear motif. I'm tired of his insistence that the chair situated nearest the telly is for his buttocks alone. Tired of Beth constantly mothering him, and tired of masturbating in the box-room cum bedroom, remembering to draw the curtains.

They haven't yet asked me what went wrong with my marriage. A blessing, I suppose. Nor about my financial situation, that has precluded me from having a drink at The Bull. It's worked for a while. I should have got the shakes but didn't. All I've got is this apparently eternal boredom. And an uneasiness I can't put a name to.

I need to see my kids. That's what I need.

I arrange through a phone call to Sonia, whose voice has a strange tinge of unease, to see them in McDonalds. A typical single parent's thing. Get the kids on my side via strawberry milkshakes. That's the sort of thing that agony aunts suggest. The norm. The desperation. Buy them baseball caps, designer jumpers. Tell them things. Tell them what they want to hear. What their father tells them. That they will grow. That anyone could get money then buy a car. A recipe for happiness.

Sad, really. Everything's sad. Sad. Sad. Sad.

My daughter has long been straining at the leash to have sex with someone, to find out what it's like and fuck the exams. I know she has. And my son? Well, he's like his father. Except for his eyes. Everything except for the eyes. They're complex. Accusing. Lovely. He's the best kid in town, and I don't give a shit who knows it. It's drizzling. There's a muddy dampness creeping in through the sole of my left shoe, and a dryness into my brain. I'm a failure. That's what I am. Didn't even go to the last Open Day at Gaynor's school, because I was too sober and pissed off to bother. It's not her fault she's gullible and not ultra-intelligent, at sixteen. All mine. I'm walking down Queen's Street telling myself these things, and wishing I wasn't. Wishing I was taller, richer. Sane.

I spot them standing on the corner near Barclays Bank.

They greet me with wary smiles, as I expected, and joint requests for money for shell suits. Gavin asks me what's wrong and I can't answer. It's optimistic of him to think that I could. The poor little sod's mind hasn't been turned yet.

Then they tell me in unison that the shell suits have to be purple and black because that's in vogue.

I smile. Nothing more. Mustn't alienate them further. We perch on white chairs and eat cheeseburgers quietly. Occasionally exchanging glances. I feel like kicking myself, because this is the set routine. Explain that their father and I have split up because we couldn't go on tearing at each other like some creatures from seventies American movies. Then I decide to ask them.

'Do you swallow this shit, or what?'

They stare at me blankly. They've swallowed it. God, what I wouldn't give for a drink.

'You're both alright then?' I ask. When I find somewhere to live

I'll collect them, I know that.

'Sonia's helping to take care of us,' says Gaynor, spitting crumbs. But there's something in her eyes. Something I don't like.

'Oh?'

'She's a good friend to Dad. And I need some sanitary towels,' she adds miserably.

Jesus Christ, what have I done?

'You shouldn't have left us,' she says angrily, twisting the serviette in her lap.

The sun, licking the window, highlights her still blond hair, and Gavin is fidgeting in his chair like a whippet wanting to escape from a trap. 'Dad says Grandad is going batty,' he says. 'So he'll never teach me chess will he?'

'Do you want to play that?' I ask, surprised.

'Yes,' he says.

I don't know him do I? Don't know either of them. My daughter is watching me.

'You've got to do something, Mum. I'm now a one-parent family.' Thinks she can manipulate me. And she can. But there's sadness in her face. Flesh of my flesh.

'I know,' I say, irritably. 'For God's sake, I know.'

It's not a happy day. Sunday has never been a happy day.

'I love you both,' I say, as they get up to go in hunt of a number twenty-nine bus. 'Don' t forget it.'

We've said nothing to each other. 'Childhood's gone,' I say. And I wish that it hadn't.

They feign embarrassment. I offer a smile. Feel guilty, because I should. I'm a cunt.

They've gone, without saying anything. And I need a friend. Phil, maybe. I'm thinking I'll have a few respectable lagers with him in the warmth of The Fleece, tell him about afterbirths and stitches, kids vomiting. About making Easter bonnets for school parades. He won't understand. That's expected. But maybe I could tell him that my dreams are starting to fade. I phone him. No answer.

It's foggy when I go back to Beth's and feel the warmth of recently ironed shirts wafting through the door towards me. She's expressionless, got an open packet of cigarettes and soup ready for me.

'Something herbal,' she explains.

I'd never thought of Beth as being herbal before. But nothing surprises me now. Nothing.

We mutter the usual niceties and I make the normal excuses, then curl up on the camp-bed in the beige of the box-room, sucking the blobs of barley sugar I've bought earlier, as a comforter. Try not to think about my kids. The sweets are soothing. More soothing than herbal. I can't afford a drink, but surely I'm entitled to some compensation after meeting my kids. I've lost them haven't I? And they're hurting. And hells bells, what a mess.

An unusually warm breeze creeps through the open window, wafting the floral curtains, plays around my cheeks, and whirls around the pink glassware on an old mahogany dressing-table. The tension eases from my jaw. There's nothing I can do about anything. What is done is done.

I'm drowsy. Now there's a blackness. A sinking. There's a voice. Then nothing.

'Nothing,' says Thomas, liquid gurgling at the back of his throat. 'We've got nothing. They threw us out. Locked us out. Do you understand?' His hands are shaking my shoulders.

I'm standing in the yard, holding wet linen to my bosom, intending to peg it on the line. It's important. He knows that. The things at home are important. Like I am. I've had a pain in my side for months, like some glowing, unwanted, flame. But would Thomas know? How can he?

His mind is still behind the black bricks of Foster's.

A woman from three doors away came to my gate this morning to listen to my woes and suggested that what was wrong with me was a retention of blood, a common fault of childless women. Prescribed a liquor of marjoram and mustard, boiled slowly. It hasn't worked. Nothing works.

Now here stands Thomas, hands dirty, moaning about work. His work.

'The office,' he frets. 'They threw us out of the office.'

'You're too stubborn,' I snap. Then try to change the subject, because there's no sense in crying. 'There's stew in the pot and warm blankets on the mantle. And some piggin' vermin' must have been chewing at my shoes last night. They're all soggy.'

I shrug his hands away from me. It's midsummer. And the voices of the members of a Bible Class in a mission down the street move like laughter through the still, darkening air.

'Don't bother me, Thomas. I've got sewing. There's your shirt. Always a shirt turned to rags.' My voice doesn't seem normal. Not like mine. Strange that. But then the vapours can take you that way, I'm told. And nothing's going right for me. Nothing. How could my brother come home talking such silliness and not understand my pain?

'Complain,' I grumble. 'Why do you and your kind have to spoil everything? Why did you have to complain?'

'Because Foster is still employing boys under nine years of age,' he growls at me. 'It's illegal, sis. Has been for years. We've got to make a stand. Big Bert says we've got to make a stand for those poor little beggars.'

'Oh, I know all about big Bert,' I say dryly. 'Everybody in this town knows all about big Bert.'

Thomas's jaw is clenched tightly. He's determined not to listen. I know it. He walks towards the scullery.

'If you got to know him,' he grumbles, 'you'd like him. I know you would.'

Then we've nothing to say. There's a man outside the yard dragging his cart along cobbles and swearing at dog faeces sticking to the red painted wheels. He's stinking of fish. Yellow and white eels wriggling in a bucket of green water.

I tramp to the gate. Dip my fingers into the pocket of my apron, notice the tic in one of his brown eyes. He drops a portion of coley into the rusting scales and says with seeming lack of interest. 'I see your brother is one of those supporting big Bert then.' Nothing more.

Tomorrow, I tell myself, tomorrow I'll sort Thomas out for good.

He still takes too much notice of others. Still has a kind of fever.

In the cool of the house Thomas is poking the coals in the grate, watching them singe the potato peel I tipped in earlier. He seems to be thinking. No, not thinking. Dreaming. He's staring at the sparks, his mind still contemplating work.

'You know they can't keep the kids working,' he says. 'They can't. Althorpe's bill was passed years ago. Years. They can't keep flouting it.'

I press the back of my hand onto his brow and feel silly for doing it. We never were ones for touching, my brother and I. Then I feel the clamminess. His cheek rests on my bosom and relaxes a little. His neck bends easily. He's still not well. I know he isn't. Even though I know the polluted water he drank from was pumped away six months ago.

'Big Bert's not too bad,' he yawns, then still on his knees and clutching me sleeps, or seems to.

A cockroach scampers across the hem of my skirt and heads for the wide-open window. Thomas spots it through half-opened eyes and winces, wondering how long we've been crouched there. I keep still and hold him. Hold him until the knock on the door. A man in brown boots stands in the stoop. Fingers hidden inside huge fists beside him. He's from the mill. I can smell the lanolin.

'Bert?'

Of course it is. Who else can it be?

'Come to see Thomas,' he says crisply.

'He's sleeping in front of the fire. And God knows he needs it after the stuff that you've put into his head.'

He nods, and asks for water. I make him tea. Thomas has crawled without knowing it into a corner, is leaning one of his cheeks against the coolness of empty stone storage jars. He dozes.

'You're corrupting my brother,' I tell Bert. 'And he's not well. Needs to work.'

'And he's a child,' Bert says slowly, perched on a stool beside the embers of the fire, and clasping his fingers between the knee patches of his oil-stained trousers.

'He needs to work. Needs to live,' I tell him, picking up my darning as if I need to prove that I care.

'The lad needs more,' he says firmly. 'Much more.' His expression darkens.

'And me? What do I need? I need to survive. We all need to survive.'

He gives a deep sigh. 'God preserve us from mother hens,' he mutters. 'Do you know what some of these kids do to survive? The risks that they take? Do you, Princess?'

'What?'

He looks at me blankly.

'You called me Princess. Someone called me Princess.'

'Who?'

'Who, I don't know. But I can smell vodka. Don't know what it is. Taste vodka.'

There's a voice in my head, 'Darling, I don't give a damn. Come up and see me sometime.'

I can feel a strange stretching of cloth across my shoulders, tightening. Tightening.

'What's wrong?' Bert asks.

'Why did you call me a Princess?' I scream. 'Why?'

I reach out to touch Thomas's arm. Can't reach it. I shout to him to wake up. Shout, and shout. And twist my head so that I can look at his face. His nose is familiar. Not his. Dad's perhaps.

'Don't call me a fucking princess,' I shout to Bert, 'DON'T call me Princess.'

Beth is standing over me, her Avon talc wafting up my nose. It's supposed to be daisies in autumn but isn't.

I can smell coffee and stir, stretching my spine uncomfortably. Beth has already drawn back the regency-style curtains, coughed up her morning nicotine residue and pushed on her slippers. She's holding a letter.

'I've brought you coffee, but it's instant,' she apologises.

I'm not really listening. I've had a dream, I tell myself, another pissing dream. I smile up at Beth's dentures as if nothing's happened and try not to let my tight grip on the foam-backed pillow look obvious.

Hyper-tension.

I've got to appear normal, so yawn, stretch the nylon sheet, give the usual smoker's cough to the centrally heated air, then slit open the envelope with a chewed down nail. Can't remember when I didn't have a chewed down nail.

'Who do you think the letter is from, then?' I ask, knowing she's curious.

'I don't know the handwriting,' she says, seriously. 'Could be Rod's, could it?'

Of course it's Rod's, I can smell his aftershave ghost on the cheap stationery. The stationery I bought at a school's Christmas Fayre.

I let my toes touch the cold floor and dress slowly, pushing the dream with difficulty to the back of my mind. Imagine it swimming in the greyness like a malformed tadpole.

Time to arise. I swill my face in Beth's pink bathroom, yank on my fading bra and throw on once expensive, and brown, Oxfam clothing, folding over the waistband of the skirt because it's too long, and I hate to not show my knees, because they're part of me. Like the hardness of my nipples, the birthmark on my buttocks. Something to stop me from disappearing.

I brush my teeth. Gargle away the nightmares and rinse vigorously.

Alcoholic dreams, for God's sake. Withdrawal symptoms. That's all they can be.

Beth is watching as I return to the bedroom and read Rod's signature on the bottom of the letter. No need to read the other words. Not now. I've got to find Dad. Don't know why but I've got to visit him. See him. See his eyes.

If he's not incarcerated in some institution because of lewd behaviour, that is. No-one I've spoken to has seen him for days.

Got to get some air.

Plus I'm missing Phil. Can't explain why. Even to myself.

On my request, Phil, with a morsel of toilet tissue stuck to a portion of badly shaven chin, meets me at the police station. Without speaking he grips my fingertips, then when I look annoyed says the tips feel abnormally cold.

Full marks to the prick, I think, because I've been on the vodka.
'Surprise surprise,' I mutter.

What am I talking about? I wonder if I should care. I feel so weak.

'I need half a bottle of sherry,' I tell him. 'That's what I need.'

'And to find your Dad?' he asks, looking at me accusingly.

'Yes, I need to find my Dad.'

We are ushered into a room. The station Sergeant chews on his menthol and tries to make my eyes meet his. Then he tells me a tale, called the truth, watching my figure swaying. I've been pigeon-holed, like Dad.

He tells me, in a tired voice, that Dad, shirt buttons unfastened, has been on walkabout for four days, through Howarth, Holmfirth and more dark places.

'It won't do him no good,' he mutters.

So I nod.

He doesn't decorate his words. 'He was picked up in the Woodhead pass, rambling on about children and pissing in a hedge.'

I stare at him in silence.

'The man needs taking care of,' he grunts. 'He's in St. Luke's hospital now. He's suffering from a bit of hypothermia, like.'

Phil, who hardly knows Dad, nods his head knowingly. Am I the only one who didn't know about Dad getting weaker or what? Another lie. I did know. I just couldn't accept it.

There's a slow drive to St. Luke's, with swallows and sparrows swooping from treetops and juggernauts honking on their way to motorways. I've got an irritating anal itch. And a feeling that I shouldn't be here.

The driveway to the hospital is lined by newly planted oaks, planted out of some sort of Council policy. Our feet crunch along the gravel to a loud, red painted doorway, where I hear people coughing out lungs. A man sits here, coffee mug on the desk in front of him, reading a Daily Mirror, his collar crisply ironed, by himself in a bedsit, I've no doubt, or some woman in an apron escaped from nineteen fifties movies.

Can't stop judging.

There's an unspoken agreement that one should whisper.

'Dad could be a cow fucker for all I know. But who would think he'd ever come to this?' I quietly ask Phil.

'Who would think?' he says, because it's expected. 'Little kids, old men, what's the difference? Everyone has a breaking point, Princess.'

'Why did you say that?' I snap, hunching a bag of fruit I've brought for Dad under my armpit. I know what is expected really. That Dad has to be incarcerated somewhere. Sensed it.

'Why did I say what?' asks Phil.

'You mentioned little kids.'

He shrugs his shoulders. 'I'll be damned if I know why. Does it matter?'

'Yes,' I say. 'It matters.'

I'm beginning to notice things. Like his hands are larger than average. I noticed that when he pulled the bus fares out of his deep pocket in town.

'I've always been the champion of the underdog,' I find myself saying, as we push open an internal swing door. 'Haven't you?'

He sniffs. 'Well, I try to be. Us underlings have to stick together. Even have to open our legs to each other.'

'Shit,' I say. But I'm not sure how much of what he says is merely banter and how much he says is what he conceives to be the truth. Have got to know. 'Do you believe in reincarnation?' I ask him as we enter the elevator.

'Jesus, Princess, what sort of question is that? We came here to visit your Dad didn't we, bring grapes and stuff and words about his Council Tax demands? We know where he is, and that's what matters.'

His arm stretches easily around my waist. 'Don't worry darling, I'll buy you a couple of brandies later, I know just the place.'

'Reincarnation,' I insist. 'Shit, you must have read some book about it, somewhere.'

He tells me to stop saying the word shit and says, 'No Princess. Not me. Don't know what the hell you're talking about.'

We pad along the scrupulously clean tiles. See a woman sat in a basket chair staring into space and cursing 'Fucking homos'. Rivers run down her laddered stockings. I wonder if I know her from somewhere.

We find Dad. He's sitting in a huge brown chair in a small grey room, mumbling to himself.

Phil looks at me quizzically.

'Well you'd mumble too, if you was in a place such as this,' I say. 'Hello Dad.'

He's staring straight through me. Clearly not seeing. Doesn't even recognise my voice. Or is it that he doesn't want to acknowledge it? Cat and mouse? Is that what he's doing? Because this mouse has got a hell of a toothache, and a hell of a short fuse. His blue pyjamas smell of scrambled eggs and disinfectant. His breath has the odour of Pethadin. I know because I took it once, twice, to kill the gloom of a miscarriage.

'It's all fucked up, Dad,' I say, kneeling on the carpet and taking his hands between mine, and feeling an idiot because Phil is nervously watching me. 'What, in Christ's name have you been up to Dad? Why are you doing this?'

He doesn't answer. Can't answer. I've got to jog his memory.

'You remember when my daughter Gaynor was born? Gaynor? Do you remember her name? You came into the hospital and said she looked like a dead rat with extra toes? That nothing should be born so helpless? Said she should be rubbed off with a rough towel? Remember, remember, later you carved her a parrot, painted it all green, and it rocked on its dowel perch for ages and ages? Remember how she loved it, thought you were special? Remember how it mattered. To her, to me and to you?'

There's silence. Phil shakes his head as I turn to him. Feels he's an intruder. But then men always are intruders. He says it's not right that I should torture the old man this way.

I can't stop. I carry on talking and clutching Dad's fingers.

'Dad, remember we once spoke about someone called Mark? We didn't know if he was real did we? Still don't. But remember the conversation. You knew something, didn't you? Still know it now. You mumbled something about horses and high locked gates. You must remember them. It was long, long ago.'

He doesn't answer.

Phil is behind me. Watching.

'How can he remember?' he asks, unsure of what the questions are about. 'The old man's gone and locked himself into his head. You can see that. Maybe he's trying to preserve bits of his brain. Who knows? Or perhaps there's some sort of guilt hidden there.'

I'm sure there is. Dad is hiding. That's all I know for sure.

'I borrowed the door key you left with your next door neighbour and fed your fish. Even watered the plants, though the bastards haven't felt moisture for years,' I tell him.

His eyes don't flicker. I place the fruit on his bedside locker and his eyes still don't flicker. Remove my hands from his and press onto his shoulders. His bones are brittle.

Phil moves towards the door, then taps his signet ring on the gloss paintwork. 'Come on Princess, come on,' he says.

Dad is still staring at the wall, his breathing shallow like he's in some sort of trance.

I try to take him by surprise, to bring him out of it. 'Do you smell apples?' I ask loudly.

Dad doesn't even blink.

Phil says, 'What the hell do you mean?'

'It's funny really, but I can smell apples,' I say. Always had a keen sense of smell. No sense in dwelling on it. It's time I visited Rod's home. And it's still my home isn't it? The blue glass ornaments on the lounge window-sill are mine, the black cherry yoghurts that will still be in the ageing fridge, the underwear I left behind still in the laundry basket. It's my nicotine breath staining the embossed wallpaper over our divan bed.

My place. Has been for twenty years.

The place where my official feller lives. The man of the stubble. Too stingy to spend on his family. The penis without a brain who once knew when I was in pain. I'm wondering when that empathy stopped. Could have been the first time I questioned him and didn't accept that he knew best. Or when my breasts started sagging. Or when I tried to stop the kids turning into little Rods. Or when I stopped loving.

No way of knowing. Can't understand why I still care.

Maybe I'm being unfair, I decide, as I push open the gate. I can hardly have an objective view of the situation. Know that for certain. I need time to think, to smell the hydrangeas, to go over my fingerprint-scuffed trainers propped against the wall in the hall.

I need time to think about the shit I'm in.

Time to collect things.

No-one in the house disturbs me, challenges my presence.

In silence, I drag coffee-stained and wine-anointed skirts from under grubby would-be laundry in the fish-odoured kitchen. Then notice the cat chewing cornflakes from a striped bowl by the sink. Poor sod. No-one even thought to buy it a tin of food. Yet it hasn't really missed me. I know that.

I go upstairs to pack forgotten bras and make-up. Open a window because I can still smell the long ago dried semen on the floral bedsheets. It hasn't occurred to Rod that he should have changed them. Of course not.

I know damned well that he's standing behind me. Feel his shadow, catch the scent of his aftershave, his breath hitting the back of my neck. I feel like something from a failed Mills and Boon. And I'm thinking, what the hell does it matter? Telling myself I should stop questioning. Should shape up. Know the chances are nil.

He'll be wondering where the family allowance book is. He looks older, somehow, thinner. But maybe that's because that's what I want to think. Who knows? He doesn't speak. Nor do I. He's remote. Unforgiving. Like he ought to be wearing garlic threaded on a string around his neck.

I can't be written out of his life easily, I think, grinding my teeth. But I can. I search through the drawers of the dressing-table, yanking at the white painted chipboard. Know I'm being a bitch. My perfume is missing.

'Where the fuck is my perfume?' I shout.

His breath on the back of my neck slows, cools down. Or perhaps I'm wrong and I've been reading too many True Romances. A pillock, I am. Only came here to collect my clothing, not to make waves. And yet. What I really want to do is knee Rod in the balls.

The cat has followed me, looks at me through yellow eyes. She's old. Too old. Wipes her long black fur against my legs. Then there's my annoyance with the TV getting to me, Channel Two screaming up the stairs about the instability of a volcano in Madagascar. It's on. The TV is always on.

I'm feeling sick because I've been compelled to eat Beth's full English breakfasts. And my ankles are swelling. Don't know why.

Rodney is following me from room to room, bleary eyed. It's only 8am after all. Until I left he never liked or had to get off the mattress at such an early hour, the bastard.

He finally speaks. 'You're alright, then?'

'Of course I'm pissing alright,' I snap. 'I've got a lovely place to stay. Have you ever listened to someone knitting from dawn until dusk? Therapeutic, that's what it's supposed to be. Apart from that, I'm fine.'

What more can I say? I try not to let my eyes meet his. I'm a black sheep, a failed Methodist. A pillock of a mother. A drunk. That's what he wants me to think isn't it? Well he's got what he wants.

'You don't miss me?' he asks.

'Why should I?' I pull dusty handbags from the gloom of the wardrobe. 'I can always masturbate.'

As his spine stiffens so does the air around us. Or perhaps that is pure imagination. Why the hell am I goading him?

Can't apologise now. He wouldn't believe I meant it. Neither would I. I want to hurt him. And why shouldn't I? He's hurt me often enough. Never even offered to taste the curries I made. Never massaged my neck when it ached. Never carried my shopping home. Never knew what I meant when I mentioned premenstrual tension. Always screwed up his nose in disgust if I inadvertently left a sanitary towel floating like a half-skinned fish in the blue of the loo. Never listened to me. Ever. Why the shit did we marry?

But I know the answer. We married because we were expected to and I wanted to get away from a mother who was a baker of apple-crumbles and a father who pissed in his special chair every evening. The usual stuff. Rod wanted to find a home for his illegitimate son and it turned out the kid's mother wouldn't give the boy up anyway.

Plus he wanted to get his end away on a regular basis without any hassle. I know why we married and so does he. No illusions. Yet we had some good times didn't we? And the sex was a bloody novelty at first. Feelings? Yes, there had to be feelings. There were. Weren't there? Too late to think of this bunkum now.

Rod throws my toothpaste onto the top of my bag, asks if I'm ok for money. And why should he care? He wanted this piss artist out of his house didn't he?

'We could try again,' he says self-consciously, 'for the sake of the children. If you want to.'

'What pissing children? The children have grown. Or haven't you noticed? And why should I want to try again?' I ask.

I can't explain what I'm feeling because I'm all choked up, haunted by something I can't explain.

Can't explain that my brain's in a mess and that he smells, to me, of horses. That I've got this preoccupation with odours. And that any minute now I expect him to drag me into our fitted kitchen and try to get up my skirt. Doesn't make sense, my sudden hatred of him. Doesn't make sense at all. It's all a dream. Within seconds he could be part of my dream. He's Mark. Got to be. He's got the eyes. I should have noticed that long ago.

I try to tell him. But he doesn't understand. Can't. Doesn't want to.

'You've obviously been ill,' he says, confused.

'Do you mean I've been off the booze?' I ask. 'If that's what you mean then the answer is mostly. I'm almost off the drink, and behold.' I'm waving my arms about, feeling pretty melodramatic by now. 'I haven't even sucked cocks in the alley behind the Jug and Bottle since I left you. Haven't even been tempted.'

He doesn't comprehend what I'm saying. Can't do. He stares at me blankly. 'As for money, I can do with some,' I say flatly.

The kids will be home soon and I don't want to meet them. Can't spend a whole day in this house. Not anymore. I've got nothing to offer my offspring but unwanted motherly advice, and a glimpse into some strange kind of madness. Can't draw them into that. Could never.

Chapter 11

I've got this arrangement.

Phil is waiting outside for me in a taxi. Sipping something from a hip flask. He promises to take care of me. Promises. Says he's got an unopened bottle of whisky in his bedside drawer. Go home with him and drink it? Why not? I've no problem with this 'eat me, drink me' stuff.

'How did it go with Rod?' he asks, as I ease into the back seat.

'How do you think? I left him about to iron handkerchiefs.'

I want to get to the warmth of a flat. Anyone's flat. Disrobe.

I patter around Phil's bedroom. Run my fingers along a badly pasted seam in the red and white wallpaper. Throw one pair of creased trousers from the bed. There are trousers all over the place.

There's a face in the dressing-table mirror. Mine. Too pink to be healthy. Small pimples around my mouth, slightly sunken eyes. Mine. Women of my age always have slightly sunken eyes. There's a nicotine stain on the small hairs above my top lip. When caught in fluorescent light they're noticeable.

I think of what has just been done. When Phil shafts me, or anyone else, he really shafts. Pushes and pushes. I pretended. Then didn't.

'Why not go to sleep now?' he had said.

'I can't,' I replied, 'just can't.'

I'm worried about Dad, shutting himself out of the world for good, or because of bad, about my children, the distant ones. About non-existent Thomas. About my sanity. Once read, somewhere, that if you think you're mad you can't be. But I've still got the overwhelming odour of crab-apples swimming in the mucus of my nostrils. Can't be normal, that. Just can't be.

'Get some sleep,' Phil kept insisting. 'You're looking pale.'

'If I sleep I'll dream,' I kept telling him. Now I'm counting the purple bluebells on his trendy wallpaper.

There's something happening to me that I can't explain. Don't like. Life's a mess. Nothing more than a packet of cigarettes and a joke in a bottle.

'I did try and take care of Dad,' I mutter lazily, feeling the weight of my eyelids. 'And Rod. And the kids.'

Phil has his arms around me. He mutters then sleeps again, his legs stretched across mine.

It's warm again.

Thomas is running along the sun-drenched cobbles of the street, avoiding dandelions and stubborn grass pushing through the cracks. When he can't he kicks at them with his metal toe-capped boots. He's teasing some kid bragging about his hoop.

It's Sunday. My brother should be on his way to the mission. But he shouts back to me when I holler to him to get a move on that he's not going. I'm leaning on the gate leading to our littered backyard. The boy never meant to go to the mission, I realise. He's heading for Farburn Hills, from where he can watch the trains.

He's stupid, I'm thinking, utterly stupid. All he can do there is pick a few bluebells from a stretch of forgotten, stunted greenery, if he crawls down the banking to reach the shade of the viaduct and clutches the stems in sweaty, calloused hands. Then he'll climb, breathless, up the hill again and fall asleep in the haze of dusk, only to wake up when some southbound train far below whistles its warning. I've seen it before. It's hopeless. I've told him as much.

I call to him again. He runs, his heels clicking on the stones, then I try to fight my way through the breeze-tossed cream sheets hanging on weakened rope lines.

There's the smell of forgotten, skinned rabbit, turning charcoal black in a nearby oven. A baby screaming, because babies always touch their red gums and scream.

There's the sound of an inconsequential marital argument coming from the open door of number fifty-nine, mingling with the laughter of marble-playing children in the shade of a derelict warehouse, their spittle hitting the ground. They curse, in imitative manliness. And there's an unease that I can't understand scratching to get out of my brain. I slow down, and try to think. Men need freedom. No point in suffocating the young ones, it could only lead to trouble.

But that knowledge doesn't help. I'm ten years older than my brother. Have some sort of responsibility. Can't escape it. And, just lately, I haven't felt comfortable letting him out of my sight. Something to do with a crazy dream with strange odours and flashing lights. I've even walked with him to and from his work, with a sense that something is wrong. Or about to be wrong. I never even felt ashamed when, hearing the sniggers of his friends, he flushed up in embarrassment in front of me. But I can't get away from it, there's something strange going on.

Can't analyse it. Can't stop it. This sense of foreboding.

Thomas has gone, as he usually does when he gets outdoors, leaping like a donkey on heat. I pick up my basket of washing from the stoop and feel this shadow hovering over me. Look up to see the shoulders of big Bert. Oddly, I'd expected to see him today.

'Front door was wide open,' he says.

The cat skims around his ankles, moves nervously past him to find its usual spot in front of the fire.

I know how to frown. 'If you've come to fill Thomas's head, even with the best of your nonsense, you're too late. He's out.'

Then instantly regret snapping. Bert has been living here long enough to know that the only place around here to go to is the hills, and he'll follow him. I know he will. Can't let well enough alone, his kind. Always want something more, like a perfect life for his kind. Silly talk. Some poorly defined mission to keep kids from turning to the ale. In the words of gossiping, neighbourhood women, wiping their hands on grubby aprons, he is not to be trusted.

Yet I know him, slightly. Knew his father, a man with gigantic whiskers, a deaf and dumb man with the soles of his boots permanently flapping. Ironic really, that Bert should be sired by someone dumb. Because Bert rarely stops talking or, supposedly, thinking. He's one of those radicals, the men with red necks and worn boots who spread their gospel in the butchers' shops or on Sundays in shady corners of the park whilst, unknowingly, the band is playing in the pavilion.

What does he want us to do? Draw blood? Or starve? Is that it?

He hasn't caught my thoughts. Wouldn't listen to them if he did. He coughs.

'I've been contemplating the fate of the younger ones, the ones whose job it is to crawl underneath the working looms and clean up. But you wouldn't know about that, never raised your head underneath that throbbing iron in an effort to rid the oil from your lungs by way of spitting, then caught your hair in the machinery. It happens. You and your like never heard that moaning. Thomas has. He knows all about it. And all about the beatings they get from their beleaguered dads when they go home a penny short in their wages.'

I'm examining my cracked fingernails in an effort to escape his lecture. Everyone, hereabouts, knows about his hopeless and senseless lectures. He's hitting his head on a stone wall. It's a fact of life.

'The young ones like Thomas,' he continues. 'He's already been treating them to arrowroot. They'll listen to him.' He's scowling, the flames from the fire throwing light that enhances the dust in the lines of his forehead. He's older than I thought. 'The lads have got to stop work and find the guts to complain. Otherwise they'll be broken and dead before forty.'

Now it's my turn. Can't resist it. 'And if they stop working?' I snap. Who does this pig think he is? 'What do they eat?'

We've had this conversation before. Troublemakers like him have no concept of life. None at all.

'It's not only the small ones at the mill I'm thinking of,' he says, as if he hasn't heard me. 'There are the kids working next door to it, Lingard's Phosphorus Products. Even you must have heard of the place. Have cousins working there? It's a bastard of a hole.'

'So? What has it got to do with you?' I say. 'Want to put them onto the streets do you? Starve them?'

We shouldn't have to keep going over this. And he shouldn't pick on Thomas merely because he's got intelligence.

I tell him so.

Bert pretends to listen. Grinds his teeth.

'The boy has got intelligence,' he agrees thoughtfully. 'Can look up at the sky, can that lad.'

'And see stars through the smoke?' I smirk. 'Is that what's coming next?'

He shakes his head. Never had a similar point of view, me and Bert, not even when we were in schooling. I doubt if he remembers me from that time in our lives. I offer him some water. The longer I can keep him here the less chance he has of catching up to Thomas and filling his head with rubbish.

He's sitting motionless, his large buttocks spread over the padded seat of the low stool by the oven, he's swamping it in coarse, brown, trouser fabric, and for some inexplicable reason his jacket is steaming in the mild heat. He appears at ease.

I stand before him and look down at this fool clasping his red, hairy, hands, and think he reminds me of a bear in a monkey suit, itching and scratching, like the one I saw when I went to the circus. His clothes are far too small for him and I don't like his eyes, they're far too probing. Belong to a trouble-maker, and no mistake.

'Leave my brother alone,' I say. My voice is supposed to sound like fire. But doesn't. 'What I'm thinking about is something called survival.'

There's irony in his smile.

'You should realise the price of survival. The word is going around that you're seeing yon Mark, Foster's lackey, the bloody little bugger. Don't think he cares about you. I've seen him with lasses on Sundays walking out. You don't realise.'

'I realise and want to know nothing,' I scream. There's a pinching sensation in my arm.

'Don't you understand. I know nothing at all. Leave me and mine alone. LEAVE us.'

My arm is red and aching. And all the time there's this invisible pinching of my skin. A pinching.

He gets to his feet, scuffing his soles on the still unscrubbed tiles.

'Are you well?' His voice is fading.

I can smell undercooked bacon and an aftershave named Adore.

'Do you want the breakfast I promised you or not?' asks Phil. 'Jesus, getting through to you is like trying to wake the dead.'

Dead is perhaps what I am, I'm thinking. I decide not to move for a while, to let the blood thrashing through my brain like a trapped whirlpool settle a while. I watch the sway of Phil's hips as he moves towards the bathroom. He looks fragile. Almost as if he's faded away too. He's not really solid anyway. Not what I think of as solid. I'm wondering if he, or anyone else, will ever understand how my mind works. Can't even understand that myself.

A snivelling little brat. That's what I am.

Phil's spectacles are parked in front of the digital clock on the white bedside cabinet enlarging the numerals behind. The numbers on the clock change slowly, angrily clicking reluctance, it seems.

That's all life is about. Different ways of shrinking it, of stretching it, of killing it. Time.

It's time for me to get out of this concrete. Go walkabout. Imagine I'm a Yorkshire native covered in woad and treading the ground in search of the echo of voices. Not lizards. Not water. But voices. In a time when there was space.

'Well,' says Phil, when I slip on my heavy coat. 'That seems to be it for now, then. You know where I am if you need anything. What with all your troubles and that.'

I raise my eyebrows. 'Troubles? Who says my troubles are any different to anyone else's?' I'm simply too intense, I'm telling myself.

There's my father to worry about for instance, him and his melting mind. What can I do about that? What the fuck can I do about anything? Phil loans me a tenner and then click-closes the door behind me.

Time to buy a packet of cigarettes in a cut-price supermarket. To keep counting coppers. Then I've got to find company in The Prince and Horse. The trivial kind. The murmuring kind. The kind who, mercifully, don't listen, but still buy a half a bitter for anyone who stands close enough and smiles. The kind who glance into patrons' shopping bags in search of a chance of scrounging something, who scratch their head and wonder about students in short black skirts buying white wine and soda, ignoring their own ages because fairy tales could happen. They're wondering about the size of their penises, the statements from the banks and the Income Support and the book clubs.

They're the stupid kind. Like me.

I sip on my lager and cross my legs under a near-to-the-door round table. Because it's expected.

Anything could happen in a place like this. Someone could offer me cut-price meat. Someone could offer to let me take them around the corner and give them a quick cock suck. Not that I'd do it. Men should sense things like that. But they've got to try it on haven't they, because of the ego thing? Then try to get up women's skirts.

I'm cold again. Know that if I let myself I could spend the day thinking about the Mark thing again, and that guy angers me. I can see him brushing down the horses, walking into a hay yard and then yawning in the air, scratching his crotch. Then he'd go with other women of the parish and tell them that they mattered, meant something. He'll poke them anytime.

How dare he?

I sip on my cider. Take a deep breath. My mind is playing ridiculous games. Always has. I'm feeling randy about and getting angry about a figment of my imagination. That's all it is, imagination. I've got to convince myself of that if I don't want to have a mind-melt similar to Dad's.

I could comb down my hair, have a game of dominoes with two middle-aged women in tweed who pretend they never cuddle each other and a guy, on medication, who used to play cricket for Yorkshire, a practical animal who always wears a long scarf. Could phone Rod. Lie, tell him that I'm dying, get him to come and get me. Or I could simply behave myself and do the crossword in the Daily Mirror.

Could weep into my beer, watch the bubbles and think something sensible.

Think of what? There's nothing left for me to think. I've been through the list.

After I offer them a bogus lecture on Philosophy a young couple in matching mustard coloured sweaters offer me a Baileys. Probably think they've found themselves a substitute for a mother. I've seen their kind before. They probably have a home computer and an ambition to adopt some kid suffering from an incurable disease and give generously to Save The Rainforests. Can't blame them for that. They probably have mothers. The girl possibly has PMT. And he, of the shiny blond hair, surely holds her hand when she goes for a smear test.

They smile at me, haven't twigged that my expensive looking jacket is cut-price Oxfam.

Well, they're not meant to.

Their heavily-voiced joint complaint about the tardiness of planning permission for their expected patio and the weakness of their Baileys doesn't last for long. But long enough. Time to move on to The Queen's, where middle-class shoppers sip sweet sherry and listen to their husbands sucking on rosewood pipes.

Feeling nasty I am now. I've only enough money left for two fucking halves. The fading picture of Queen Victoria over the bar makes me wince. Can't do with things like that. Never could.

It occurs to me that Big Bert never could either. Then I feel like scratching L-shaped scars on my wrist. There is no Big Bert, I'm trying to tell myself. Never fucking was. Got to get away from it. Stop slipping back.

The beer goes down my throat slowly. It's meant to. If I bide my time, sooner or later one of the likely lads who just happens to have had a lottery win and his weekly Giro is sure to come in and offer to buy me something stronger. Is bound to. Then I'll have to smile and feel obliged to say thank you.

I slip off my shoes and peer down at my stunted toes. Always have strange shaped toes, my family. Every single member. I nod at a few faces, then cadge a bag of crisps off the ageing barman. He says I'm looking a bit down in the mouth.

'Jesus Christ, if this is living I could just as easily forget it,' I mutter.

I hear Rod's cough and smell Sonia's perfume, before the couple come into view.

Not into the pub-crawling, is Rod. It's got to be a one-off. Sonia will be picking at her gums with one of her long pointed fingernails, as usual, and killing time before one of an endless number of dental appointments. And Rod? He's not difficult to understand. Probably trying to make me jealous. He's like a twelve piece jigsaw puzzle. His smile fades when he sees me. Good actor at times. Watches a lot of television.

Sonia nods to me and tells Rod to buy me a whisky. He looks uncomfortable, because he's never bought me a whisky in all of his life. He hasn't ironed his shirt properly, I can see that, and there's a speck of blood from a hurriedly shaved chin on the crumpled, checked, collar.

'So?' says Sonia, throwing off her C&A coat and seating herself, uninvited, beside me. 'What brings you here?'

'Fate?' I don't want to talk to her. Her conversation is bound to be unimportant twaddle, not even humorous. Then it occurs to me. Like a flash of intuition. And I have to voice it. 'Are you fucking Rod?'

She laughs uncomfortably.

'I don't mean right at this minute,' I snarl.

'I'm taking care of him,' she says in a quiet voice. 'That's what you asked me to do isn't it?'

'You're a cunt.'

'Darling, please don't turn this into a circus. You didn't want him. It was obvious that you didn't want him.'

'So? Did you? Or is it just a game?' I can feel the blood pulsating through my neck.

'Make up your mind,' she sighs. 'He's a pussycat pretending he can chase tigers. Some men are like that. And you either want him or you don't.'

I glare at her.

'I thought you two were finished forever,' she continues. 'I thought we were adult friends, you and I. And I've told you the troubles I've had with my man for long enough. Surely you must have listened?'

'Have you ever really stopped being a prostitute, Sonia?'

A bitch. That's all she is. A bitch. So why aren't I more upset? Maybe I'm no longer capable of being upset. It's possible. It's well pissing possible. But for Pete's sake, I've still got my pride.

I catch the nervous flicker of Rod's eyes as he walks towards me clutching drinks. He knows that I know, and I know that he knows that I know. Can't live with someone for so many years without developing some morsel of telepathy. Can't be done.

I smile sweetly as he puts the single measure of whisky in front of me. 'Is she better at sex than I am?' I ask quietly. 'Does she move better? Or maybe she doesn't mind getting undressed in the dark, then getting out of bed the next morning to pretend it was only a dream. Is that it? So desperate is she?'

Well I'm supposed to say such things. Strange that I'm not enjoying it though.

Sonia jumps to her feet and shakes her head at me sadly. 'There's no need for all this darling,' she says as if she's something out of *Gone with the Wind*. But she's flinching. She can't hide that. 'After all, you owe a lot to Rod. Like the children?' she suggests.

Jesus, my children. That bitch is not having my children. The alcohol is cooling my brain, as it should, pushing me into another thought.

I say, 'You'd like to put them into strait-jackets. To give my kids a yen for mortgages and holidays in Spain. And shit to their souls.' Then I begin to laugh. Don't know why I'm laughing.

Someone is trying to steal my kids, but nobody can, can they?

Rod is watching me closely, running his tongue along his dry lips and wondering with apparent concern if I'll start throwing glasses about. I couldn't if I wanted to. Apart from the normal thing of not wanting to give him that satisfaction, I'm knackered.

I know he's watching as my head hits the table and sense that he's nodding in what he thinks is wisdom because he can smell the alcohol in me.

Then nothing.

I don't remember getting back to Beth's. But suddenly I'm trying to sleep it off in her inherited, floral-patterned rocking chair in the corner of her dining room. I don't know if, somewhere in the blackness, I've been rambling on about Rod and playing the woman betrayed. I don't know anything anymore.

'You need a good long sleep,' she says uneasily, throwing a blanket over me. 'Forget everything for a while.'

'Forget?' I slur. 'Do you mean forget? Or remember?'

I remember. Things I don't want to. Then the wooden arms of the chair. I'm falling again.

'Like Alice in fucking Wonderland,' I scream at her. She hasn't heard me. Nobody can hear me.

The purr of the central heating system has gone. I can feel my knees pressing hard against stone, and wind around my face when there should be none. I've got a vague sense of unease, like I shouldn't be here. I shrug it off. What else can I do? It's common knowledge that women of childbearing age get attacks of nerves.

Of course I should be here. There's something rough and splintered in my hand dripping soapy water onto my skirt. I'm in the midst of doing what I'm supposed to be doing, I tell myself. I'm scrubbing the steps of the mission. A job I always hate. It's my turn. I have to remind myself, once every calendar month it's my turn.

The townhall clock strikes in the distance. There's a faint smell of dog piss. And varying appetising odours of lamb or vegetable stews emitting from open doors along the dusty street.

I must have been tardy in my work, dreaming a little, perhaps. Without my having noticed, the sun's turned from an irritating glare into a small ball of jaundiced yellow casting a chill onto my shoulders. The autumn warmth is fading for now. It's almost seven o'clock, or perhaps later. I can't remember.

But the workers are coming up from the factories, having cut across the fungi-coated viaduct, laughingly pushing their fists into their hastily repaired pockets. Some have earned good money this week. I can tell by the way they're carefully carrying white jugs brimming with ale, or throwing caution to the wind and sharing tobacco. All except for Old Gilbert, who's well known for being badly with some bone disease. Their clothing smells either of lanolin or sulphur, never a mixture of both, and nervous voices tell coarse jokes and chuckle with relief.

It's Saturday, I have to remind myself, pay day.

A man carrying a parcel of meat, the blood dripping from the newspaper wrapping down the side of his jacket, nods to me in recognition. Nothing unusual, for haven't my family lived around here for more than fifty years?

Self-consciously I push straying locks of hair away from my face, then find my head full of unwanted reminiscences. Of me sitting on the doorstep imagining what my father must have been like. Came up from Cornwall looking for work and a wife, he did, found both, and built me a cradle. Then died of typhus twelve months later. Then I wonder about Thomas's father. No-one still living knew who he was except, perhaps, for the woman who delivered him from Mother, dragging out his screaming head. But, silent or not, Mother's privacy was always respected. She was always respected. The soap's stinging the webs between my soggy fingers, but I still remember that. Never harmed a soul, did she, and no-one could fault her lacemaking. A dying art, that.

Thomas could be the son of an Earl or a tinker. Not that it matters. Now there's only the two of us left. But when he's not behaving foolishly and talking nonsense we get on well, I'm telling myself, putting more power into the job in hand.

Today he's late in returning from work. Should have passed me ten minutes ago, at least. I've got an instinct for such things.

But not to panic.

He could have become entrenched in a game of marbles, or foolish spitting contests to see whose spittle was strong enough to knock down the dandelions growing through the cracks in the corner of the mill yard. Or he could have leaped over the low, dry-stone wall that separates his workplace from the phosphorus factory to flirt with the girls there. Thomas is at a strangely disturbing age. I know more about him than he thinks.

A voice behind me startles me. Pulls me back from such thoughts.

It's Big Bert, the troublemaker, again. He's even been thrown out of two perfectly respectable lodging houses because he stumbled home late and drunk and cursing. Now Mrs Roberts, who lives half way up Castle Hill and indulges herself the whole day long in some strong brew, is the only one who'll tolerate him and let him have a room.

Word gets around in a small town like ours.

He's muttered some kind of greeting to me.

'What do you want?' I ask impatiently. I had been hoping it would be Mark who was passing, because I haven't seen him for five weeks. I've kept telling myself that his duties preclude him from having much time to himself, but still, he could have sneaked out to see me for a short while couldn't he? He was never as thoughtless as this before he got up my skirt.

What was it the older women always said? Keep it for the marriage bed or else you'll find the bastard's fled? Well, that could be Mark. Maybe.

I feel a pang I can't describe to myself. Something akin to bile. Bert clears his throat, then thoughtlessly puts a foot on a stoop I've just cleaned. He explains that he's come to apologise for upsetting me and that he can't think how he managed it.

'And to walk you home before it gets dark,' he adds.

How did he know that I'd be here? A wild guess? But he knows, right enough. He's probably been and waylaid Thomas at the side of the looms, been filling the boy's head with nonsense again. And probing like a flea's tongue. Always probing and wanting to know everything, this one. As if working wasn't enough for any right thinking man.

'Since when could the likes of you upset me?' I retort. But it's useless. He knows he upset me.

He shrugs. Lifts up my bucket and empties the grey water into the street, then walks slowly beside me towards my home. My hips hurt. They've been hurting for months. Something to do with the damp of a changeable summer. What I need to do is get some powders suitable for the pain. I never have been good at tolerating pains. Not even minor ones. They always put me in a dark mood and slow my thinking down. Today I feel bathed in a kind of dullness, like the clouds slowly following us, and like the huge worm stretched out on the cobbles in front of me must feel. Everything feels something.

I realise that I'm grinding my teeth. Haven't done that for years. At the age of twenty-four I should have more sense.

'I'm not trying to corrupt Thomas or any of the other boys,' Bert is saying. 'I'm trying to tell them what is going on and what isn't, and what their rights are. I know, you see, girl.'

'Oh, you know do you? And how do you know?' I snap.

He's paying no heed to my manner. Takes my elbow and guides me past the green, wide-open gates of the slaughter house and the weekend queue outside the provisions store.

'I haven't forgotten the summer strike of forty-two,' he's saying. 'I travelled all the way to Shropshire on foot to support it. We should have won. Got higher wages. Could have won.'

He's expecting me to say something. Anything.

I take a deep breath. There's going to be no getting away from this. 'So what happened, then?'

He shakes his head. Expected the question. Typical of his type, I'm thinking.

'We marched from establishment to establishment to drum up support,' he scowls, 'from town to town, girl. Town to town. Plundered potato fields to keep going. Even managed to unseat a detachment of cavalry by pelting them with sticks. Believe it, girl. That's how strong we were.' Now he's puffing out his chest, unwittingly. 'And who started the rumour that the Queen had been assassinated? We did.'

'And it failed,' I sigh. Had to fail. What sort of fool did this man take me for?

He's still not listening. He's going to try to lecture me.

'Men trickled back to work. Stupidly.' He emphasises by gripping my arm tighter. 'Like mules. A farce. The Chartists blamed the Anti Corn Law League. The League blamed the Chartists. The government blamed both and added the unions for good measure. Many arrests, there were. Many. And then we battled over the cholera epidemic. Some of us,' he adds. 'The outbreak that started in Sunderland in thirty-one is still going. It's known that dirty water spreads the thing. It's known.'

'Then you failed again,' I say flatly. But for some reason, I feel sorry for him.

Suddenly he turns me towards him and takes my shoulders.

Grips them so tightly that it hurts.

'Take care of Thomas,' he warns, needlessly. 'Just take care of him. He's got a head on his shoulders.'

Chapter 12

Beth stands over me with a china mug of instant coffee and then the sun screams through the nylon curtains, licks the toes of my highly polished shoes and tinges Beth's supposedly naturally black hair with purple.

I try to lick the dryness from my mouth. Feel the crick in my neck. Morning.

It's got to be morning.

Beth tightens her chocolate-brown dressing gown self-consciously around her sagging breasts. Tells me Fred has gone to put a few bets on, almost ashamed, embarrassed. Says he usually breaks even. And reminds me that I asked to be prodded into life early this morning because I had promised to visit my father.

I can't remember it. Promises? Was I still making promises? What the hell did they mean to me? Or to him, anymore? His mind has gone.

And I've still got the uneasy feeling that mine is going. But what the hell? A father is a father, just as a dream is a dream.

Beth coaxes me downstairs, poaches an egg for me, then stares across the formica-topped table at my unwashed face, with a look of genuine concern. I'm a mess. And I know I look it. My badly permed hair is standing as far away from my head as the roots will let it. I've dribbled down my chin during the night creating the beginnings of spots and my poorly fitting dentures hurt like hell itself, or how I imagine it to be.

'I've had another of those pissing dreams,' I tell her, not knowing if I've mentioned them before. 'Don't know why I did. And I don't know what causes them.'

My sudden announcement has no effect on her, whatsoever. She doesn't understand. Can't.

'Do you understand what I'm saying?' I ask her. 'I think they're something more. They've got to be something more. Ordinary dreams aren't like that, not like disjointed passages from the same story-book.'

She looks at me blankly.

'Either I'm going totally mad or there's something in the past trying to get to me. Do you think I'm talking crazy?'

She pours me more coffee. Of course she thinks I'm mad, with luck a borderline case. There's no reason for her to think otherwise.

High View Rest Home has tall iron gates and a cat sitting permanently in front of them, licking his genitals. There's a path soldiered by oak trees and still elms leading up to the newly varnished door. My heels bite into the gravel. I spot a squirrel in the growth of rampant pansies. The sun glares down like an over-ripe melon with a sense of humour.

I'm here now. No choice but to visit Dad. I'm from his sperm. It's no fault of his that he's going off his head.

The entrance hall smells of urine disguised in a thin veil of pine disinfectant. I never expected anything else. These places all smell the same. I've read about it. And I've always had a keen sense of smell. Not my fault. Just a quirk of nature.

I'm still tired. My shoulders ache. There's no virtue in having slept in a rocking chair. The narrow-waisted matron who greets me weighs no more than a nine year old child, and smiles like a whippet who once won a race. She says my dad may ramble a bit. It's to be expected, so I shouldn't feel disturbed.

I'm thinking that I don't remember a time when I didn't feel disturbed.

So I follow her, through spotlessly clean corridors lined with collapsible wheelchairs and metal walking sticks, and crocheted cardigans covering stoop-backed women writing letters to granddaughters on pink notepaper, or knitting something yet to be decided.

Dad will be in his room. Of course he will. Not exactly his scene, is this. He'll venture out into this strange community if the Saturday stew smells nice or the Grand National is on the telly. No great mixer is my Dad. At least he's got some fucking sense.

The matron smiles at me sweetly, pushes open an avocado coloured door identical to every other and asks if I've bought flowers, because if I have they'll have to be put in a jug.

I tell her, 'No, I fucking haven't.' That's the way I feel. Can't help it.

'Took your bloody time coming to visit me,' says Dad. Despite being told that it wasn't the done thing, he's got out of his highseat chair, undressed himself, and got back into bed again.

I've nothing to say to him. Nothing to anyone.

Matron sniffs, and tells us she'll leave us together. It's clear she's seen it all before, rotting father, embarrassed daughter. 'Together,' she emphasises. What kind of a word is that? No two people can be totally together. One of the great media-created illusions, is that.

I pull a red plastic chair to the edge of the counterpaned bed and stare at the curtains, a restful, medium green with fine white stripes running through them. There's a chipboard wardrobe in the corner. An unused urine bottle leaning against a box of pink tissues and Dad's spare slippers on top of a small chest of drawers. Then a portrait photo of Mother sporting a blue-rinse perm and a snap of me riding a rocking horse to hell. Both are perched on a ridiculously high shelf welded to an anaglypta coated wall.

Dad's reading my mind. 'It'll do me,' he says challengingly. 'What did you fucking expect?'

I didn't expect anything. Don't want anything.

'You're looking pale,' he says.

I raise my eyebrows, and he grinds his teeth together. 'Well, I'm supposed to say things like that aren't I? Have you bought me any fucking grapes?'

'Don't be bloody ridiculous, Dad. My head aches. You can't know how much it aches.'

He doesn't want to know, more like. Old folk are selfish buggers. Well known is that. He re-adjusts his pillows so that they throw his spine forward a bit and make him look fragile. Contrary to the impression he's trying to give, the place is getting to him.

'Can't understand why my legs gave way on me,' he says. 'Just like that,' he tells me, trying without success to snap his fingers. 'They gave way just like that.'

'Just like what?' I say. 'You've had those leg ulcers for years. Ever since...'

'Ever since what?' he demands.

I shrug. 'Since about the time of Mum's funeral, I suppose.' I shudder. I shouldn't have said that. It was an old wound. But Jesus, the old man can be pathetic. Yet there's no way that I can help him. No point in beating around the bush. Whatever is still living in the undergrowth of his brain knows that as well as I do. My mouth is dry. I'm about to try pulling wings from a fading butterfly. There's something I've got to know. I've been rehearsing it in my mind during the journey here. Mad or not, I've got to pursue it. It can't be ignored any longer.

'I've come to ask about Mark. Mark and Thomas and possibly Big Bert. You know what I'm talking about don't you?'

'You're talking about your soddin' dreams,' he says, trying to twist his wrinkles into an acceptable expression of disgust. 'I don't know anything about them.'

'Don't you?'

He turns his face away from me. Of course he knows. He's looking at the wall and not seeing.

'Dad, please,' I beg. 'Talk to me. You recognise the mill in my dream. I know. And you knew about the smell of crab apples, that I can't escape it. When you were dozing in your chair one day you mumbled, without opening your eyes, that I should be wary of Mark. Screamed that you'd say no more. Don't you remember?'

'I must have been tired. Old men talk nonsense when they're tired. Make your mind up to believe that.'

He's looking old. Older than he really is. And suddenly uncaring. Doesn't even bother to brush away a small fly that lands on his forehead and lazily washes its feet in his sweat. We sit in silence for five minutes, then Dad's hand clutches the top of the sheet that grips his neck, holds him there, where he thought he was supposed to be. He squeezes the cotton, rolls the edges between what I used to think were pianist's fingers.

When I was young he drove that thought into me and I imagined that he was some disowned bastard son of some great Hungarian musician. It was a fantasy grown out of childish silliness of course. But I was proud of him. Still am, in some weird sort of way.

'How can I believe what you say,' I sigh. 'You talked to me about tooth fairies and Santa Claus. The older I get the more I realise that you're a liar.'

I've hit a nerve.

'Then ask Mark about it,' he spits. 'Or Rod.'

'What the chuff has all this got to do with Rod?'

He turns to look at me again, sees the bewilderment on my face. 'What you're hearing is the ramblings of an old man,' he snaps. 'You shouldn't ask me things. Can't leave well enough alone can you?' His cheeks redden. He's becoming more and more irate. 'You want to fucking know about the dream? Then I'll tell you. It's a family thing, see? Rod is Mark. Mark is Rod. I know,' he shouts, raising his head. 'Nothing changes.'

I'm shaking my head in disbelief. He's off his trolley. He's glaring at me. He starts to cough and it becomes louder. It's uncontrollable for a few minutes. He's fighting it. Forces himself into a slouching position so that he can uncomfortably suck in air and line his lungs.

The coughing subsides as quickly as it came. He slouches back onto the pillow. His eyes are glazed. He's not with me. 'Watch out for Rod,' he warns loudly, his voice curiously croaky and his venom hitting the pillow in hot spittle. 'He betrayed us lads. Betrayed us. You could have stopped him. Could have listened to Bert.'

'Dad, I don't know what you're talking about,' I insist.

'Don't you?' he shouts. 'Don't you? This is just the ramblings of an old man's mind, eh?'

'That's what you told me,' I say.

'Listen to me,' he booms insistently. 'He betrayed us before and he'll do it again. Betray you. Betray me.'

'You? How can he betray you?' I'm perplexed. He doesn't make sense, but neither does the damned dream.

He presses his head into the softness of the pillow and sighs.

The audience is over.

'Dad?'

He waves me away with a fine-boned hand. 'An old man's ramblings,' he mutters before closing his eyes. 'Just an old man's ramblings.'

Matron escorts me down the gravel path leading to the main gate, looks at me askew when I enquire about Dad's medication.

'Just a mild pain-killer for his arthritis,' she says. 'Nothing that can affect his mind,' she adds reassuringly. 'His ramblings, as you call them, are simply the result of old age.'

'Are they?' I ask.

I'm not so sure anymore. I've got to escape, I'm telling myself. I mean REALLY escape. I can't do with Dad's craziness anymore, nor mine. I can find some amber nectar. That will do the trick. Always did. Should put Dad's problems on the back burner for a while.

Got to go.

Some fool is having a birthday party in the function room of The Royal. Some fool in corduroy trousers whose name I can't remember. Free vol-au-vents and champagne perry. I need some liquid courage so that I can confront Rod and Sonia to talk over the custody of my kids. My young ones are the only people on earth who can help me keep a sensible grip on life right now.

I really should feel guilty about that. About the way I treated Rod, pushing him out of my life because he wasn't perfect, had stopped trying to be. Me thinking sensibly. Or the drink maybe. But I decide I'll do that tomorrow. The drink's going down smoothly. Another couple of barley wines and I'll have the speed of mind and tongue to confront anyone.

I'm swaying to the music, head back, watching action on a forgotten spider's web hanging from a corner of the high ceiling as it sways slightly in the rising cigarette smoke illuminated by the busy disco lights. Now I'm wondering about the destiny of flies. Perhaps they realise that disappointment is inevitable, close their compound eyes and don't struggle to disentangle themselves from the death sentence thread.

'Believe in reincarnation?' I suddenly ask this guy I'm dancing with.

'No,' he shouts back above the noise.

'I bloody don't either,' I yell determinedly. 'So let's have another drink.'

Two more drinks and I know my head will come back down, that I'll fall into one of the inexplicable bouts of fear that I've been stricken by lately. And then what?

We sit down and the guy's leg touches mine under the table.

He fancies himself as a philosopher. 'You seem to be having some sort of problem with life,' he sucks on his bottom lip, thinks he's tapped the nail on its head.

'Life damn well haunts me,' I scowl, 'and if you'd like to meet me tomorrow, man whose name I don't know from Rasputin, you'd be wise if you bought me another drink.'

My voice is crisp. Hoarse. Hell I'm coming down a lot faster than I thought I would, and behaving like a typical drunk. If I'm not careful I'll end up labelled as a Huddersfield bicycle. No hoper. What chance of rescuing Gaynor and Gavin then? I keep telling myself not to worry, that I'm as tough and as quick as old miner's boots, then decide my problem is that I keep telling myself - another drink.

Can't go to visit Rod in this state. My brain has sunk too far, swimming in cockles and sherry and nonsense. So I teeter to the bar, pick up the phone and shout to Rod above the din that I want my kids.

'You're not going to put one over on me, you bastard.'

So he says, 'I want a divorce,' because he's been watching too many American movies.

And I say 'Fuck off', and put the phone down.

'That's no way to behave,' says my new drunken companion, breathing in my right ear. 'Why not forget everything and have a game of darts?'

Now he's looking uncomfortable, expecting that I'm about to burst into tears and that he'll have to pay for a taxi to take me out of here. Take me where? I'm asking myself. Then I decide that it's the Grand Scheme of Things, and it doesn't matter.

'Does everyone know,' I say loudly, 'that every religion is built upon the belief that no-one ever dies? It's either about the choice between heaven and hell, or a certainty that everyone,' I hiccup, 'and everything, goes around in circles. Circle after circle after circle. It's meant to make the mind boggle.'

I lean over the table of a woman who's nibbling on a chicken leg, her dark red lipstick staining the bone. Between gnawing she's managing to scowl.

'Even the teeny-weeniest little fly,' I tell her nostrils. 'I know because I read a lot, learned that trick from my mad father.'

Then something occurs to me.

'I've got a question. If you drop your knickers in one life do you drop them ad infinitum? Or do you get to the point where you wear no knickers at all?' I'm pointing towards myself, wishing that I could stop this. 'See what I mean, madam? That is the quandary we're in.'

Someone starts to pull me away. I can smell the tobacco stored in the top pocket of his outdated, tweed jacket and the delicate scent of his Steradent-cleaned dentures, and just a hint of whisky.

But I keep talking to her, part of my mind still able to observe her carefully plucked eyebrows. I'm not going to be daunted.

'I think we've lived before. You and I, and just about every bugger. Now how's about that? We've probably pestered and fucked each other time after time. Cogs in the workings of a fucking doomed big-wheel.'

Now the feller in the jacket has got me to the door, and the guy I've been dancing with has disappeared through the haze into the lavatory.

'Doomed to eternity,' I call back to the silent woman, who has now stopped chewing. 'That's what we are.'

I've got silence now. A foot on the pavement. Should never have tried to clear out my mind in public, I decide. Never.

What do the fuckers know anyway?

There's a fountain in the park. A pigeon with a damaged leg, hopping around it, tossing a discarded Chinese noodle into the air with its ageing beak. It notices me. Doesn't care.

'Why should you?' I slur softly. 'I may come back as a firefly tomorrow, and you as an archer fish. Get yourself a good, a bloody good solicitor, mate, 'cos I won't cave in.'

I might convince myself to believe all this shit, I'm telling myself as I kick off my shoes and, cursing a ladder in my tights, stretch my legs out on a green, paint-chipped, bench. Could be a real turn up for the books, that. There's a cloud in front of the moon. Always is a cloud in front of the moon when I try to look at it, I reflect.

Or is it smoke, the apex of rising smog?

There's someone laughing. Or is it something? Hard to tell. It all seems so far away. There's sulphur in the air, and the sound of an approaching fishmonger's cart.

My mattress is hard, harder than I remembered it from the rainy night before, and the wooden slats beneath are sagging. There are hurried footsteps of heavily clad feet crunching across the frost, and the occasional rustlings of skirts outside the window I neglected to close.

Can't sleep with the windows shuttered anymore. Not since the pain in my side started disturbing my slumber. I've needed to feel the fresh air of night ever since I watched Thomas struggle for breath. I covered his chest with mustard plasters and, listening to his ramblings, turned my face to one side to avoid the staleness of his breath.

But that was two years ago. More. His survival was unexpected. A miracle, almost. Now he's fit and almost a man. Fitter than he's ever been, and showing signs of developing muscle around his neck. His shoulders. Tomorrow is his entitled holiday, and I've saved up enough from his wages to be able to take him by train to the seashore. He's earned it. We both have.

I try to slumber again. But the female voice from across the street is shrill. Her words strike me at once. Make me sit up with a start that causes my ribs to press painfully on the inflamed swelling nestling on my waist. The voice belongs to the strange, Jewish woman living at the end of Buck's row. Her words are like something from a story in a penny newspaper. Hard to believe. I don't want to believe them.

'The phosphorus factory,' she's screaming. 'It's afire. Burning. Oh, the poor kids.'

There's a stunned silence. A strange smell in the air. Then there are more voices. More accents. Masculine feet move, metal toe-caps hurriedly kicking against the frozen cobbles. There's a soft falling of snow.

'God forbid, not that awful place,' a woman groans in an Irish brogue, resting her buttocks against my cold window ledge and folding her arms. She's a woman who always folds her arms.

'Some of the bairns sleep there at night, they'll be roasted alive.'

She lets out a steady stream of breath that curls its way into my room and swears to me that I'm not dreaming.

'Roasted alive,' she says more quietly. Her sadness dulls even the sound of the feet.

I'm out of bed quickly. Move quickly. Pulling on my bodice with a haste I didn't know I could muster. 'It's impossible,' I'm telling myself out loud. 'Ridiculous. Can't be happening.' Part of a dream. Yes, that's it. Factories don't catch ablaze in this day and age. There's an involuntary tightening of the muscles of my stomach. But it does happen doesn't it? Accidents at work happen all the time.

I stub my toe on the nail of a floorboard.

Got to go. Follow the others from the street into the mist.

Foster's mill is next door to that dreaded factory. And Thomas is working his shift. Whatever happened he wouldn't turn tail and run home leaving the more timid, younger boys there. I know that. And some of the smaller boys wouldn't move for fear of losing their jobs, with the talk of a slump on the cloth market. I know that too. Everybody knows that.

I slam the door loudly behind me, as if that would suddenly wake me up. But there's no waking up is there? Not from the truth.

I'm gasping in the chemical-poisoned air before I reach the top of the hill. It's scratching the back of my throat. Footsteps slow down. And the voices of the handful of people, some carrying blankets, and all moving in the same direction, are almost murmurs.

'Nothing to be done.' Was that my voice or someone else's? No way of knowing.

We can see the yellow and blue flames rising, almost lethargically, from the factory now. It's gone. All but gone. A cat gallops away from the heat, heading for anywhere.

'Foster's,' an old man with a walking stick grumbles, determined not to let himself panic. 'The fire's bound to reach Foster's, if it hasn't already.'

We can't get near the heat. Men are carefully pushing us away from the heat. Pushing. Then pushing more. I begin to cough. Sharp intakes of smoke-flavoured air are aggravating the pain in my side. And I've forgotten to put my shoes on. Without shoes I can't push through the arms and the smoke and run towards the gates. I just can't.

Best not to panic about it, I tell myself wildly, best not. I could wake up within minutes.

Stones are biting through the melting frost to graze my numbing feet.

Not real. None of it.

If it was real, the men and boys would be flocking out from the mill like stunned sheep, and hurrying down the hill with sensibly dampened sacks wrapped around their shoulders. If it was real I would be able to feel my toes, my fingers.

Suddenly Bert's at my side, gripping my arm like a vice. 'They won't let them out,' he pants, sweat glistening on his forehead. 'They have the gates locked.'

'What?' I'm still fighting for breath and can't quite take in what he's saying. I'm fighting down panic. 'It's my brother we're talking about here. Almost a baby. All I've got,' I scream at him.

He's annoyed with me. His wide belt hangs unfastened around his waist and his hair stands almost straight up from his scalp in oily, unruly strands, as if he's spent the early hours of this night tossing and turning on too thin a pillow.

'Listen to me, woman. Foster ordered the gates and doors to be locked. He says it's to stop panic. That the fire can't possibly spread. That the men are safer in there. But the fumes from the factory are still drifting across, getting in there. Probably filling the weaving sheds.'

I'm looking at him, frightened and perplexed and shaking my head. 'They'd never do that.'

'It's your Mark,' he explains impatiently. 'They've put Mark and his friends on the gate to keep people in, or out.'

I'm shaking my head again.

'Your Mark,' he shouts.

'But there must be a reason. The plan must be right,' I say in desperation. 'Mark would never put people in danger. Never.'

'Feel the heat,' he's screaming, 'feel it. Go and speak to this man of yours. Climb over bodies if you must. Tell him. Explain his folly. He won't listen to me. Won't.'

Almost before he's finished this sentence, before the brown and white pigeons start flying away from nearby, no longer cold rooftops, before my gasp, there's a strange rumbling sound, like barrels being pushed across the cobbles in their hundreds. Unexpected sparks hitting the spirals of black air like fireflies in fear of death.

There's another sound. The rumble of falling brickwork and rubble hitting dandelions like a fist on a gnat. Someone's sharp elbow hits me in the side, that place again beneath my ribs. Then there's a solitary scream. A woman's scream and a surge forward. She's at the forefront, up against the brown painted railings surrounding Foster's.

She's menstruating and the shock of this fire has made her careless. The bloodstain on the back of her skirt is like a map of Indo-China I once saw whilst at school. I don't know why I should think of that now. My mind should be on Thomas, and his rescue. Fully on Thomas.

But none of this is real is it? Don't want it to be real.

I'm closing my eyes. Pressing the lids tighter and tighter together, seeing stars under their cover and watching them depart. Someone's talking but I can't make the words out.

'Shout, God damn it.' A husky voice calls from behind me, through the dense smoke to vague figures on the other side of the gate. 'If you know what's happening tell us.'

A baritone answers, somewhere ahead, his voice like a ghost in a dream. One of my dreams. Strange dreams I remember vaguely. But now is not the time for such things. Now is not the time for anything. A dead time. I feel myself swaying from one foot to the other. Life's not like this. It can't be.

'The weaving shed is gone,' says a voice. 'Only the weaving shed, thank be.'

Bert lets loose my arm. 'They're opening the gates,' he mutters with relief.

'And Thomas?' My voice is loud. Louder than it has ever been before. 'Would Thomas still have been in there?'

I feel the sting of hot spittle on my left cheek, and the nearness of a woman smelling of camphor and peppermint. 'You naive bitch,' she's saying. 'You bloody naive bitch.'

Bert is still by my side, shuddering. The disturbed air is licking my neck like a luke-warm curse. He knows something he's not telling.

'Don't stay to watch,' he's saying softly. 'Just don't stay to watch.'

My eyes are still closed. My legs still trembling. I want to shit. To shit badly. Shit all this nightmare out till my blood is as thin as the rain on the field. Yes, that's the answer. To shit all of this stuff to the ground.

I can't.

My brother is gone. It's a dream, for God's sake. But I'm crying. Dying.

Chapter 13

Something is crawling up my leg, and I glance at my laddered tights. Always hated laddered tights. But I'm not where I think I am, am I? Not in the park. And not outside the mill.

I'm in a centrally-heated room with baby-blue walls and a gleaming white hand basin beneath a double-glazed window. There are voices, echoing, crawling along the floor. A notice on the door stating 'Thou shalt not'.

There's a fly on my forehead licking sweat and a memory in my mind of a pop record spinning. Cliff Richard's 'Please Don't Tease.'

But that was dredged up from long ago. Long, long ago, when I wore a beehive head and the last of the starched underslips. What age was I then? It's so long ago I can't recall. There's a phone ringing somewhere, insistently. And my feet hurt like they've got splinters of glass stuck in their soles. Splinters like ice. Ice coated cobbles.

So what? I'm always hurting, somewhere.

There's someone crouching down beside me, showing fleshy thighs beneath a black nylon skirt. My cell-mate. If she doesn't get a cig right now, she says, she'll die. There's an off-white pot of cool milky tea on a small metal table, screwed down, by the side of my bed. The cell-mate has Huddersfield type dreadlocks and appears to be emptying her soul in a deadpan fashion she's anxious to perfect. I've missed the first half of the conversation.

'I wouldn't let any John go up my arse without a Johnny, would you?' she's saying. 'I mean, considering.'

I'm considering. Telling myself that I know where I am and that everything comes out logical in the end. And I'm struggling to be practical. Sane. Thinking that some men may have gone up my arse in their imagination, and that I never got paid for that.

'Where do you come from?' she asks, like a child meeting another on their first day at school.

Suddenly I don't know where I really come from.

But I'm not thinking sensibly. I'm hung over aren't I? There's nothing more certain than that. I must have got picked up in the park for trying to sleep it off. IT. The big IT.

I've got a vague memory of the figure of a boy in front of me crying. Of looking at the nape of his neck, a familiar yet unusual shape. He could be Thomas, couldn't he? But which world? What time? My mind's starting to wander, and I'm thinking of a boy I knew when we were children. Could have been a next-door neighbour.

I have a mental picture of him unfolding a sheet of silver paper, the wrapping from a Cadbury's Milk Tray, of him burning things on a rusty spoon by aid of Swan Vestas while I watched and said nothing. Then he breathed heavily and clung to the dampness of a splintering tree. I watched and watched him. Then he became quiet. Silent.

He had odd socks on I noticed, as he slithered to the ground. His mother wouldn't know, wouldn't care, I remember thinking. She probably painted Passion-Red onto non-existent lips and the lines engraving her forehead were Sweet-Beige. She pulled rhubarb from hillsides in her younger days, complained to the Council regularly that her cooker hadn't worked for months.

The Council had probably buried it. Him. Funny, that. He could have been Thomas's twin.

I haven't the heart to follow this line of thinking through. Not while I'm still slightly pissed. And would probably have less heart whilst sober. Gone to pot, in the old-fashioned sense, that's what I have done. No need of narcotics.

Then there's a fresher memory stirring its head. That of unforgettable scents. Of a foetus-stained toilet, in the red of the bus station on a bustling Saturday afternoon, of recently painted yet rusting railings leading to the shopping precinct, and of a policewoman in a crisp white collar daubed in Charlie perfume, grabbing my arm. A whiff of her menthol mouthwash struggling to strangle it.

And crab apples.

Can't get away from this smell can I?

And what have I been put into a jail cell for? Aiding and abetting? It's dawn. I can see it through the high windows, feel it in invisible yawns. Now I'm walking in an almost straight line towards the desk, following the straight back in front of me, the straps of my sandals tight around the swelling of my feet.

'As you asked for, and as is your right, a phone call has been made on your behalf,' yawns the sergeant, used to all this bumph and searching through pink and white papers in front of him. 'Do you understand that? Remember it?'

I look like hell. Know that I do. Does this feller think that I'm a simpleton or what?

'To whom was this overture via the telephone made?' I ask, hoping this phraseology makes me sound intelligent.

'To your husband,' he grunts, signing forms, and taking it for granted that I'd forgotten.

A phone call to the blameless Rod. Of course it was to Rod. What would this fat sod behind the varnished desk think I'd desire more? And now Rod's coming to pick me up. Nothing surer. And now I'm a registered daughter of a pillock with thin blood flowing through maverick veins. Nothing more.

I must freshen up my face to face him. It's expected. So I'm escorted to the washroom in case I decide to carve my name on my navel. I know how it works alright. The water's lethargic, cool, does nothing to camouflage the nicotine-stained hairs above my lips, does nothing to make me care a damn whether it does or doesn't. There's a face of something staring at me through the mirror. It's expressionless. Blotch covered. Lined. Like trails have been left by an anorexic snail.

This is no surprise, I tell myself, scratching my crotch because I've no clean knickers. Then become annoyed because I'm always telling myself things and never listening.

Clock ticks. At least thirty years old.

Rod, hair still uncombed, signs for me, like I'm some piece of cheddar cheese he tried to lose on a midnight train. Mutters something to the sergeant I'm clearly not meant to hear. By now I'm well into this self-pity shit. It's got a certain strength to it. I'm expecting what's coming.

When he finally looks me full in the face his eyes show no emotion. Expected. When he wants to be, he's clever at concealing what's pricking at his mind, thank God. It saves a lot of hassle.

I'm gasping for air. Queasy. Wondering if today is one of those days when I need sanitary towels. Wishing. Wishing for what?

He takes my elbow and leads me out into the open air and towards the car park.

'I just need a bit of peace,' I tell him, as a cop out.

The woman with the Johnny complex and the dreadlocks is pressing her face against her first-floor cell window. Her voice is strong enough to cut through any glass. And possibly any renegade arse, I'm thinking. That's what I'm short of. Strength like that.

'Good on you, lass,' she calls. 'That's what all the Aussies say on TV isn't it?' She laughs. 'Don't let the fucking things bother you.'

I can't help thinking she'd make a suitable mate for Rod. They could watch all the soaps, use the right bubble baths at the right time, and chew peanuts. I feel guilty though. I should care shouldn't I? But that would mean I'd have to relish being alone. I can't do it. Never really could.

Rod looks up to the window and simply shrugs as if he doesn't know what she's really saying. Or maybe doesn't want to.

Without looking back I put my fingers in a V-sign, because it's expected and doesn't hurt. Between the Devil and the supposedly blue sea I am. That's what I tell myself.

Rod sees the gesture. 'What the Devil did you do that for?' he asks.

'Don't know,' I say, ignoring his rumbling.

As he unlocks the car door in familiar, studied silence, I stare across the carpark barrier towards the glare of the neon-lit stores lining the other side of the road, and wonder why they can't settle for the gloom of winter daylight, a fact of life.

Somewhere, in one of those shops, a woman with honey-blonde hair will be sneaking into the pink of the staff loo to examine the lump on her breast in practised disbelief. Somewhere a manager with a pair of Marks & Spencer knickers in his cupboard, with gussets just right for his waist, will be pretending to ogle a valium-taking shoplifter. There will be someone contemplating fiddling the till. And someone contemplating abortion.

'So?' asks Rod suddenly, pulling me back to the spot I'm in, with a bump. 'What about your problem?' He turns a key in the car door.

'Which one?' I say defiantly. 'Sonia?'

He hasn't noticed I've got more than one, of course. Any more than I've noticed him for a while. Looked at him. Realised he's got to have problems. It's the non-communication thing. I know all about it. The domestic stuff, the stuff of *Woman's Own*.

So what? Another marriage fucked up.

'I'd like to tell you about Sonia,' he says. His knuckles are white against the steering wheel. True Confessions business. 'A drive over Ilkley Moor?' he suggests, still without looking at me.

'Why not?' He's wanting to talk to me anyway. To sever the cord.

All women are mothers, I'm thinking with disgust. Mothers of men. Getting the blame for everything from grazed knees to premature ejaculation. I wonder.

'About this Thomas thing you keep on about,' he says as we enter the ring-road. 'Of course you know it's all down to your drinking.'

'And my drinking? What's that down to?'

He gives one of his familiar shrugs. Then we get down to the usual script thing. I've seen too many television programmes not to know about it or sense it coming. The 'We can't go on like this' scenario.

Then, unexpectedly, he sees me through the corner of an eye, and I can almost feel his breath on my flesh. Chemistry. Nothing more. Surely he can't fall for that thing again. That would be too much straw clutching.

'Hangover?' he asks gently.

'What do you think?' I ask. 'If you're really asking if I miss your cock up my cunt, the answer is no.'

He winces. Of course he winces, he's never heard me talk like that. He switches the car's engine off near the Cow and Calf rocks, offers me a cigarette. Then we sit in silence and I'm glad of it. A chance to breathe, step out of the car, stand on the grass and slip off my shoes. The ground is coarse beneath my feet, feet that have yet to heal up from their brush with imagined cobbles, or was it the bars of a police station bed?

'All those lights,' I say, gazing down into the valley, 'and those invisible people scurrying around like ants. Everyone describes everyone as ants, once they manage to find a distance. Know what I mean?'

Rod is nervously stroking the red bonnet of the car. He wants to talk. I know he wants to talk, but it doesn't frighten me, and that fact frightens him. Vulnerable, that's what he is. That's what drew me to him, once. But I embarrass him. I can tell by the reddening of his ears and the slight twitch that would be imperceptible to strangers. I'm not the fool I seem to be. And I've got to forget all this analysis shit. All this watching for body language.

I light a cigarette, watch it glow in the unaccustomed darkness. No street lamps here. No pubs. It's unexpectedly comforting. A cat, kitten in mouth, pads cautiously towards the shadow of the rocks, its own shadow growing with every step. I've done the same. Done it for years. Part of life.

'You want a divorce?' I say, without looking at Rod. 'After all, you're behaving like a whore. How many times have you prostituted yourself? Double playing. Debt collecting. You name it, shit-house. Your problem is people get to know you. You'd sell your whole family, wouldn't you? Pity you always fail.'

He seems startled.

'Oh, I get it. You want an argument about it.' I can't help but smile. 'Recriminations. The 'Oh, how could you do this to me' bit, like on the silent films the Saturday matinees used to spew out, followed by the expected boozing. That was years and years ago. Remember?'

He coughs and inspects his fingernails. Proud of his well-manicured fingernails, is Rod. 'I never went to the picture houses,' he says. 'I was more interested in horses. Used to help out at the local stables on Saturdays.'

Like Mark would have done.

'As long as you get paid for it,' I say. 'That's all you ever care about.' Like Mark.

I've nothing to say to him. Nothing to feel but an emptiness in the pit of my stomach.

'It's the first time you've mentioned this, but I already knew,' I mutter. 'And you'd always obey orders from someone you thought had a little money, wouldn't you? Obey people like Sonia, for instance? I mean, she hasn't been keeping her toyboy by feeding him a diet of milky pobs has she? You're mercenaries, you lot.'

He glares at me, and then his spittle hits my face, cooled instantly by the dampness in the air.

'You'd always obey wouldn't you?' I continue. 'Even if it hurt somebody's soul. Mine, for instance. Human. Albeit damaged already by fucking drink. Even if it killed someone, you'd obey. Even if it meant some folk burned you'd obey, wouldn't you Mark?' I can feel my voice rising.

'What the hell are you talking about?' he asks.

'I can't explain what I'm talking about. Even to myself,' I tell him quietly. 'I wish I could.' Then it occurs to me to ask him something.

'Have you ever had dreams, Rod? Strange dreams about people who won't leave your head? Odd memories that don't fit?'

'No, but I've got a bloody drunken wife.'

I can't pursue this line any longer can I? Can't.

'I want the kids,' he says suddenly. 'Permanently. Legally. Sonia and I.'

I cut in.

'Sonia and I? Do you want to know what Sonia and I means? It means temporary. It means until she gets tired of shagging you and realises that, like the rest of us buggers, you've no prospects.'

Then he throws the cigarette butt to the ground, watches it sizzle on the frost and presses it into the hard soil with an experienced heel. Tells me that Sonia has been having a hard time and that's all. That she loves him and the kids, takes them to McDonald's. Buys the boy computer games and microwave popcorn.

'When did you ever do that for the lad?' he spits.

'Never,' I say.

'Well now they're getting what kids want and they're happy,' he tells me. 'With me and Sonia they're happy,' he repeats.

He's got a point. No point in telling him that he never gave me money for such things.

So I ask 'What about me?' because that's another thing I'm expected to do.

'You? You're a lush and need help.'

'Perhaps I'm also neurotic?'

He looks confused. 'Don't fight me,' he says. Lights another cigarette, then tells me. His body close to mine. 'I've got ammunition to fight you with, beat you. Your dad? The mad old man who stinks of piss. You're out of him. He let your mother die. Do you know that? Have you any idea about what's gone on around you?'

I look at him startled. I remember. See a picture in my mind.

'Think back,' he insists, 'think and remember.'

I remember. Mother in cream-coloured linen, her vertical frame almost enveloped in green, candlewick bedspread. Her spitting into a gent's handkerchief. She had a supply of them on her bedside table, leaning on a never empty bottle of Lucozade, close to her worn dentures wrapped in a tissue. How long had they been wrapped? Two weeks? Three?

I remember no words she uttered. And why should I? She was simple as they came. And there never were words. Not at the last. I remember Aunt Eva perched on a kitchen chair pulled close to Mum's bed and glancing at her watch, while I sat nearby in a pink basket-chair, scratching a scab from my left knee. Of course I remember.

'Your fucking lovely dad withheld her medication,' Rod is saying. 'Understand? He let her die. You watched but never noticed. But I was there too. Saw it. The poor bugger had no bowel left inside her. No bladder. And her breath smelt like hell.'

I'm shaking my head. Hurting.

'You didn't want to notice did you, woman? Didn't listen to her rambling or changing incontinence pads. You just sat there, in a corner, smoking damned cigarettes. All of your life you've been sitting in a corner. Watching. Waiting. You didn't see the look your mother exchanged with the old man, didn't notice him slip her bottle of capsules into his pocket. You didn't want to, did you?' His voice rises.

'It's not true.'

'Oh yes, it's true,' he says, pulling my face towards him and gripping my shoulders tightly.

I can see the tiny remnants of a long lost baked bean on the stubble on his chin. He's determined to say his piece.

'A mercy killing, that's what they call it. Whether you agreed with it or not. I've kept quiet. But give me a hard time, girl, and I'll fight you. Use what I know. What you refused to know. Whatever it takes, I'm going to keep the kids. If I have to open my mouth and, in the process, kill an old man, I'll do it. What happens now is up to you.'

He lets go of me as quickly as he grabbed me.

'Got it?' he snaps.

I nod. He's wrong about me. I knew about Mother, of course I did. Just hid it from myself. Buried it. But never deep enough, did I? Never deep enough.

'I'll keep you from my kids,' he says, pointing at me. 'I'll keep custody, whatever it takes. Whatever I've got to do.'

I can't fight him now. Got to think. And walk. And walk. He's got me cornered, has Rod. Or is it Mark? No, it's shitting Rod. Or could be both. I just can't think, any more. Mark was instrumental in causing Thomas's death. They both existed, I know. Have stopped fighting myself. I simply KNOW. And now there's Rod. If he opens his mouth to the wrong people he could destroy what's left of Dad's sanity. Worse than death.

Parallels. That's what life's all about.

'Crab apples!' I call over my shoulder. That's all my mind can think of and hear, first from Thomas's mouth, then from Dad's.

Then I hear my voice, muttering to myself, a strange kind of madness. But I don't believe what I'm saying. Not anymore. My feet meet the pavement and my eyes the neon lighting of the shops. I've just missed a bus into town. 'Fucking bastard!' I call after it, as it turns the corner. 'You fucking bastard.' I'm feeling watched. Being watched whilst sober. Not me, is this, not my style at all.

Dad's killed Mum? I don't believe it. But supposing he did? Just supposing? Whatever the stupid old feller's actions were, life killed Mum, I tell myself firmly. I'm muttering to myself and hastening towards town.

I'm outside Phil's door. Can't think how or why I got there. Drunk, it wouldn't matter. But sober? I should know. He'll listen to me, I realise. He can't help me, but he'll listen to me. And I've always felt comfortable with him. There's no complications there. No undertones. What you see is what you get.

He answers the door in his black nylon dressing-gown. He's never one to dress tastefully, I reflect, never one to care if he does or not.

'Trouble,' he states, looking at me but smiling. 'Black coffee?'

'Coffee with milk,' I say.

I kick off my shoes in the doorway, go into his lounge to lounge on a polka-dot sixties bean-bag. Then wait. Then sip the hot liquid he hands me. He's the only truly honest man I've met, is Phil. Crude, but truly honest. Never landed himself with baggage such as people.

He sits opposite me, knees tightly held together in case I should glimpse between the flaps of his gown his genitals by daylight. Some embarrassment there. Strange. I never thought of him as the type to feel embarrassment.

He raises his eyebrows, like an artist. 'Well?' he asks, as I stare at him in silence. But I'm in no hurry to answer. Feel comfortable. Amused, almost.

'It's about reincarnation,' I say finally, reluctantly. Wanting to be waylaid by practicalities, so glancing at my feet to see if my toe-nails need trimming. 'Do you believe in it?'

'It depends,' he sniffs, diplomatically.

I hear myself giggle. 'You mean it depends on who is asking the question and whether they're insane or not.'

'And are you?' he asks. 'Are you insane?'

I shake my head, uncertain. No way I can judge that. 'When I had my babies I wasn't sure I could take care of them, kept thinking that I'd smother them, or kill them by becoming so desperate that I'd lay them on the stone floor of the pantry to freeze. I was frightened then,' I explain, 'of responsibility. I didn't know what it was like. OK, so I overcame it. But I was really frightened. And I'm frightened now. Like I'm possessed.'

'Frightened about what?'

I don't answer. About the sins of the fathers of the fathers, perhaps.

Phil jumps to his feet as if he's had a brainwave. 'Are you religious?' he says, as if that answers every question except how to make puddings. He forgets to offer me another cigarette and lights his.

'Am I fuck,' I say. Then I tell him. About Mark, and Rod. Dad and Thomas. The lot. 'You could even be Big Bert,' I muse.

But I know that's not true. 'You haven't the hardness of Bert,' I say.

'How do you know? Maybe I've simply got more sophistication than him.'

'Are you humouring me?' I ask.

Now it's his turn to give no answer. After a while, he yawns. Tells me I need a rest. And I know I'll get none. Unless.

'Unless you let me stay here,' I say 'I won't eat anything. Won't touch anything.'

Phil shakes his head, 'It's not time,' he frowns. 'Don't you see it's not time? You've got to take time to sort your head out, and to give me the chance to find the fucking courage to take you on.'

'Then you won't let me move in?' I ask flatly.

'Should I?' he asks.

He grabs my elbow and leads me to the door.

'If you need help with this Mark thing let me know,' he says suddenly. He winces.

'You believe it. You know it.'

'I know nothing,' he says, and then tells me he's expecting some female to visit him. 'She needs my cock up her badly,' he says, but he's watching my eyes, searching for something I can't grasp.

Instead, I grasp his hand and feel the heat.

'Will she turn up?'

He doesn't answer. And why should he? I don't know the man. Don't know him at all. Know only the scent of his shirts.

So I'm walking back to Beth's place. Nowhere else to go. Wondering whether I want to go back to Rod's. Whether I could.

And should I? No dispute. I've blown it. But I was safe there. No questions asked, no questions answered. And I was good at embroidery wasn't I? Cooked brilliant dumplings? Great baked apples?

Apples. Whatever happened to apples?

I can hear Thomas screaming. Feel a whitewashed, stone wall through his own clinging fingers.

'What do you want of me?' I shout, clinging to park railings as a flickering street-lamp buzzes and some bloke with a stolen car stereo hurries past me.

'What the hell do you want? You're dead.' I'm screaming.

No-one's listening. But someone has an idea he's caught my screaming. A limping man with evening papers glances at me and scurries by.

How long have I been walking? I don't know. Time to come down to earth. Come to terms. I'm a wife who deserted her husband. Her kids.

Got to fight with practicalities. The problem of having nowhere to live, an impending decree nisi. A feeling. A feeling that I'm somehow being used. Have got to be used to get rid of my guilt.

A silly cunt, aren't I?

Beth is sitting, legs curled beneath her broadening hips, on her moquette settee. Tells me she's seen a cheap blouse at Marks and Sparks. And what do I think of that?

Then she looks at me. Falters a little.

'I'm not drunk,' I tell her. 'Only worried. A turn up for the books, that.'

She sighs. Tells me, 'I don't know what you want. But you certainly want too much. Your Rod...'

'My Rod what?' I interrupt. 'He used me. All my life he's done that. Don't you understand that? He used me like a washing-up mop, for his own satisfaction. When he thought my body was coated in jewels, and when he didn't.'

'No, I don't understand.' She's genuinely puzzled.

My mouth is dry. 'He haunts me,' I say. 'It's as if he's someone else playing a stupid game. Someone I despise. Sonia's made her mark on him. But Sonia's only an incomer. It's all about him and me. Retribution.'

Beth sighs again. She's read a lot of women's magazines.

'Maybe you should seek help,' she says.

Maybe I should.

'Your kids miss you,' she says.

'No, they don't. Not now they're weaned. They're chained to their dad. He's softer than I am. Oh, he pretends not to be. But he's got them. History repeating itself. He's got power. Not ultimate power, but the little man's idea of power. And my children follow him.'

'You're just tired,' she says.

Her husband, Fred, walks in, his suede shoes moving silently across the beige nylon carpet and his fingers clicking nervously, as they often do. He's started looking at me, grudgingly acknowledging me. He's had a good dominoes game, he's telling Beth. It all went well. It's a pity his bifocals don't work as well, I'm thinking.

Then he turns to me. Looks at me quizzically. His eyes give out the message. He wonders why I'm still here.

'Yes, I am tired,' I reply to Beth's earlier question.

It's the only polite thing to do. Now for the bed, and the dream. The final chapter perhaps. I've got a feeling about that. The duvet cover is purple and blue. The curtains, tinted magenta. The ancient clock on the white chipboard chest of drawers by my side, tick-tock-ticking.

I've got to get back to the dream. Got to. No force. No fear. None, I decide, closing my eyes. No fear. There's got to be no fear.

The fungus is high on the wall. Probing. Always probing. And the menstrual blood heavy on the rag between my legs. It's almost midnight and the lamps are dying.

There's a knock on the door. I expected it.

Can't answer. Am cradling my elbows. No point now. No point in anything. Thomas has gone and the fucker betrayed him. It's the fucker at the door. I know that.

But the smell is all wrong. There's something strange in the palm of my hand. I can see it. It's an old plastic clock. And there's a smell of chop-suey up my nose. News at Ten, from a distance, touching my ears. Jesus Christ, I'm still awake.

Or not.

Which earth am I on?

I can hear Beth asking if I still want Horlicks, her pink nylon mules padding across the floor. Wrong time. Wrong place. But more. I can still hear more. Follow it. Go back. Back.

There's Mark's voice. He's knocking on an unpainted door, pressing the latch. Stooping to enter.

I'm there. Barefoot, on the tiles. Now he's standing in front of me. Standing. Still standing. Shaking his head and drooping the sides of his mouth in probably feigned sadness. It's a practised expression. I know it is. Know everything about him.

He opens his mouth to gulp air before speaking, and follows me across the room. Looks as I curl up on a horse-hair stuffed chair. Watches. He's always watching. I should have realised that before now. He's unsuccessfully trying to get my eyes to meet his. Then hesitates. But only for a moment. He's not indecisive. That's well known.

'Thomas?' That's all I can say.

'You know he died. An unfortunate accident. Act of God.'

'God?'

'Life is like that,' he says. 'Now someone must lay out the body.'

'Must they?'

He's looking at me bemused.

I've got to ask him. 'Do you know what death is like? Do you? I know. I'm certain of that. And Thomas knew.'

He's shaking his head.

'You knew he knew,' I insist. 'About the burning? Burning flesh? Perhaps you can't picture that in your mind. But I can picture it. And he lived it.'

Now Mark's sighing. Bored. 'That's how life is,' he mumbles, 'best accept it.'

'And death?' I ask.

I know he can't answer. Not now. But he will soon, I've been thinking. The knife I placed beneath my cushion is still there. Can't go anywhere else.

I push the blade under his ribs, the natural armour, feel the warmth of his blood spurt forward. Watch it shoot up on a gust of air from his punctured chest to the fold of his chin. It's not unpleasant.

'Know how vulnerable we are now?' I shout. 'Know how vulnerable?'

He's not listening. Can't.

He'll cool down quickly. I know that.

Beth is still shaking me.

I'm still. Listening.

I killed Mark because he killed Thomas.

What if Rod, with his words, destroyed Dad? What if I killed him? What if I had to? I struggle up from the camp-bed loaned by Beth, my spine stiffer than I thought it would be. Then search beneath the perspiration-scented duvet for my watch, and feel the dampness from my body skimming the floral sheet like milk.

Something wrong here. Something terribly wrong.

'Another nightmare?' Beth asks, scowling. She's wearing a see-through housecoat, which surprises me.

I nod. 'Yes, another nightmare,' I mutter. Then take the mug of coffee from her neglected, unsteadily cupped hands and thank her, watching her push a straying strand of greying hair away from her unpainted forehead.

'You think all of this dream shit is due to my drinking, don't you?'

She doesn't answer. Can't know what I'm talking about. Wouldn't want to know.

I can't bring myself to say any more to her. The exercise would be useless. I stumble to the bathroom to vomit, hit the inside of the toilet pedestal with my bile, and watch the splash-out run down the shiny enamel and onto the patterned cushion floor. Then wonder if Beth swills the bathroom down with Dettol every week. It would fit wouldn't it? Fit her patterning.

I'm feeling envious, and furry tongued. Where's my patterning? Got to have some. Everybody has. I can't give way to the idea that mine is purely based on self-destruction.

I'm hungry. And trembling. I think I should feel cold. But I'm hot. Terribly hot. Sweat runs down my chest in a stream.

I peer at my reflection in the sparkling mirror. The eyes are blacker than they should be, the skin around my lips more grubby, showing the slow sprouting of hairs around the curves of the mouth that all menopausal women get.

I'm a mess. That's what I am. And frightened. Getting off the booze might cure it.

Could it?

Beth comes up silently behind me. Offers me the use of her toothpaste.

Chapter 14

Suddenly it's another Saturday. Flat, and black. Can't remember the last two, but two giros for my upkeep must have dropped on Beth's mat, and I must have spent them. Mad fourteen days of nothing.

I critically re-examine my eyes in the bathroom mirror, also examine my breast with hot red hands in the search for lumps. Nothing there. I tell myself to believe it.

Death is inevitable, but not now, not for me. I haven't earned it, not yet. Some people have. Deserve to go to hell.

I'm becoming accustomed to such mornings. To Beth's motherly concern, to the calling of the peacock kept by a farmer in a nearby, neglected field, as a status symbol. Its shrill voice cutting through the frost and breaking my sleep from a distance. Dissolving the screams of Thomas. Spreading its echoes like arrows through my head.

This has gone on for two abstinent weeks.

I can feel the boy burning. Can no longer put this down to my own crazy mind. I've been dry for days. That should say something. Mean something.

I'm doing what I've done before, put on the floral dressing-gown and saunter into Beth's kitchen, with its flickering strip-light. Then I put some butter onto some off-gold toast and listen to her talk about old Fred's tax bills.

I tell her, 'My head hurts. I could be mad. That's a comfortable straw to cling to, don't you think?'

She scrambles some eggs and looks nervously through her kitchen window, watching for a feral cat that keeps performing its ablutions on top of her radishes.

'I can't bear to chase it,' she mutters.

She doesn't want to listen to me.

'Beth, I'm scared,' I tell her when she turns towards me.

'I could loan you another blouse, should you want to go out and about,' she suggests, avoiding my eyes.

I nod knowingly. My sanity is seriously in question. I know that.

'I'm going to sort it all,' I say, feeling an unexpected surge of adrenalin, and thankful for a dumb chemical reaction. Something to laugh at. 'I'm going to sort everything out. And I mean everything,' I stress.

Beth's blouse fits me fine. Enhances my almost non-existent breasts.

Got to walk. Got to get out and walk.

The air is damp, filled with the sound of pigeons' wings, angry cars, screaming kids.

My feet hurt. Swollen ankles. Water retention.

If I'm really going to confront Rod, I need a drink first. And I know just where to find it. At The Plowman. Back door open at nine-thirty. No problem. I even know the guy I'm looking for there. Too young to be as grey and broke and as knackered as the rest of the early morning drinkers. Too old to be naive.

He danced with me didn't he? Held me and swayed in front of the juke-box.

Doesn't know about my madness yet.

A dispassionate viewpoint, I'm telling myself, as I push open the door. That's what I want. And this man doesn't know me from Eve, but could remember my eyes. What was his name? God, I can't think. The acid from Beth's poached eggs clings tenaciously to my ribs, and my corns are playing up like kids demanding ice-cream. But the man with no name is there. Where I expected him to be. He pulls his elbows from the bar and looks at me and smirks.

'Want a lager?' he asks.

'You can bet I bloody do,' I say.

Wilf, the landlord, standing behind the bar and, for once, not staring suspiciously at his optics, looks at me suspiciously, a vulnerable man in a white shirt and braces. Used to own a transport cafe, he did, and can't see the difference. He's sipping on a miniature whisky, between gently nibbling on a bacon teacake.

'So,' he says, when I've gone onto barley wine, 'how's Rod?'

Occasionally came here for a pint of lager, did Rod.

'How the hell do you think he is?' I ask.

So he shrugs. Gets the idea. The man with no name offers me a cigarette. Tells me that he's just finished the night-shifts.

'Doing what?' I ask. 'Digging graves?'

Then I laugh. Tell him that I'm fucking mad. Then watch his eyes. He's no expression. Nothing.

'Thank you,' I say. Then commence to tell him the usual thing. He's obviously been around. Must have heard this thing a hundred times before.

'My husband is a pillock. I never had a chance with him. Not without stitching myself to embroidery etc etc. Never could bake sponge cakes. Either of us. And he kicked me in the crotch etc.etc.'

'I suppose he dressed in the dark, too,' he says, with a wry smile.

'Sometimes,' I say.

And he's heard it all before.

'I'm fucking haunted,' I add. 'Don't know what to do about it.'

Then I watch his eyes, half expecting him to say 'What? By Omen 2? or Jaws 4?'

He doesn't. 'I've seen more hauntings than you've sucked hot cocks,' he says.

He's impressed by the lack of reaction from me. Buys me another drink. I've got to open up to someone. Find help. 'I'm frightened,' I tell him. 'Crazy. I want to kill my husband because he was responsible for my brother's death, you see. His sort kill everyone who thinks or feels, like we're committing a crime.'

There's tears running down my cheeks.

'Like we should all be sat in some shit and not sneeze. Got to kill them before they kill us. Thomas should have known that, poor kid.'

'Thomas.'

'Oh, forget it. If I told you, you wouldn't believe what I'm on about.' Wish I wasn't talking so crazily.

'I see only the stars, girl,' he says, draining the liquid from his glass. 'Us Dublin men are awfully romantic.'

'Romantic enough to know what I'm talking about?'

'What?'

'My husband destroyed my brother a hundred years ago, when

the bastard was my lover. Kept him locked up in a burning mill. How about that? Can you understand that? Can you?' Then I laugh. After all, it is hilarious. 'What do you think, then? With a mind like mine I need carting away? I'm telling you, he died in pain,' I grip his arm so tightly that it should hurt. 'Understand? UNDERSTAND?' I raise my voice. 'I even dreamt about the fire. Thomas, my brother. He was the first to become unconscious. His lungs were bad. Then they all followed. Still holding damp rags against their faces. But they all went. One by one.'

Wilf has been listening. He's leaning across the bar.

'You two cunts either lower your voices or leave,' he says. He takes my drink away. Says I've had enough.

So I move closer to the man with no name, feel I could be still in a dream. Know I could be.

'Car keys?' I ask.

He looks startled.

'Look, I know you've got a car. I've got a clean licence and I need to borrow your vehicle for an hour. That's all.'

'So you think I should loan it to every bitch off the street?'

'No. To me. Just to me.' I hold out my hands and stare at him squarely between the eyes.

Wilf mutters sarcastically. Something about damsels in distress.

I haven't time to retort. Haven't time to think.

Got to sort this thing out before it ruins my life completely. And my children's and my father's. And I'm drunk, for sure, inadvertently banging my thighs against pub stools and past worrying. I leave my watch and family allowance book as guarantee I'll be back. Get the loan of an idiot's car. Have the feeling he was about to weigh it in to the man with notorious greyhounds in a yard down Cooper Bridge until I told him my sob story, and hinted of payment in flesh on my return. I've missed my way. Have come to the conclusion I could have made a good liar, had I put my heart into it.

Wilf leans across the bar and says, 'Take care.' Doesn't care.

So I say, 'See you.' Feel the worn steps under my feet as I slam the door against the smell of Tetley's bitter. Find the car, steel grey, appropriate colour almost for my need, find the ignition. Whose car is this? I can't for the life of me remember.

The windscreen wipers work, and there's a steady drizzle. There are roads of greyness, punctuated only by an occasional scurrying pink mac, something with trainers on a blue mountain bike, and a frightened neutered tom-cat.

And, Jesus Christ, I'm pissed. If I never have been before, I am now. A waste of space.

I'm waiting in the dampness for Rod, and chain-smoking like they do in the movies. The engine is still running and there's some damned silly opera blurting out from a tape in the car stereo, unintelligible, a status symbol.

I'm thinking of Thomas and about what happens now. If what happened before should happen again. Mark never really cared for me did he? Never noticed my limp. My pain. The lack of meat in the cooling stew-pot in the dust of the grate. Never listened, nor heard the moans.

Rod's out in the avenue, hosing down his car. I can see him clearly. Know that the boil on the back of his neck will be still aching. Yet he's only a small denim-clad peanut in the distance, wiping his hands on his pockets and pushing the windblown, gingerish hair away from his face. Never took much pride in his appearance, did Rod. That was one of the reasons I liked him. Loved him? I'm asking myself the questions. Maybe I was only grateful that he desired me. But that gratitude has been repaid in full. It's over.

It's almost lunchtime. Soon he'll be going indoors to ignite a flame underneath the chip-pan, then he'll take off his wedding ring, roll his sleeves up, then carefully scrape potatoes under running water, scratching out all of the eyes. After that he'll examine his fingernails for splits. Won't find any. Then he'll probably place his stained handkerchiefs and underpants in a bowl of hot water and bleach, leave them to soak. He'll switch on the telly, fall asleep in front of it.

I know him. I know him too well. He should never have become mixed up with me. Never.

Enough of this.

Tears running down my cheeks don't matter. Don't solve anything.

If I'm going to run him down I've got to do it now. Now. While I'm still intoxicated. No court would deal harshly with a drunken, emotionally upset, estranged housewife who came to speak of reconciliation to her husband and couldn't think quickly enough to push on the brake pedal in time.

And my tears? Tears of what? Sorrow? Because I thought we had something once? Felt his thighs on mine and expected something more? Not Rod's fault, that. Not his fault alone. They could be tears of guilt because I shit the marriage up. Didn't I? And Rod, the bastard, didn't know it hurt me. Refuses to know. Refused to.

'Simply because a man doesn't show his feelings, it doesn't mean that he hasn't got any,' he once told me.

I can hear the words now. I shouted at him and he changed the subject under the duvet, mentioned he felt very much alone, rabbited on about finding fluff behind the toilet pedestal, and about my sponge cakes never rising. A midnight argument of long ago. And all that has gone now. Gone. Like the reason we got together. If reason there was.

My fingertips are numb. I haven't been behind a steering-wheel for years. I haven't been allowed to, on account of I'm not trusted. Makes sense.

And what if I kill him? What if I do? What happens to my kids? Bloody melodramatic, this, I'm telling myself, too much like frigging American TV. But I'm sweating alright. Under my armpits. Beneath my breasts.

It will only take seconds to kill a man who killed Thomas. The man who screwed me up, stole my kids, would be no longer. In less time than the Big Bang took. Easy. Too bloody easy.

I switch on the car radio and listen to a sixties record. Then light a last cigarette. No cigarettes, no money. Nothing new. A part of my life. I'm feeling sorry for myself. No warmth in my memory. What the hell am I waiting for?

The foot is working in death spasms. So is the radio. Guitar music punctures my ears. I stab the accelerator.

Six yards. Three yards...

The bastard turns and sees me. There's the expected look in his eyes. The look of a cornered fox. He knows.

And I can't see for those fucking tears.

'Those fucking tears,' I scream, 'you did that.'

I lift my foot from the accelerator. Slam it down on the brake. Then look at him. Watch.

He's had a lucky escape and knows it. But he recovers instantly. Moves quickly around the side of the car. Yanks at the door, his mentholyptus breath filling the cavity, crawls over the mock-leather passenger seat towards me.

'Pissing idiot,' he yells, then drags me from the car. 'You pissed up idiot. That's what you are, pissed up.'

'You should be grateful I left you with your legs,' I spit back, feeling the pavement against my knees. 'You should be dead.' Then I go off my head. 'Maybe you are dead. Maybe we all are.'

He's grasping me like a whippet breeder might hold a runt puppy. 'Black coffee, that's what you need. There's no way you can run me down. You know that.' His grip tightens.

A neighbour opens the door to find out what the shouting is all about, then closes it quickly.

'Yes sir, no sir, three bags full, sir,' I scream.

'Say what you mean, you bastard,' he shouts back at me. 'Say it.'

Then I'm in his kitchen. My kitchen.

'Well?' he asks. 'You want the kids? You have them. Spoil their lives.'

'Spoil their lives?' I yell. 'They don't know what life is. They've never even seen you touch me. Don't know what affection is. And now you say I'll spoil their lives?' He's glaring at me.

'And what about Thomas?' I ask.

'What?'

'Thomas, you twit. You wouldn't unlock the door and let him out.'

He shakes his head. 'You are fucking mad, you fucking cunt.'

'Then you've never dreamt,' I say flatly. If he had it would be so much easier.

'About what?' he asks.

Now it's my turn to shake my head.

There's a silence. 'Look, take the kids,' he eventually mutters. 'What Sonia and I had is finished. For God's sake, it was only a fling, a bit of fun on both our parts. A laugh between the sheets. But then you don't know what a laugh is do you? You've never laughed in your life. Any woman with her head about her would realise that was all it was,' he puts his face closer to mine. 'It was all about sex. Because I was bored with you and your constant whining. I was bored with all your demands. The shit you talk.'

I know all about psychological warfare. Try to look away, because I'm supposed to.

'Oh no, you don't,' he says, 'you're going to hear me. You are a mess. A bloody mess. One step away from being crazy.'

'You mean I'm paranoid?'

He sighs and shakes his head. Lowers his voice. 'For some reason the kids miss you. Why they should, I don't know,' he adds loudly. 'They shouldn't.'

'Because I'm a drunk?'

'Because you're a drunk,' he nods. 'A bleeding, Council estate, piss artist. A clone. Future stamped out. In a few years you'll be going to the bingo in wet knickers, sleeping in the afternoon and complaining all night. You probably won't even have enough about you to change the bedding. I've seen it. I've seen it all before. You're either respectable or not.'

'Or mad or not?'

He glares at me, making it obvious he thinks that he's talking to himself.

'So who drove me to that?' I ask, frowning.

He shrugs his shoulders again.

'It hurts does honesty,' I spit. 'Doesn't it?'

He turns away, grunts. 'It's done. Finished. No turning back the clock. You've gone too far.' Then rinses some striped towels out in the sink, his spine stiffening. He's making it clear by his silence that it's time for me to leave.

'Nothing more to be said is there?' So I get to my feet, feel the toes pushed together in ridiculously tight shoes and notice the tiled floor must have been washed regularly since I left. Nothing's wrong, everything, down to the striped sugar bowl which I've kept meaning to wash out, is in its place. The cat's red plastic dish is sparkling with cleanliness and filled with fresh food. Nothing wrong. Nothing wrong at all.

There's nothing of me about. No plastic, hollow frog I bought from a door to door salesman for a ridiculous price and kept scouring pads in. No pot-pourri. No plates of my half-eaten meals on the draining board, the sausages waiting to be nibbled at by passing mouths. Well, there wouldn't be.

There's nothing to be said. So I move my feet across the tiles. Watch them.

I can't take the kids. I know that. Not until I feel better. Am better. I'm admitting that to myself, as I zip up my anorak. You're something of a drunk, girl. But there's more. Much more. Things misunderstood. No-one understands.

I let myself out, in silence. Memorising the scent of lemon cleansing gel.

Don't apologise to him.

Can't.

Time to write off my losses. Take the car back to the man I got it from, buy him a drink, pat his hand and make up an excuse to get away from him. I could tell him I've got the shingles in my eyes, and been diagnosed as HIV Positive. Easy. Then time to walk to Beth's semi-detached via the green of the park, teaching myself not to think.

That's been my downfall. Thinking. That was Thomas's downfall. A nightmare.

Just what is the nightmare? Maybe this is, and I'll wake up in some hovel knowing my place. Even liking it. There's a lot of satisfaction in lying prostrate and thinking about the possibility of being a murderess. I've tasted it.

But time passes. Pain passes.

And here I go again, I'm telling myself, walking past the fungi floating on the boating lake and kicking up leaves. There's a sick duck, with water-worn feathers, limping around the surrounding tarmac. Around and around it goes, occasionally glimpsing me and not caring. I'm thinking. Can't stop. Thomas must have been thinking in the fumes of the flames. Thinking and hurting.

Beth, clad in unexpected crimson, is waiting on her doorstep. Looking up and down the road of white light, anxiously. Waiting for me. I'd told her I'd be home. I'm half expecting her to have my blue suitcase in her hand, and an apology on her discreetly painted lips. The late afternoon is licking her hair. Lighting up the strands of grey. Strange that I've not noticed that before. The passage of time.

I'm smiling to myself. Time. The great con. The more of it you have, the more of it you want, and the more it hurts. The vicious bloody circle.

My trouble is that I keep slipping and going back into the sphere of its grasp, anti-clockwise. It's time to stop. Time to get my footing.

'Don't tell me,' I say to Beth with false joviality. 'There's soddin' liver for tea, the ceiling's fallen in, and Fred has murdered the cat.'

She shakes her head and takes hold of my shoulders because she thinks she's supposed to. Poor Beth. Always does her best. She's always well-behaved and feeling at her best. Happy.

Poor me. Poor everybody, I'm thinking.

She's got her stereo on in the living room. Songs of melancholy and tripe, songs of lost love the artists never knew.

She takes a deep breath. 'It's your dad,' she explains. Then her words come out in a nervous stream. She's been trying to find me. Phoned everyone she could think of, including Phil, who is walking down the path behind me, I realise.

'Rod?' I ask Beth. 'Did you try phoning Rod?'

'Well, why should I?' she asks bewildered.

'Why indeed.'

'Your father is really badly, luv,' says Phil coming up behind her. I don't want to hear it.

In the taxi, Phil keeps his distance. Doesn't touch me. Clearly thinks it's appropriate behaviour.

'Doctors can work wonders, these days,' he says, because he's read it somewhere.

I nod in appreciation, because he's trying to display concern and feels uncomfortable about it.

'Old folk die,' I find myself saying. 'And not only old folk.'

There's silence.

'That's a callous way of thinking,' I conclude.

'Not for me to say, sweetheart.'

I glance at him. He means that. I can see he does.

'Dad and I don't always get along,' I explain. 'Something to do with genes, I suppose.'

'But you love him?'

'The part of him he lets me know about, I do. But he keeps so much hidden.'

'He's not dead yet,' Phil reminds me.

'Oh, he knows all about dying.'

'You're talking about this Thomas thing?'

I nod. It doesn't matter whether this man believes what I'm going through or not. I believe it.

I've got to. Thomas is dead. Dad is dying.

The old man's got his dentures in, I notice as soon as I see him. Hates to wear dentures in bed. Always thinks they'll choke him in his sleep. And I feel annoyed. Why should the so-called ladies in green make him do that? They probably pushed them onto his gums with long, lily-white, disinfected fingers and told him to act his age. But what age is he? I'll be damned if I know. Just how old is anyone?

He's breathing quietly. Drifting in and out of consciousness, I'm told. On his bedside locker is a half-eaten orange resting on a tissue, the usual jug of untouched water, foot powder, and a photograph of me whizzing down a playground slide thirty years ago and scowling. A touch of the past. Should be long gone.

But it's never gone. I know that.

Phil is gripping my hand, offering to go down the corridor to the coffee machine, when Dad stirs and dribbles down the stubble on his chin and weakly tries to wriggle his toes beneath the blankets. He's moving his shoulders in irritation, annoyed with the thickly woven cotton. He's never worn pyjamas in his life before. That's something else I know about him.

I'm standing by the side of his bed. Still. Quiet. Watching. Watching him use depleting energy to glare.

His words are unexpected. 'You forgot to take me to see your mother's grave.'

There's not much time left. He knows it. Yet he's still struggling with pettiness, trying to leave me a guilt trip.

'You promised. You promised.' He's shouting.

'Why did you let Mother die?' I ask coldly. 'I think I know. But I want you to tell me.'

I'm expecting silence. The shutting out again. Instead he looks me in the eyes. Hesitates.

Then speaks. 'It was the pain she was in.' He's trying to raise himself to his elbows and fighting back a threatened spasm of coughing. 'I know all about pain,' he says.

I can't let him off. Can't let him go that easily. I don't want to do this but I can't stop myself.

'And the nightmare? My nightmare?' I'm surprised at how easily I'm managing to control my voice. There's no emotion in it. None. 'Will you tell me about it now?'

'Best left alone,' he coughs. 'Best not to burn again.'

'So. You dreamt about the mill fire, didn't you?'

'Lived it,' he coughs again. 'Long ago. Long, long ago. I had a different name then. Can't remember what it was.'

I take his hand. 'Thomas,' I say gently. 'Your name was Thomas.'

He's losing consciousness. I've got tears in my eyes. At last I've got tears in my eyes. I know about this. Think I've always known about this. At least he hasn't burned again. And I haven't killed again.

The wheel is broken. If there ever was a wheel.

Dad's gone.

Phil and I walk down the gravel drive. He asks, 'What now?'

I shrug. 'Time to sort my life out?'
'Can you?' he asks.
'Maybe. Maybe I can this time.'
There's a chill in the air.
A strange foreboding.

Other Titles From Springboard Fiction

Annie Potts is Dead - Available Sept 1998
by M Y Alam
ISBN 1 901927 03 2   Price £6.95
It's not easy to write when you work in a shop, customers can tend to break your concentration. It's not easy to deal with rejection from an editor either, especially when you imagine him to be like the little fat bloke from the film *Deliverance*.
Amjad has a plan to get himself recognised and when Annie Potts gets dead one day, the police come knocking wanting to know exactly what he has been writing about.

The Righteous Brother
by Adrian Wilson
ISBN 1 901927 00 8 Price £6.95
For Crown prosecution solicitor James Turner there is a clear distinction between right and wrong, and before the local magistrates he's usually right. But what of his wife Sally, and her admirer Kevin? Or his courtroom adversary Colin Chatterton and the ambitious journalist Jo Hinchliffe? How have these people forced James Turner to be so suddenly and murderously wrong?

Miasma
by Chris Firth
ISBN: 1 901927 01 6   Price £6.95
Deserted. Lonely. Sad. Going bad. Going slowly mad. Anna Fisher can only take so much. In this darkly humoured first novel, Chris Firth leads us into the murky world of Anna Fisher - where nothing is quite what it seems.

The White Room
by Karen Maitland
ISBN: 1 898311 23 4   Price £6.95
They have surveillance cameras in the White Room, watching every move you make. In a Britain of the future where social and cultural conflict has sharpened, Ruth is drawn into a disturbing exploration of the forces that shape her life: her cultural identity, her family history and a society that she no longer feels a part of.

Flood
by Tom Watts
ISBN: 1 898311 12 9   Price £4.99
Bob is back in the home town he hasn't seen for thirty years. A remarkable first novel which moves us into an adolescent world fraught with underlying passion and danger. A demanding, disturbing and rewarding read.

The Labour Man
by Jim Wilson
ISBN 1 898311 01 3   Price £3.00
Can there be honour in politics? Harry Beamish, a lifelong socialist, wrenches a marginal seat from the Tories in an election which returns a Labour Government with a majority of one. Unfortunate then he's done a bunk. A pre-Blair Mania novel where the future of the Government and socialism depends on Harry.

Tubthumping - Available Nov 1998
ISBN 1 901927 04 0   Price £5.95
Short stories from a selection of the most promising young writers in the Yorkshire region.

Ordering

Annie Potts is Dead	£6.95
Dark Places	£6.95
The Righteous Brother	£6.95
Miasma	£6.95
The White Room	£6.95
Flood	£4.99
The Labour Man	£3.00
Tubthumping	£5.95

Title: _
Quantity _ _ _ _   Price _ _ _ _   Total _ _ _ _

Title: _
Quantity _ _ _ _   Price _ _ _ _   Total _ _ _ _

Title: _
Quantity _ _ _ _   Price _ _ _ _   Total _ _ _ _

20% discount on orders of 5 or more of any individual title. Postage and packing free in the UK only.

You may pay by cheque or postal order made payable to Yorkshire Art Circus Ltd. We also accept payment by Access or Visa.

Card Number (Access/Visa): _ _ _ _ _ _ _ _ _ _ _ _ _ _ _ _
Expiry Date _ _ _ _

Name _
Address _
_ _
_ _ _ _ _ _ _ _ Post Code _ _ _ _ _ _ _ _ _ _ _

Please allow 28 days for delivery.